Praise for *Plausible Deniability* by Robert Gilbert

I've seen flacks up close and personal (including my Dad, wife and a sister). I've seen big-time journalism, too—my Dad, a brother and I totaled more than half a century at the *Wall Street Journal*. So, I can assure you that Robert Gilbert nails the nuances of both while exploring the sorts of tensions and offbeat characters that pop up in those intertwined worlds. (Not that I ever personally saw anyone use alcohol as a crutch, of course.)

—Paul Carroll is a Pulitzer Prize nominee and author of *Big Blues*

Simply put, you are there. Robert Gilbert's intimate, evocative storytelling of corporate malfeasance and human frailty pulls you in to a point that it's almost impossible to not feel like you're in the room. It's a story both unfamiliar and all too familiar, of good people finding themselves in situations that expose their vulnerabilities and challenge their moral fortitude. There is a gentle, compelling honesty to his prose and to the inner truth of his struggling hero Pete Wendell, a person and persona that we all have something in common with.

—Chris Colbert is the former Managing Director, Harvard Business School Innovation Labs and author of *This Is It*

Robert Gilbert has done what few writers attempt anymore, and even fewer pull off — he's written a great American novel. *Plausible Deniability* is as funny and tender as its heartbreaking hero. Blue-blooded Pete Wendell, raised in superficial privilege and emotional scarcity, thinks he's found salvation when he moves with his new bride into the upscale Connecticut town where he grew up. But what this young business writer discovers is that no story is so simple or so sweet. Following in the tradition of Richard Yates and John Cheever, with a dose of John Irving tossed in, Gilbert has written a big novel — about love and loss, about the individual within the corporate workplace, about responsibility, big and small. Ultimately, *Plausible Deniability* is a book about the very nature of truth, and one man's long and winding road to finally owning up to his.

—Rachel Basch is the author of *The Listener*

This first novel has the stylistic maturity and cleverness of a career novelist. I fell in love with Robert Gilbert's New Canaan and with Pete, who gallantly struggles with all the frailties of being human, including alcoholism, love, and the great struggle to survive in a corporate world which has lost its moral compass and its soul. Told with great humor and insight into both the corporate news world and the human heart, *Plausible Deniability* is a tale for our times that shows what's possible when a cog in the wheel, who could be any one of us, takes on both his own personal demons and those of the almighty corporation. The result is one hell of a ride.

—Karen Osborn is the author most recently of *The Music Book*

Thoroughly original, Robert Gilbert's page-turning *Plausible Deniability* reveals the complex machinations of corporate skullduggery as ordered up from within corner offices. In Pete Wendell we find an unlikely protagonist: part Hildy Johnson in *The Front Page*, part Raskolnikov in Dostoyevsky's *Crime and Punishment* and part Cato, the incorruptible Roman stoic. In the sordid world of business today, how far will one man go to survive while trying to hang on to his own human dignity? Or as a company lawyer asks him in the midst of a national scandal, "Do they pay you enough to lie?"

—Veteran investigative correspondent Willy Stern has reported from six continents.

In *Plausible Deniability* Robert Gilbert gives us a protagonist, Pete Wendell, who works in the business communications field, otherwise known as "flakdom," a field he knows only too well. The people in the corporate world and the reporters who follow them come vividly to life in this novel, but it's Pete who makes the deepest impression as he tries to surmount profound personal loss and who emerges in these pages as a sort of corporate Everyman, someone who has seen through the chicanery and manipulation yet who has given it his grudging assent. Pete's struggles are deeply human; his insights are both witty and painful in this utterly convincing book.

—Baron Wormser is the author of *Tom o' Vietnam*

When did corporate greed reach the point where any story could be faked, as long as the corporation had "plausible deniability" in case things went wrong? When did some journalists become corporate shills? When did truth become "truthiness" and facts acquire alternatives? In Robert Gilbert's wordly, witty and wise debut novel, these things are happening in the 1990's; caught up in the middle of it all is *Wall Street Bulletin* reporter Pete Wendell, a man with denial issues of his own. Pete is running from his own skewed vision of his perfect upper-crust Connecticut childhood; his grief over a terrible loss; his selling-out of his journalistic ideals; and, most of all, his out-of-control drinking. Pete is a classic anti-hero, human and flawed, a guy who keeps trying to do the right thing, keeps getting screwed, and keeps on keeping on anyway. Gilbert's own background as a journalist shows here, in his sharp, precise and graceful prose. He's a fine writer and *Plausible Deniability* is an enlightening and entertaining novel. That's undeniable.

—Hollis Seamon is the author of *Somebody Up There Hates You* and *Corporeality*

Plausible Deniability

By Robert Gilbert

Published by Piscataqua Press
an imprint of RiverRun Bookstore
32 Daniel Street
Portsmouth NH 03801

ISBN: 978-1-950381-29-6

It seems, as one becomes older,

That the past has another pattern, and ceases to be a mere sequence —

T.S. Eliot, *Four Quartets*

To my wife Margaret, who introduced
me to spirituality,
and to Willy Stern, who gave me the
opportunity to discover my true self.

Acknowledgments

The common image of a novelist depicts some tortured soul isolated in a garret, agonizing over every word. The latter may have been true of me as I labored for more than five years on the book you hold in your hands. But I wasn't alone. Indeed, an extraordinary group of people personified the old cliché of "I couldn't have done it without you." Chief among these were some generous MFA mentors: Karen Osborn, Baron Wormser, Rachel Basch, and Hollis Seamon. I also want to thank Sergeant Keith Beebe of the Stonington Police Department; Tim Evers, a retired prep and high school teacher; and Mike Greene, a careful reader of an early draft. Finally, I wish to thank my publisher and ultimate editor, Tom Holbrook.

Prologue

My iPhone sounded a hollow ding, pulling my attention away from Judy Woodruff's progress report on the 2016 election campaign. The text was from Camille, my daughter, who is also in the news business, though less grandly as a reporter for the Newark *Star-Ledger*. I muted the TV and read:

> Hey Pops, I just saw this piece saying that Trump's Art of the Deal originally made the bestseller list because of gigantic bulk purchases made by his executives. Sound familiar? It's in some guy's biography of The Donald. Apparently, he did it again with his campaign book.

Because my hands shake, it took me a while to respond:

> Aha, is the new political tome called Make Fakery Great Again?

The little dots at the bottom of the screen danced as she composed a reply:

> LOL. But isn't this just like your scandal?

> Actuallu

Damn tremor. I tried again more deliberately:

> Sounds crude. My villains knew exactly which bookstores to buy from. We were also the first to get caught.

BOOK ONE

Libby, 1989

CHAPTER ONE

Boner

"Oh you think that's *funny*, do you?"

I barely knew her, but as Libby glared up at me from the old copy desk at the *Wall Street Bulletin* there was no mistaking her loathing.

"Yes I do," I replied, more than a little taken aback. I'd been joking with Frank Fallon, the desk chief.

The other editors on what they called "the Staten Island Ferry," so-named because of the massive copy desk's ovoid shape, had now taken a keen interest. All twelve of them—enough to comprise a jury. Beyond the workplace windows shone the endlessly rising aluminum façade of 2 World Trade Center; inside, upturned faces. Standing there, the sole center of attention, it dawned that I was on trial for stumbling over some feminist trip wire.

What I'd noticed most about Elizabeth Lindquist was that she was no-nonsense. She was the best editor, fact-checker, grammarian, story-logic imposer, and what-the-hell-*were*-you-trying-to-say error blocker on the desk operation. Yet, reporters respected her fairness and decency. She had a habit of walking back to a miscreant's desk to discuss problems in private, instead of phoning from the desk with loud embarrassing questions for the entire newsroom to overhear. In her customary slacks and closed-face demeanor, she was the kind of formidable professional woman I steered clear of.

"But it *is* funny when you realize the double meaning," I insisted. I held up the paper and repeated aloud the three-deck headline:

Grantland Avoids
Ketcham's Boner
In Overexpansion

"Don't you get an unfortunate mental picture of what's going on?" It was a story about a female CEO who did *not* make the same mistake as her male predecessor, who had nearly bankrupted his company by pushing for breakneck growth.

Libby's eyes narrowed.

"Frank," I appealed to the slot man in the middle of the Formica-covered enclosure, "help me out here. Didn't you once say it takes a dirty mind to put out a clean paper? This thing is going to wind up as a joke in the back of the *Columbia Journalism Review.*"

"No way are you dragging me into this, Pete," said Frank. He opened a gurgling pneumatic tube and shoved in a copy-filled receptacle. A pair of these clear-plastic conveyors snaked up from the middle of the desk. With a clunk and an echoing whoosh, the cylinder zipped across the ceiling and disappeared through a glass wall into the operations center.

"Well, most of our readers are men," I said in an appeal to the entire desk crew. "You know, alpha males, sexist pigs—and a lot of them are probably chuckling at this two-faced headline." My reasoning was flawless, but I wasn't winning the argument.

"You *sniggering* little boy," Libby said.

The others put their heads back down, sniggering themselves, and resumed their line editing. Case lost.

Her rebuke stung, even more for being so unexpected. I certainly hadn't meant to insult her personally; I wasn't even talking to her. It kept nettling me. A day later, around three in the afternoon, I approached to apologize—for what, I wasn't exactly sure. The desk was standing down before the flood of stories at deadline. This was back in the old days, before the rise of online journalism, with its buffet of fact-free opinionating. Everyone still worked on paper copy, dead trees, making pencil edits signed as an aid for management's identification of the guilty. Enough errors and they fired you. Investors bet serious money based on what they read in the *Bulletin*. Mistakes were not tolerated.

The New York newsroom in that era was on Van Zandt Street, five stories above a large retail pharmacy. It was between the Trade Center towers and the downtown Brooks Brothers' branch. Incredibly, no exterior sign revealed that the largest-selling newspaper in America bustled with activity not far above a giant pharmacy filled with toothpaste, laxatives, and Ace bandages. This disregard for appearances carried through to the newsroom. The wide shabby expanse proclaimed the owning family's parsimony: duct tape repairs across the rips in the coffee-stained blue carpets, battered desks and filing cabinets overflowing with annual reports and filled-up notebooks, and the occasional mouse that skittered between refuges at night. A visiting journalist from Russia, who observed us for several months during this Glasnost era, had some suitable mockery for our outmoded operations. "You kopitalists," he declared, "are leaders in backwardness."

"May I have a word?" I asked Libby, straddling an office chair and putting my arms atop the swiveling back.

"Got some more sexist double entendre?" Her blue eyes smoldered. What was she so sore about?

"No," I said. "I just wanted to say I'm sorry that I offended you. As you pointed out, I'm not entirely grown up. Please excuse my thoughtlessness." It was the sort of surrender that had always gotten my father off my back. Strange how much emotional clout I gave to contempt, displaying the people pleaser's need for approval.

"Well-raised, aren't you?" she said. "Nice party manners."

"I'm simply trying to apologize for being sexist and insensitive," I said. "I hope you can forgive me." She remained mute and I started to rise with diminished dignity.

"Oh, sit down," Libby said, pulling me by the hand. She brought her face close. "*I* wrote that headline," she hissed. I drew back to apologize further, but she yanked me forward again. "Frank says the publisher is furious. One more 'boner' like that and they're going to let me go. The whole place is laughing at me."

Without thinking, I pressed her hand in sympathy. She yanked it away, banging the underside of the desk. "Ouch!"

Heads turned our way, but her fierce glower turned them right back around again. "Why should the publisher be mad at you?" I asked *sotto voce*. "Frank's the guy who cleared the headline, right?"

"Wrong." She dropped her head to expose a meandering part. Shafts of gold and sandy brown were mixed within her long blond hair. I wanted to touch it. "I was filling in for him on the slot that night," she said, contemplating the soiled carpet and her equally stained prospects. She glanced up. "It was my big chance."

"Oh, I'm so sorry." I was more aware than ever of the intensity of her eyes. They were a deep cobalt blue.

"I come from a tiny community in the Upper Peninsula of Michigan," Libby said, answering my unasked question. "As bizarre as it may sound, I've never heard that puerile expression before."

"I see," I said, making a mental note to look up "puerile." A whole new persona materialized: sensitive beauty from the sticks, on guard against ridicule and the unwanted sexual attentions of louts. No wonder she always wore that game face.

"I always thought the proper little-boy nomenclature for an erection was hard-on," she went on. "And, of course, I was under a brutal deadline."

"Yes, well, regardless of the, ah, usage, they wouldn't dare fire *you*," I said. "You're the best copy editor we've got. Anyway, everybody makes mistakes around here. Take me. I'm still getting grief for my million-billion blunder. Thanks to my careless typo, I reported a company with bigger earnings than the U.S. defense budget, and it somehow got through, remember?"

"You *are* gallant, aren't you?"

"Years from now you'll tell your grandchildren this story and laugh."

She appeared unconvinced.

"At holiday dinners on the Upper Peninsula," I suggested.

"Bonehead granny, huh?"

"Exactly." I grinned at her.

"I could use a good laugh right now."

"How about a drink after work? On me, as amends for being puerile, whatever that means. I can get you laughing. I *guarantee* it."

"'Childish,' and I'd much prefer a cup of tea," she said, maintaining her steely lookout. "You do realize that I'm not done here till ten o'clock, don't you? Is anything even open around here at that hour?"

"Let me worry about that. Meantime, I'll wait for you downstairs in the library. It'll give me a chance to, uh, bone up on my Standard & Poor's reports."

Libby's lips quivered and then the mask fell back in place. "You're not too stupid," she said. The phrase was the highest compliment *Bulletin* people gave each other. "I don't have to do much to edit your stories," she elaborated, "and Tom Dorsey thinks you're one of the best reporters we've got."

"High praise from a Pulitzer nominee, but vastly undeserved."

Tom Dorsey was the kind of reporter who lived to expose wrongdoers in the business world, people like Wall Street's infamous junk bond swindlers, whom he'd helped nail. By this time, he'd moved over to covering the National Computing Company, the high tech giant. He particularly enjoyed beating up its PR flacks over incomprehensible industry jargon. You could hear him shouting into his head set mic as he typed notes: "What the fuck does 'virtual memory' mean? Christ, you don't know either! What do they pay you for?" He was my best friend and a kind of role model, though I didn't have his instincts for the jugular and never would. His legendary rudeness made me uncomfortable. When I thought about it, I realized Tom's ego was the mirror of the executives' he covered. Or maybe his cynical attitude stemmed from his father, who'd been a New York detective.

Libby and I had tea together that night, sipping out of sky-blue paper cups trimmed with an ivory Greek key pattern. They were omnipresent in New York lunch counters back then. We sat on hard plastic seats in the empty PATH subway station beneath the Twin Towers. As promised, I made her laugh, though only politely, at a dreadful grammar joke. It involved a Harvard man telling a hick arriving on campus to never end a sentence with a preposition, so try it again. The punchline: "Can you tell me where the li-berry's at, asshole?"

"Is that your best material?"

"I can do armpit farts."

"No thanks. But tell me, why do you keep staring over my shoulder?"

I nodded toward a boy of maybe ten. Libby turned to see. "I'm worried about that kid over there. He looks like he's in trouble. It's eleven at night and he's all alone. I'm going to go talk to him."

Benny Glazer was actually twelve years old, but acted much younger. He informed us that he was waiting for his Aunt Sophie to pick him up. We took seats on either side of him. How long had he been sitting there?

"My train got in at six," he stammered. "What time is it now?"

"It's time to phone Aunt Sophie," I said. "Have you got her number?"

Benny fished a folded slip of paper out of his backpack. "I already tried calling but nobody answered. She said to wait here in Penn Station until she came, and not to go off with strangers."

Libby and I traded glances. "This isn't Penn Station, Benny. It's the World Trade Center. You must have gotten on the PATH subway somehow. How did that happen?"

The boy couldn't answer.

"Let's try that number," I said, leading them to a nearby pay phone. But I had no luck either. Benny appeared on the brink of tears.

"Not to worry," I said. "I'll stay with you until we can get ahold of your auntie, even if it takes all night." Libby couldn't help checking her watch. "You'd better make your train." I advised. "Like you said, the next one's not for an hour."

"You sure?"

"Absolutely. And I'm glad you don't hate me anymore."

"Hardly at all."

"Good. Hey, Benny, want to play tic tac toe while we wait?" I pulled a small reporter's notepad out of my jacket and sketched the game's grid. "Here, you go first."

"I'll be the Xs," he said, grasping my pen and selecting a box.

"Whoa, you stuck it right in the middle, you can go a lot ways from there."

"I know," he gloated.

Libby watched me let him win and seemed to make up her mind about something.

"What?"

"Wouldn't *you* like to know." She stood and touched the boy's shoulder. "You're in good hands, Benny. Goodnight, Pete."

"Goodnight." I watched her walk away with her bouncing strut.

"She's beautiful," said the boy. "Is she your girlfriend?"

"I wish. Where do you go to school, by the way?"

Benny's face brightened. "I go to the Deron School in Montclair. They're nice there."

CHAPTER TWO

'I think I'd like that'

Libby came in early the next day and dropped a note on my desk. "Meet me in the library," it said.

"So what happened to Benny?" she greeted me, once I got down there.

"Eventually, and I mean very eventually, I reached Aunt Sophie. She was frantic and had already called the police. As you probably guessed, Benny's a special education student. The next problem was how to get him home. She has cataracts and trouble with night vision, so she trusted me to bring him in a cab down to her place in the Village."

"That was nice of you."

"Yeah, I guess, but I wish it hadn't kept me up until one."

"You take on other people's problems, don't you? You tried to save Marcus Anderson's job last winter when he got in trouble."

"He was a good guy."

"You rewrote his pieces right on deadline. I saw you back there at his desk, flailing away with a rip stick and glue pot."

"He always buried the lede."

"But he got the axe anyway."

"They didn't give him time to develop."

"It's a nice trait, empathy."

"I'm not so sure. I think I'm really a sap, a soft touch," I said. "I give money to bums, too. My father tells me I'm a sucker."

"No you're not; you're simply kind—yet ashamed of it. You're hard to figure because you come off as standoffish."

"I'm shy."

"Yeah, right." She started to head toward the stairs, but then turned back. "Want to have lunch? I haven't got a thing to do for hours."

"Sure," I said, surprised. "And I know just the place."

I took her to a little take-out shop farther down Van Zandt Street—a dimly lit, narrow walk-in where the Greek owners hollered and gesticulated at each other, and only seemed to sell subs and pizzas.

"*Omorfi gineka,*" said one, no translation needed. The man's eyes bugged. "What can I get the beautiful young lady?"

She was taking her time studying the big plastic wall menu, with her back to him.

"Howzabout a pair of spinach calzones?" I suggested. Libby didn't respond. "Trust me, they're great. And we'll take them with legs, George."

"You got it, lucky man."

"Hold on there, George," she said, holding up a countermanding hand. "Make mine a grinder with meatballs and marinara."

We ate them sitting on a bench in City Hall Park, hot cheese dropping to the ground between our legs. Hesitant pigeons strutted back and forth on red legs to peck at our crumbs. We talked shop at first and then traded life stories. I was surprised that she was four years older than me. She'd gone to the University of

Michigan and the Missouri School of Journalism, like her mother, a pioneer woman in the 1940s world of Chicago newspapering. The original Elizabeth Lindquist had won a Pulitzer for her coverage of unemployed black defense workers, stranded in hordes in northern cities after the end of World War II. Libby was serious about her editing career and wanted to move up to the Page One Department.

"I already had you figured for an Ivy Leaguer," Libby said after I delivered a brief CV. "The whole candy-stripe shirt bit."

"I'll burn them."

I began to hang around the office late for our tea-fueled conversations at the PATH station. Waiting for her after work in the library, I could hear the little building creak like a wooden ship in pirate movies.

"So how were things up there on the Staten Island Ferry tonight, matey?" I asked Libby as she descended the threadbare stairs a couple of weeks after our initial conversation. "Frank keeping the crew sullen but not mutinous?"

"Arghh!" she said. "We're plotting bloody deeds. Grab a pneumatic tube and join the mutiny."

I got to know a person I never expected. I learned that she wasn't so much worried about what people thought of her as she was angry with committing errors. Unlike me, Libby had no need for approval. She didn't judge her insides by comparing them to others' outsides.

Starting out to impress someone I'd imagined—distant, judgmental, self-contained—I found I liked the real person. She heard me out patiently, had thoughtful answers, seemed to just enjoy being with me. I also could always make her laugh. The more boyishly I behaved, the very character flaw she'd accused me of, the more Libby enjoyed me.

One day, she winked at me across the newsroom and didn't seem to care if anybody noticed. Tom Dorsey, who witnessed this, told me I reacted with a "really dopey expression." He gave me a knowing look through his steel-rimmed glasses and said that he could tell me a few things about Ms. Lindquist from personal experience if I wanted to hear them.

I said I didn't.

The flirting stage ended the night she invited me to dinner in her walkup condo in Hoboken, perched high above the Hudson. Each landing of the four floors had a different smell: curry, mustiness, dirty diapers, and hers—lemon-scented Old English floor wax. I halted at the top, breathing heavily. "Yellow roses to match your hair," I panted, holding out a bouquet as the door swung back. She gave me a tolerant smile.

Libby was a good cook. She made lamb chops with mint sauce and asparagus with Hollandaise. Adorning the chops were little paper frills like tiny chef hats. She bustled around preparing things and asked me to lay out her mismatched flatware as she melted the butter and stirred eggs into the ochre-colored mixture. She handed me a glass of red wine. But even though I'd brought my favorite merlot, I didn't want alcohol in my system. I'd gone bashful. Worried that I'd blurt out some truly unforgivable boyish faux pas if my tongue was loosened, I had the same empty-chested feeling I had in grade-school speech class, when the dreaded Mrs. Simmons called on me to stand and recite.

I was twenty-eight years old and had never been in obsessive love before. I wanted to know everything about her, but was afraid of what she'd detect if she really got to know me.

"You're very taciturn tonight," Libby said, bringing over the plates of food as I swirled the maroon liquid in my glass. "No witticisms?"

"I want to propose a toast," I said, heart racing. I held up my glass. "Here's to Grantland and Ketcham, those wonderful people who brought us together."

"You're blushing," she marveled. "And here I thought you were such a slick operator." She held out her own glass and said: "Let me tell *you* something, buddyrolls. After Grantland and Ketcham came along, I was planning to stumble over some torn carpet into your lap." She put the glass to her lips and gave me a hard-to-describe look, something between challenge and entreaty.

"You're kidding."

"Didn't you ever wonder why I came in so early the next day?"

"You wanted to know what happened to Benny."

"Actually, I wanted to know more about you. I always liked your looks, but your sweetness was a revelation."

I wasn't myself after that. Incredulity fogged my mind through dinner and the sparse conversation that culminated with Libby leading me by the hand into the bedroom. Was this a dream? Our clothes came off and, arching her back, Libby moved her breasts across my chest. She peered into my eyes with a questioning smile. I smiled back, probably in a manner described as dopily. Demure and brazen at the same time, she reached down between my legs, but it was no go. I rolled toward her and buried my face in the hollow of her neck.

"What's the matter?" she grunted, freeing her head to look at me.

"It has something to do with Bernoulli's Law."

"Who?"

"Hydrodynamics and the theory of lift. Can we just hug?"

"Okay."

She circled her arms around my neck and I clung back. Kaleidoscopic globs of color flashed as I clenched my eyes in a fit of longing. I squeezed harder.

Libby's gasp brought me back. "I can't breathe," she complained.

"Uh, sorry about that."

"What was going on just then?"

Face flushed with embarrassment, I said, "I guess I was realizing something."

"And that was?"

"I'd rather not say."

"Perhaps you don't find me attractive?"

"God no, just the opposite. I wanted this to be perfect."

"You don't need to impress me in that way, you know."

"Yes I do, because I love you… Oh shit."

Libby exhaled a breathy laugh. "Well, you needn't be so upset about it."

"But we just met. You must think I'm a maniac." I pictured the next scene in this farce: my hasty departure.

"No I don't, not at all." Her eyes held a mischievous shine. "And I just thought of an appropriate headline for the wonderful thing that's happened tonight." She rocked her hand back and forth as if placing the words on shelves: "Lindquist—Avoids…" Her hand dropped to the next level. "Wendell—Boner."

I sat up. "Now wait just a damn minute!"

She guffawed. "Oh, come on now, it's alright. We can make love anytime—when you calm down and get over your performance anxiety. Can't you see the humor in this?"

For an instant I was black with hurt feelings. But as she shook me by the shoulders, kissed my cheeks and forehead, and tilted her head from side to side so she could catch and smile into my eyes, I let it go.

"Your headline is inaccurate," I said.

"How so?"

I pointed to my crotch. "No boner, which is interesting because I've *never* had that problem before. Maybe it's due to…"

"Would you please just stop nattering? It's okay, because I love you, too."

"You *do?*"

"Hey, where did *he* come from?"

Two days later, I asked Libby to marry me.

"I think I'd like that," she whispered.

"You sure? You sound uncertain."

"Don't push your luck, buddyrolls."

We made a pact to wait three months to make certain that the violence of our attraction wasn't infatuation. In the interim, we couldn't keep our hands off each other and assured ourselves that constant sex proved our love would last forever.

The small ceremony took place near her home in Michigan, with a reception in the basement of a timber-and-plaster-covered Lutheran church. The pastor had a bad comb-over. My father, the CEO of a global oil company, looked testy and bored. Resplendent in a bespoke tropical wool suit, he sipped the raspberry punch and engaged in a condescending conversation with Sven Lindquist, a building contractor. My stepmother Lucille didn't come. Father explained that she had to attend a dog show that weekend. He handed me a check for $5,000 and told me not to squander it. Once he was gone, I tore it up and dropped the pieces in a trash barrel among the paper plates and half-eaten pieces of wedding cake.

"Why couldn't you have at least endorsed it over to the church?" Libby asked, when I told her. "And what's your big beef with old Aubrey anyway, besides his being a stuffed shirt? You guys barely acknowledged each other all day. Don't you like him?"

"Some other time, okay? It's complicated. Let's just say our goodbyes and blow this pop stand. I'm looking forward to the honeymoon part of these proceedings."

CHAPTER THREE

Not Letting Go

That night I revealed to Libby that my mother died of alcohol poisoning. I hadn't meant to, but it followed my explanation of how South Sea natives catch monkeys.

"They drill a small hole in a wooden box and put a banana inside," I said. "Then they chain the box to a palm tree. The monkey can just barely slide his hand in, but can't get his fist out with the banana in it. He won't let go even when the natives arrive. He's too greedy."

Our one-night honeymoon—all we could swing—was at the Grand Hotel on Mackinac Island, a gargantuan wooden structure both historic and exorbitant. Our second-floor front room had its own small balcony. The French doors were open. Carriage lamps around the rolling lawns cast luminous parallelograms across the darkened walls. A screech owl, sounding like a monkey, was trilling from one of the large ornamental gingko trees bordering the wide Mackinac Straits.

Libby came up on an elbow in the post-coital snarl of sheets. "Do they eat them?" The relentless fact-checker had emerged.

"The bananas?"

"No dear heart, the monkeys. Do the natives eat the monkeys?"

I could see her picturing what I'd described. She leaned back on the pillow and put her hand behind her head, flattening a breast. We'd been making love for hours. The room had acquired the mixed aroma of jasmine perfume and mud flats. Hopelessly in love, I remained astonished by her beauty, locked in wonder over her cupid lips, thick brown eyebrows, unusual against her brilliant blue eyes, golden hair, and translucent Scandinavian skin. I couldn't get over my good fortune; I felt like giggling half the time, as if I'd gotten away with something. Yet I sensed an inexplicable sadness; this intensity couldn't possibly endure. I'd mess up for sure.

"Do they, Pete?"

"Do? Oh, I don't know. Maybe they sell them to zoos for medical research. How about another smooch there, hot lips?"

"It sounds like an urban legend. Where did you hear this?" I leaned forward to kiss her, but she pulled her head back. "Hold on a second. Did you just make this up?"

"I heard it in a sermon, a long time ago, haven't thought about it in years. Good old Reverend Elway made the analogy when he was preaching about letting go of possessions. You know: the parable of the rich young ruler? Jesus told him to sell all his possessions and give the money to the poor. But he turned away." I emitted a mirthless grunt. "It stuck in my mind because of how rich and grasping that congregation was."

"The Bible calls greed idolatry, but I didn't know your family went to church."

"We were Episcopalians for maybe six months."

Libby's eyes glazed over like someone staring into a fire. "That makes total sense. I can just see you guys: 'the frozen chosen.'"

"And we certainly qualified. In my father's house were many

mansions—if you count the pool cabana and the detached garage where he kept his car collection. But the interesting bit is I picked that church…sort of."

"I'm wide awake now, monkey face, so tell me this 'interesting' story."

"With pleasure." I assumed a basso profundo: "It was a dark and stormy night…"

"Pete!"

So I launched into it: My mother had been in an alcohol detox facility back when I was in grade school. I had to shift for myself until Dad came home at night from White Plains, where he was chief executive officer of Middle Atlantic Oil Company. Libby knew the bowdlerized version of my childhood—Despicable Dad, the corporate kahuna; Mental Mom, moribund in middle age. Instead of taking the school bus home, as I was supposed to, I'd walk down tony New Canaan's tree-lined South Avenue to a luncheonette named Ginger's.

"And you're about to tell me she used to tap dance with Fred, right?"

I informed Libby that Ginger was a *he*, Angelo Gingerella. He had curly dark hair that stuck up like he'd slept on his face. He was a benign, smiling man who let kids sit around his establishment nursing Cokes. To get there, I had to walk past Saint David's. One afternoon, the Reverend Timothy Elway fell into step beside me and that's how I had my introduction to God. Libby's doubtful expression told me she was anticipating lame humor.

"No, I'm not kidding. This really happened. He asked me where I was headed, and I got all self-conscious. All I could say was…" I imitated a young, timorous version of myself: "town."

"How old were you then?"

"Maybe Benny's age, or a little younger, ten or eleven."

As I told the story, I recalled Father Elway's patrician WASP face, reminiscent of New York Mayor John Lindsay, and how he gently probed. He wanted to know where I lived, which was way out past the country club on Smith Ridge.

"That's a long, long way, son. Why doesn't your mother drive you?"

"She's at Silver Hill," I'd confessed, like the artless boy that I was, and immediately suffered a searing pang of guilt. Silver Hill was a high-class mental hospital and sanitarium. Marilyn Monroe had dried out there once. Mother had warned me never to reveal her secrets, some of which were pretty obvious—like the fact she was always half blotto from nipping at her bottle of red phenobarbital.

"She sounds so sad," said Libby. "Growing up did you think all women were as troubled as your mother?"

"No, but I guess it made me avoid female attachments; I mean I never really got that close to any girl before I met you."

She tapped my nose with a forefinger and made a face of commiseration. "Lucky for you I came along; lucky for *me*, too."

The honor bar's compressor started up with a rattle. Rising from the king-size bed, I walked over, genitals sticky and bobbling, and extracted a beer. I pulled the tab with a pffft of pressurized gas and turned around, naked, to face my new bride—Ms. Elizabeth Tanya Lindquist, who had insisted on keeping her maiden name. ("That's my name, bub. You got a problem with that?") I held up the foaming can. "Want one?"

"Finish the church story."

I needed to lighten up. Honeymoon lugubriousness is a turn off. "The Rev must have contacted Dad," I said, "because all of a sudden we were attending that church. When Mom got out of the hospital, she came too. I even sang in the kids' choir, had this dippy red robe with a big white collar. Couldn't read music, but there I was, singing like a bird. So that's how the story ends…on a high note."

"But why did your folks stop going if you were such a chirping choirboy?"

"My voice dropped with puberty?"

"Look me in the eye, Pete."

"I suppose I ought to mention that was right when my Old Man divorced Mom." I hesitated. "She died a year later in Chicago."

"Of what?"

"Alcohol and pills, but the coroner ruled out suicide. There was no note."

Libby gave me an incredulous stare. "How come you never mentioned *that* little detail before?"

"I was going to get around to it. Does it matter? I mean it was decades ago."

"How did your father deal with the news?"

I rubbed my temple at the resurgence of an ancient despair. "He got my uncle Janush to take care of the funeral arrangements out there."

"Janush?"

"Yeah, I'm half Polack, didn't I tell you that? Dad flew in from some big deal in Saudi Arabia to speak at the service. As I recall, he said she died of a disease that he'd 'failed to help her enough with.'"

"That was quite an admission wasn't it?"

"I think he was reading the audience. Mother's relatives were furious."

"What did he say to you on the way home?"

"Nothing. He headed back to the Mideast. I flew home by myself. We never talked about it later, can you imagine?"

"Yes, it's called denial. And you never went to church afterward?"

"I tried once or twice when I was older, but it always reminded me of being in calculus class, hoping no one would call on me. Everyone knew the right responses, and I just mumbled along."

"We need to talk more about this," she said, and then erupted into one of her jaw-dislocating yawns. After lovemaking, sleep usually overcame her as if conked by a mallet. She snapped her mouth shut.

"Nothing more to discuss—especially on our 'abba, dabba honeymoon.'"

"Oh yes there is, buddyrolls, like how you always joke away your feelings."

"I always crack jokes when I'm deliriously happy. Banana fanna fo fanna."

"But right now I'm too exhausted." She rolled on her side. "Bananas," she murmured, "sheesh, *you're* the one who's bananas. Oh, and don't drink any more tonight. We need to get up early tomorrow, long trip ahead of us: Home to Hoboken, and back to work at the good old *Wall Street Bulletin*. Tom says he needs your help; he's after another plutocrat."

"It's not all *that* good a place. You can't make any money there."

"Meaning?"

"I'm thinking about shoving off."

"Where to? One of the business magazines?"

"Remember Jim Daley? He's running a whole communications shop at Xerox now, makes pots of dough. Maybe something like that."

"Become a perfumed courtier, you mean?" She fluffed her pillow. "Over my dead body. Anyway, you're going to inherit 'pots of dough' from Aubrey. Don't you realize that's what helps make you a good journalist—you can't be bought?"

"Is that why you married me?"

Libby rolled on her side and mumbled something I couldn't make out. Its tone sounded derisive. Almost immediately she began to breathe heavily.

A sighing breeze came through the open doors, stirring the sheer white drapes. The owl made another chimpy chirrup. I pulled the covers up over Libby's shoulder and kissed her tangled hair. Wandering out on the balcony with another beer, I gazed out at the dark moving waters without seeing. I wasn't going to inherit squat.

CHAPTER FOUR

Homecoming

New Canaan, Connecticut, is one of the wealthiest towns in America. Once an obscure nineteenth century shoe-making center that supplied footwear to the Union army, it has a largely unheralded cultural history. Maxwell Perkins, who was Hemingway and Fitzgerald's editor, lived on Park Street, a few strides from the wooden gothic train station. From there, he commuted to Scribner's in New York, where he also worked with Thomas Wolfe and later James Jones. In the early 1900s, an artists' colony coalesced around sculptor Solon Borglum, brother of Mount Rushmore's creator, and formed the Silvermine Art Guild. During the 1940s and early fifties, when land was still inexpensive, young modernist architects like Phillip Johnson, Eliot Noyes, and other Bauhaus-influenced experimenters put up minuscule flat-topped homes using the new technologies of veneered plywood and massive windows. Many have been demolished. But Johnson's Glass House—which became a museum—and a seven-bedroom Frank Lloyd Wright home built in 1955 both remain.

By the 1990s the town had become the embodiment of the excesses of hedge fund managers and executive grandees from such nearby world headquarters as Credit Suisse, Xerox, the National Computer Company, and Middle Atlantic Oil Corporation, where my father ruled. Spec builders were tearing down ranch houses and split-levels, filling entire one-acre lots with multi-gabled McMansions, and making millions.

Are the rich really different from other people? I don't know, but nobody likes them. I tell strangers that I hail "from downstate, near Stamford," a small nearby industrial city, to avoid the sharp reappraising glances the truth always elicits. I suppose this represents a kind of reverse-reverse snobbery, or maybe some kind of guilt, though I never thought of myself as really well off. Sure, Father had bucks, but he managed Mom's household budget—our whole lives—from the perspective of scarcity. It was a legacy, I presumed, of his own father's financial devastation during the Great Depression. At the Country Club he'd order the least-expensive item on the menu for me. "He doesn't want that," he once countermanded, when I asked a waiter in a white mess jacket for Lobster Newberg. I got the Yankee Pot Roast. Nor, after the age of sixteen, did I receive an allowance. "No student princes in my house," he grumbled.

I went to work in a rival Shell station, just to jerk his chain. The owner, Ed Kerrigan, taught me how to change oil and told stories of being a nineteen-year-old soldier in the occupation forces in Japan. When I made my first mistake, emptying a crankcase of oil onto the concrete floor because of a loose gasket, Ed got up on his tiptoes, waved his fingers near his ears, and called me a "Yokohama head." Then he grinned, spread oil-absorbent granules, and showed me how to install an oil filter the right way. Ed was the best boss I ever had.

"Peter," the Old Man observed when more than once during

this period the police brought me home drunk, "you have all the traits of a leader, except the desire to be one. There's something fundamentally lacking in you." I couldn't have agreed more. The missing ingredient was menace.

He was equally disenchanted with my mother—a blond former beauty whom he'd met when they were high school nobodies in an immigrant section of Chicago—and who was embarrassed that she'd never gone to college. Her spells of depression affected me with painful anxiety. What was wrong with her? Father's explanation was that she was neurasthenic. I told him I didn't understand. "Nuts," he elucidated. She was indeed listless and despairing, spending a lot of time in her bedroom with the shades drawn, a kind of Miss Havisham of marital disappointment in the hulking shingle house she detested. I learned to avoid her because I felt obliged to defend my father. I later learned that's psychologically called "triangulation."

Example: After he left a prioritized list of ways I needed to improve on the kitchen table, she crumpled the paper and said, "What kind of man writes a memo to his son about his behavior?" Taking his side, I reminded her that he was a busy executive. "Is he *that* busy?" She tossed the ball of paper on the fancy slate floor.

One time when I was all of nine years old, I called the police when I couldn't awaken her when I got home from school. She was flat on her back in the kitchen. Paramedics arrived to pump her stomach. They must have summoned her psychiatrist, Dr. Broom. He found me walking aimlessly in the back yard. I suppose I saved her life.

"This is not your fault," the doctor told me. It took me a long time to figure out what he meant—that children soak up free-floating responsibility. I felt that her misery was entirely my fault. Poor Mother, the timid daughter of Polish immigrants who, lacking emotional boundaries, told me about my father's infidelities and problems with premature ejaculation; poor me, caught in an almost incestuous role as her auxiliary husband and consoler.

Early on I stopped trying to meet the expectations of my father, whose management training taught him that withholding praise increases employees' performance, if not a son's. All I wanted was to escape. Yet he retained one unbroken grip on my ambitions: I coveted his lifestyle and had adopted his basis for happiness—acquire more. Maybe this was the boomerang effect of privilege, of growing up owning both a tuxedo and white dinner jacket, going to dancing classes and debutante balls, and thinking that assured wealth was my destiny, too. Thanks to the National Computing Company, I came home, though not to the best neighborhood.

I was thirty years old when I took a call in the tattered news room from the NCC recruiter. The behemoth was growing rapidly, the headhunter explained. Would I be interested in starting up a magazine for a new division that handled personal computer sales? The job provided regular hours and would treble my pay.

As it turned out, Libby was becoming persuadable to relocating. the *Bulletin* was a rough place, backbiting, and profligate with talent. Despite her skills, she never moved up and, disenchanted, left to join a women's magazine and then became a free-lancer. I'd also had enough. More and more, editors punched up my stories to be humiliating to their subjects. I wasn't even consulted, and yet they carried my byline. Meantime, we tried for children as Libby's biological clock moved onward toward her thirty-fifth birthday.

"Will we have to move?" Libby asked when I told her.

"No, or at least not yet. We may if I'm successful."

And so I commuted from Hoboken to White Plains for nearly a year until Libby got pregnant. Then a summons came from corporate headquarters in Westminster to work on a monumental product announcement about a new generation of personal computers. That's when my new manager entered my life, the odious Freddy Pritchard, who considered public relations his life's work. It's also when I began a campaign to return to where I'd been a boy of promise—New Canaan's Silvermine section, named after a mine that never yielded ore. I didn't see the irony in wanting my child to have the same advantages I had.

We found a tiny nineteenth-century cottage, hung along the bank of the shallow Silvermine River, where Norwalk, New Canaan, and Wilton converge. The front door, with its lopsided horseshoe knocker, was just four steps from the winding roadway. Anchoring the house, the dirt-floored cellar was toed into the bank. The ancient pink-brick walls down there had timbered cubbies, part of their original function as a root cellar, and were handy for storing wine. An about-face yielded a view through warped French doors to the rocky stream. Charm oozed from every exposed chestnut post, girt, and beam. Yet the jerrybuilt updates were atrocious; it was a peeling, chopped-up disaster, but I had to have it.

Libby resisted leaving Hoboken, where we owned our condo free and clear. She only relented after seeing the historic and scenic neighborhood—with its pretty country tavern and noted art school—and in grudging agreement that the vaunted local education system would be good for "Whosits" growing in her womb.

"This means something intangible to you," she said, outside the lawyer's office before the closing, "evidence that you've made it, doesn't it?" We were about to take on a $200,000 variable rate mortgage. I didn't say anything. "You know we can't afford this. What happens when the interest rates rise next year? Once I stop free-lancing we'll have to live on your salary. Is that guaranteed to go up, too?"

By that time I'd received a modest raise at NCC and had finished the product announcement with Freddy. I tried to assuage her worries. "I'm bound to keep moving up, nobody can write there."

"I'm not so sure they want you to write well."

"What's that supposed to mean?"

"Some of those puff pieces in your house organ are cringeworthy. I mean, how about that hard-hitting report on how to file accurate expense reports?"

"Well, employees *do* get reimbursed faster if they do it right, and the company saves money. Nothing wrong with that."

"From a guy who used to expose corporate shenanigans?" she scoffed. "You're writing propaganda."

"I'm not doing anything dishonest."

"You're being dishonest to yourself."

Because she loved me, we moved in and I started stripping the tiny 1940s flower print in the second bedroom to make a nursery. Scraping down through strata of wallpaper, my arms grew sticky with dissolved paste. A preacher's cabinet emerged like a time capsule from above a fireplace. Its empty interior still had the odor of the pine boards it was made from. According to the custom of the time, it was where alcohol was kept to entertain a visiting parson in what had started out as a Connecticut theocracy of Puritan Congregationalists.

Working side by side with me over the weeks of her pregnancy, Libby warmed to the house with its curling brown shakes, but never stopped disliking New Canaan's upper-class uniformity, its tasteful ostentation, and its casual Republican assumption of deserved superiority. ("I refuse to wear Lilly Pulitzer to fit in with the Junior Leaguers in 'Nouveau Canaan,'" she made it clear.) She gravitated toward Norwalk, another nearby fading manufacturing city, where she volunteered at an English-as-second-language program for children. She never understood my attachment for where I grew up.

Because the Silvermine section of Connecticut encompasses portions of three towns and lacks distinct borders, people sometimes joke that it's a state of mind. Delusional or not, it always represented the epicenter of my being. I know that sounds overwrought, but after any extended absence my chest pumps full of air when I get back. Everybody has to be from somewhere and this was it for me. I never got tired of it.

While contractors refurbished his Smith Ridge showplace in the 1960s, my father rented in Silvermine's outer edges. In the riverbed above the upper dam I'd watched sunfish excavate nests with their tails in the sandy mud. They looked like rocket ships undulating above moon craters. Maybe that's the pull of childhood places: they mark where imagination combined with wonder.

Twenty-five years later, I scanned the shallow waters but didn't see any fish. I'd just gathered orange daylilies for Libby near the gentle splashing of the mossy spillway. I had to climb a chain-link fence to do it. It was a flawless Sunday afternoon, the sky a limitless pale blue dome.

"For my lady love," I said, presenting them.

She held them in both hands under her chin and posed like a bride. "For a second I thought you were going to fall into the river, buddyrolls."

Later she pressed them in a copy of *The Age of Innocence*, a gift from her mother, who wrote on the flyleaf that Edith Wharton was the first woman to win a Pulitzer Prize. They're still there, like carrot-hued crepe paper.

Holding hands, we ascended the half-mile to Forge Lane and the former workplace of Clifton Meek, a gray-haired Hephaestus who operated the Silvermine Forge. He'd started as a cartoonist, like many of the artists drawn to Silvermine at the turn of the twentieth century, and later turned to ironmongery. My father ordered exquisite carriage lights from him, works of art; the one over our garage had wide-scrolling copper volutes.

Libby's expression melded affection and concern as I related this.

As we moved slowly on, I told her how on one visit Mr. Meek had plucked a sepia photograph off a blackened wall. It showed himself and a slender man with dark slicked-back hair. Mr. Meek explained that the young Walt Disney in the old photo had just purchased the rights to his Johnny Mouse cartoon character. With his low widow's-peaked hairline, Walt bore a strong resemblance to Mickey.

The forge, now a residence, appeared embalmed with fresh paint and crisp additions. Its owner, dressed in madras shorts and a Yale Athletic Department T-shirt, was outside gardening. He ambled over as I pointed at his house. From the woods in Wilton came the pop-pop of roofers' guns. Standing under a mammoth white oak, the man shook his head and said he'd never heard of Johnny Mouse. "All I know," he added, "is that some old coot made lamps here."

"Could you have misremembered that?" Libby asked as we left. With a ponderous swing of her leg, enlarged by water retention, she kicked a bright green acorn that skidded and spun in a looping curve.

"Maybe his name was Steve Mouse."

"Just the fact-checker coming out, I guess."

Picking up her acorn, I broke off the tip. "Let's head back," I said, "you're tired, and a little cranky."

On the way home, moving her legs with difficulty, she asked about a large 1930s Colonial reproduction on a hill across from the shallow sunfish pond. She pointed it out with her drooping lilies. "So what's the significance of that impressive mansion?"

"That was the home of Vance Packard, the author of *The Status Seekers*," I said. "He was a critic of consumerism and pretty famous. His basic argument was that symbols of success had become more important than real achievement."

"Status symbols? Wasn't that a little paradoxical from a guy who lived in this elite burg? What was his alternative? Certainly not to go into debt to live here."

I whipped the acorn sidearm as far as I could into the woods.

"You angry?"

"Who me? Not one bit."

"I don't mean to hurt your feelings, buddyrolls. But I worry that you never got your boyhood out of your system. I can show you my childhood haunts too, you know: our girls' club tree fort, the spot where I found a note in a bottle in the sands of Lake Michigan, Sven's historic horseshoe pit. Do you realize you live in the same make-believe town as your odious father, and have even begun to dress like him?"

"So what was in the bottle?" I asked, imagining her as a platinum-haired girl reaching down to pick it up.

She had to think. "Let's see, two soggy lollypops and a child's note asking whoever found the bottle to report its location and write something about themselves, then throw it back in the lake, which I did."

"So conceivably it could still be floating or even have found its way down the Mississippi. Think of the stories it could tell, the Mark Twain of bottles. Maybe I could make up tales about its adventures on the river for Whosits. It bonks a bad guy on the head. It saves a castaway. It's how Steve Mouse gets to the Mardi Gras to meet his Uncle Antoine, the trumpet-playing rat. Call them 'Uncorked Corkers,' whaddya think?"

"What I think is that you're going to make a wonderful father."

"Why do you say that?"

"Because you're just a big kid."

CHAPTER FIVE

Smart PR People Don't Lie

The whole truth about corporate reputations is that veracity moves along a sliding indicator, like twisting an old radio dial. Gradations, interference, and distortions affect fidelity. That was the lesson of Jason Dinsmore's phone summons a few days after Libby and I strolled through Silvermine.

"Not interrupting any kind of emergency down there on the first floor, am I?" asked NCC's vice president of communications.

His gravelly timbre was unmistakable. Penetrating but never loud, it ranged from rumbling mirth through honeyed persuasion to whispering ire. He never bothered with salutations.

"Not at all, Jason."

"Frederick tells me you're our resident expert on the *Wall Street Bulletin*. Do you know the reporter Tom Dorsey?"

"Tom was my best friend there."

"What's his deadline for filing copy?"

"He has rolling deadlines. The first is at four o'clock, in about two hours. Re-plates can go as late as nine." None of this was secret, but I felt uneasy.

"If you're not too busy, can you come up to my office, please? I need to kick something around with you." The polite request was a command.

Dinsmore snapped me a salute when I entered his cavernous office minutes later. "Ah, the cavalry," he said. He motioned for me to sit in front of his desk beside Freddy Pritchard, who'd been promoted as his assistant.

"Here's what we're up against." He leaned back in his big leather chair and adjusted a French cuff. "The engineers in Tampa have discovered a faulty switch on one of our specialized RISC PCs. It can give users a pretty nasty shock. A dozen instances were reported, but nothing serious, that right, Frederick?"

"Correct," said Freddy. "No guys staggering around with smoking hair, though one or two were checked out at hospitals and released." He turned to me. "Do we need to get you up to speed on RISC?"

"Reduced instruction set computing," I said. "They're CAD/CAM minicomputers used in factories, warehouses, and engineering shops."

"Bingo," said Dinsmore. "The deal is that we're mailing every user a plastic safety cover with instructions on how to screw it on, and an explanation that this is to prevent what amounts to a rare hazard. Our big question right now is how to finesse this with the mighty *Wall Street Bulletin*. We're putting out a short release, but how do we prevent sounding like we're peddling exploding computers?"

"Exactly," Freddy agreed. "We don't want any headlines reading, 'Shocking Truth about NCC's Booby-trapped PC.' We can never trust that idiot Dorsey not to blow things out of proportion."

"Any suggestions?" Dinsmore asked.

Up until then, I'd been a press release writer, laboring in

obscurity, talking to trade publications about technical topics, like "speeds and feeds." Of course, the truth in flackdom is that reporters aren't *supposed* to be trustworthy, especially with the powerful people and companies they cover. That's the whole idea. But I couldn't say that. A knot grew in my stomach.

"We're all ears," Freddy prodded.

"Are we recalling these boxes?"

Dinsmore's response was equivocal: "Users can get new ones if they ask, but we're not socializing that widely."

"It'll be bad if he finds *that* out," I said.

"Yes, we already understand that," said Freddy. "The issue is how do we fence the whole thing? You know the guy, what's your advice?"

"It's not to try to pull one over on him," I said.

"Naturally," Dinsmore assured me, "smart PR people don't lie. We just don't want to give away anything we don't have to. What else?"

I felt a little better hearing this, and began to improvise amid warring loyalties. The bottom line was that NCC paid my salary. I owed my allegiance to these guys. "So if this really is not such a big deal, you might call Tom right on deadline. He'll be distracted and won't be able to call other sources. Tell him the version you told me, but assure him there's no danger of serious injury. Be up front about shocked users, if he asks, though."

"Anything more?" asked Dinsmore.

"Give him an idea of the number of units we're talking about."

"Only around a hundred," Freddy said. "An outside vendor screwed up."

"I'd avoid saying that. It leads to questions about whether they supply components for our other products."

"Good point."

"Okay," said Dinsmore, "We'll give it a whirl," he checked his watch, "in approximately an hour and a half."

At four o'clock, Dinsmore called us back in and activated the speaker phone. Tom didn't pick up for several rings. Dinsmore chewed his lip. "These conversations always feel like somebody tossed a live grenade through the door," he muttered. Freddy sat hunched forward.

"Dorsey," answered Tom in a harassed tone.

Dinsmore, his deep resonant voice warm and sincere, launched into a statesmanlike shtick: Broadcasting this warning was NCC's corporate responsibility. We've notified each user by registered letter. Only a few users have been affected. But we don't want to leave any stone unturned. That's not the NCC way. I listened in, saying nothing. Tom never knew I was there.

"Anybody get zapped?" Tom asked. The phone connection was bad. He sounded like he was holding his nose in an echo chamber.

"None that I'm personally aware of."

We could hear the muffled chatter of the newsroom on deadline: Somebody shouting, "Chicopee needs the last take of that earnings piece, Tom, pronto."

"Coming right up, Frankie, baby." Tom must have put the receiver to his chest but we could still hear him. "Let me get rid of this shit head."

Dinsmore raised his eyebrows in delight at this unintentional candor.

"Back to you, Jason: It's not worth a story; haven't got time."

Dinsmore displayed cigarette-stained teeth in a wide grin. "Okay, Tom."

"We'll run a squib on the ticker tonight. That should cover it."

"Whatever you think best, and—"

The dial tone buzzed.

Dinsmore tapped the console's button, leaned over the desk and gave us each high fives. In PR terms, it had been a masterful performance. He hadn't lied, exactly. Rather, he'd tuned the factual bandwidth dial to just shy of honesty. Strictly speaking, Dinsmore had not, himself, met any victims. Nor, for that matter, had anybody been seriously hurt. A dozen, arguably, could be characterized as a few. His immense relief was palpable. But would this hair-splitting mendacity come back to bite him? Probably not. Nevertheless, I noticed Jason's palm was damp.

My own reaction bounced between elation and shame.

CHAPTER SIX

Playing on Different Teams

"Tom Dorsey called while you were in the shower." Libby's voice carried from the kitchen into the bedroom. "I invited him for dinner tonight."

"All the way up from New York?" I was toweling my head after a post-jog shower and felt uneasy at this news. Dinsmore's artful dodging had been only a few days before.

"The *Bulletin* sent him up to talk with NCC's CEO and your great new friend Jason Dimwit. Help me straighten up this mess in the living room, will you? And throw your running shoes out on the porch." She held her nose. "They're extremely odoriferous."

"It's *Dinsmore*, and he's not my friend." I levered up a sticking sash and jettisoned my sneakers.

"Tom's writing a company profile on NCC and told me he's planning to really put it to you guys."

"Jeez, I hope I don't get dragged into this one, too."

"*This* one?"

"But why should I? I'm just a peon in the bowels of Westminster."

"What are you babbling about?"

"Oh, Dinsmore finessed something with Tom last week. I

kind of gave him some advice."

"What did he finesse?"

"It was a kind of an eensy weensy product recall, though it had—how do I put it?—a certain shocking element to it."

"Please explain that sly grin."

I gave Libby the CliffsNotes version. "So, no harm was done, really. I mean, are we supposed to blow out of proportion every minuscule danger with our equipment, even after we've fixed the problem?"

"Yes you are."

"Why?"

"Because it's the right thing to do and you know that."

"The people who needed to know found out, didn't they? We weren't hiding anything from our customers." My self-justification felt flimsy.

"What about future customers?"

"What about them? Everything's fixed."

"You're catching on fast, aren't you? Anyway, let's not litigate your tale of misdirection right this instant. I told Tom I'd have you waiting for him at the 123 Parkway exit, and you'd better get out there. Johnny Mouse's birthplace is nearly impossible to locate."

"To keep everything as factual as you suggest, maybe we should call this the alleged birthplace of a forgotten imaginary mouse. Tom would appreciate that. Also, please don't mention what I just told you. We're on different teams these days."

"Maybe I will and maybe I won't. But I do want to talk to him about some wonderful news: Tom thinks there'll be an opening for me on the new Second Front they're planning to start publishing down there—and he should know. He's gaining a lot of influence, even being mentioned for bureau chief out in my old stomping grounds in Detroit."

"Who's mentioning this besides Tom?"

"It's a whole new section of the paper devoted to good writing, the kind of stories that pull readers in by the nose hairs, as they say. They'll need editors, good ones."

"But the *Bulletin* doesn't rehire traitors."

"Unlike you, I didn't surrender to the dark side. As far as they're concerned, I just left to join a woman's mag and have a baby."

I touched her taut belly. "So who'll raise this little guy? Are you forgetting about him?"

"*Her.* And Tom said he'll start sending me free-lance work until I can go back full time. How's that sound?"

"Sounds like you've already made up your mind."

The thought of Tom reentering Libby's life didn't appeal at all. In an early confidence I wish she'd kept to herself, Libby told me she'd had a relationship with Tom that had been "just physical" and long over before we met. She explained that she wanted me to know that from her, not some gossiper. How do you respond to that? I'd mimicked maturity, saying I'd married her for our future together, that the past was none of my business. But jealousy festered like a canker sore.

"You'd better get moving," she said. "Oh, and pick up some wine while you're at it. Better yet, make it three bottles, the way you guys drink."

"You're looking at a changed man, my dear. Now that you're pregnant, I'm swearing off."

"Get going, will you?"

—

Tom stepped into the cramped entryway and swiveled his head around. "What a dump!" he snorted. "They pay you all that money and *this* is all you could buy?"

"You have to use your imagination," I said.

"Yeah, Pete's loaded with imagination," said Libby. "Get him to tell you about his idea for bedtime stories in a bottle."

"Some other time," I said.

Dinner over, Tom was growing vociferous. The lenses of his wire-rim glasses shone under the bare bulb in the torn-apart dining area. It was stiflingly hot, even though I'd opened all the windows. Cheeks flushed, he was a little drunk, too. We'd been debating the imminent collapse of NCC, the world's largest and most profitable technology company. The idea seemed preposterous on the face of it. Libby, who'd prepared the same lamb chops she'd made for me on that first night at her apartment, had been abstemious on account of Whosits. She sat like an uncomfortable Buddha, chair pushed back from the table, the empty dessert plates un-cleared. She was nodding and following every word with an almost proprietary smile.

"You want any of this?" asked Tom, tipping the California Merlot toward me.

"No, you kill it," I said.

"You're turning into a loathsome teetotaler, a disgrace to the news profession." He upended the bottle into his glass. "So, my analysis is that you guys will definitely go out of business. And before that, your CEO will lose his job. The latter might take less than six months."

"Horsepuckey, and the word is 'fewer' months not 'less.'"

"I couldn't care fewer about the right word," he countered, "all

I'm saying is that… Oh, who cares about all that?" He rubbed his hand over his face. "Let's talk about something more important. What am I going to do about you, Pete?"

"What do you mean? You don't have to do anything."

"Look, I understand why you took this gig. I get it. You wanted a good home for Libby and the kid, you wanted to be home at night to tell bedtime stories. But this bucolic love nest on the river is a dangerous illusion. You've gone from being a reporter at the center of a news operation—essentially the product—to way out on the periphery. You're like being the best pastry chef in the Marine Corps. There's no security in corporate America anymore. In the old days, NCC guaranteed lifetime employment. But they won't be able to soon. Take it from me, when the shit hits the fan you're going to be one of the first to get the heave-ho."

"So what do you suggest?"

"Why not come back, the both of you?"

"That's impossible. I heard you've got a job offer lined up for Libby, but I'm persona non grata."

"Not necessarily. I didn't mention this to Libby, but the *Bulletin* is launching a pub about personnel and executive recruiting, supported by executive-search ads. Why not try for that? You could interview headhunters and businessmen about hiring, retention, and succession issues. I could put in a good word with Deke Malloy on your behalf. He was always a big fan of yours."

"What's it pay?"

"Same as before, union scale. You won't get filthy rich, but isn't honest work what you really yearn for?"

"What I really yearn for is to get filthy rich enough to afford this 'dump,'" I said.

CHAPTER SEVEN

Googolplex Times the Universe

"Pete, we need to talk."

I'd just gotten home from work. Libby sat upright on the wobbly camelback couch, hands atop her knees. Her expression—scared, determined, angry—signaled coming fireworks. I threw my suit jacket on a chair and bent to kiss her, but she drew her head away.

"So what's the topic?"

"We're headed for a divorce," she announced, scrutinizing my face for a reaction.

"What brought that on? What did I do now?"

"Not do, it's who you've *become*."

She pulled me down beside her to get my full attention, which she already had in spades. Seeing me through Tom's eyes, Libby explained, she'd been shocked by how I'd changed (a pause as she gathered her nerve), how I'd become a yes man. How I'd begun to spout idiotic NCC jargon (another pause to make a disgusted face): "crisp staff work, boil the ocean." What did these terms mean? It was like I'd become possessed by the devil. "Sometimes," she said, "I feel like yelling, 'Pete come out!'"

"Well, 'boil the ocean' means uselessly throwing lots of people and money at problems…"

"You're turning your back on everything you stood for. You worked so hard to get to the *Bulletin*, paid your dues at all those no-name dailies, and then endured the hard grinding years at UPI."

"They were grinding, alright. We used to say 'you can't spell stupid without UPI,'"

"Oh stop that, would you? How'd you get to be this liar for hire? I'm ashamed of you. Why aren't you like Tom?"

I'd had nearly enough now, was feeling that hollow prelude in my chest to a forbidden outburst. It must be nice to let it all go, to shout and stomp and carry on. But I'd never learned how to argue honestly. My father employed malevolent silence. Mother screamed and threw dishes.

"Can you honestly say Tom is writing about truth and beauty? A lot of his stuff feels mean."

"You disgust me," she said.

The little living room was very still. A shaft of floating dust particles slanted from the window to the chestnut floor. Libby waited. I exhaled slowly. "Okay," I said, "you want a divorce, you got it. Wouldn't want to disgust you, of all people."

"Aren't you going to fight for our marriage?"

"Why bother? You just said I'm disgusting because I don't want to cover assholes like my father anymore."

"Your career wasn't all covering assholes. Remember that article you wrote about faulty truck tire rims killing mechanics?"

"Yeah, so?"

"You researched that over months, sold it to the Page One Department. That's when I first noticed you. That story saved lives, helped families win law suits. You won an award."

"But no bonus check."

"Tom says…"

"Fuck Tom."

"Pete?"

"Go fuck him like you used to." I was breathing hard now.

My side of the couch fell with a clunk as Libby stood and scurried on swishing legs for the bedroom. I kicked myself mentally. Way to go, Peter, object lesson in the pitfalls of venting. How was this going to end? I heard nothing from her for hours. Finally, I sneaked into the darkened chamber and lay on my stomach at the far edge of the bed, so as not to wake her.

"Pete? Can I say just one more thing?"

I jumped at her voice. "Let me say it first," I said, rolling over. "I'm very, very sorry. As you know, I'm still that sniggering little boy you pegged me for."

"Oh, Pete, I was trying to help; I'm so worried about you. You're really such a fine person."

"If I am, it's because you make me that way."

She threw her arm over my shoulder, kissed me, and breathed warm air into my ear: "You're a goofball, you know that?"

"As they say at NCC, 'I non-concur.'"

"You trying to provoke me?"

"I promise we'll hash this out when I get back from California, okay? I'll even take Tom's advice and talk to Deke. Get out my kneepads to beg on his office floor. But if he tells me to take a hike, would you be proud of me if I wound up on the Obit Desk at *The Podunk Bugle* and we starved?"

"Of course I would. I'm proud of you right now, but call Tom—and then call me. I also may have some exciting news about Whozits when you get back. Actually, you can drive me to the obstetrician's office if you return in time, and we can find out together. Won't that be exciting? It's Thursday afternoon at two. Think you can make it?"

"You bet. My red-eye gets in at eleven, and I'll come straight here."

"Be there or be square."

"With bells on. One vital issue remains, though: tell me I'm a lot better looking than Tom."

"Way better."

Libby's VW Rabbit was gone when I got home. It was half past three. Missing her doctor's appointment wasn't going to help me make up with her. But I'd stopped off at a favorite seafood shack in Norwalk for a quick bite. Two bags of airplane peanuts were all I had in my stomach when I landed. Gobbling down fish and chips at the bar, I'd gotten into a conversation with a sun-wrinkled lobsterman, who related a tale of lobsters migrating to Maine's colder waters, dwindling catches, and onerous state regulations. The reporter in me kicked in. Had he done this his whole life? Yeah, he answered, his father had been a lobsterman too. It had once been a great living. Way back, his grandfather had dragged Norwalk Harbor for its once plentiful oysters. But pollution and overfishing had wiped them out. One beer had led to another and then another and yet one more. With the sunlight glittering on the Norwalk River as we spoke, I told him I kind of envied him. His rugged outdoor calling seemed honest and worthwhile. He offered to sell me his boat, cheap.

Home at last, buckets and tools littered the rosin paper-covered floors where I'd laid them down. I was half buzzed and feeling conscious-stricken. Dropping my canvas travel bag, I was putting on a pot of coffee when the horseshoe knocker banged. Its loud whack indicated that Libby was extremely pissed, but why hadn't she walked right in and bawled me out?

I swung the door open to reveal Ritaldo DeMarco, a New Canaan cop and former football teammate. We'd been drinking buddies in high school, or at least close enough to share personal insults. As we'd sat in the dim taproom of the Three Pines in those distant days, he liked to grab me by the back of the neck, shake my head, and tell me with spittle flying what a great fucking guy I was—even if I was a rich kid. I'd played tennis with him several times since I'd been back, and we'd been talking about sharing dinner with our wives.

"Hey Ritzy baby," I greeted him. "Where's Gail? Is tonight the night we're all going out to the Peking Palace?"

"Pete, I need to…"

"Know what you call veal in Chinese?"

"Listen, Pete…"

"Young cow. Libby hates that joke, thinks its racist. Hey, why the long face, buddy?"

A state trooper stepped into view. The Statie wore a gray Stetson, which he removed by lifting it from the back. Its ornamental gold-embroidered acorns tapped against the brim as he brought the hat down to his chest.

"Mr. Wendell?" he asked.

"What's going on, Rit?" I said.

"This is Lieutenant Castigliano, Pete," Rit said. "We've been trying to reach you all afternoon."

"I just returned from a business trip."

"May we come inside?" asked Lieutenant Castigliano.

"Just tell me what this is all about."

The lieutenant and I locked eyes and I started to bargain with God: Let her be alive.

Lieutenant Castigliano forced himself to speak. "I regret to inform…" He paused. "I'm sorry tell you that your wife, Elizabeth, was killed earlier today in a vehicular crash on the Merritt Parkway. She was headed southbound near the exit to 123. She must have been going very fast."

I heard what he said, but it didn't register.

Rit touched my shoulder. "Come on, Pete, let's go inside." He led me to the couch. It rocked sideways as we sat. The trooper came in and stood beside an empty five-gallon plastic bucket in the corner. A hooked wrecking bar protruded from it at an angle.

My mind seized on a triviality. I'd been meaning to wedge some wooden shims under the couch's short leg. I had bought a package of them at the hardware store. They were around here someplace. In the kitchen, probably.

"It happened at about two this afternoon," the trooper said.

"She was scheduled for an ultrasound then. She'd probably waited for me and then tried to get there on time."

Rit cringed.

Snippets of phone conversation returned:

Now come home right away. And don't stop off at the package store.

"The operator of the other car was driving under the influence," said Lieutenant Castigliano. "It was head-on. He was killed, too."

"Oh, God."

"Pete, is there someone you should call?" Rit wanted to know. "Parents, brothers, sisters?"

I shivered involuntarily. "Her parents and brothers are out in Michigan."

Tom says you haven't called him yet. Don't be proud. Please call him or Deke Malloy directly from out there.

"Where is she now, Rit?"

"Norwalk Hospital."

"Can I go see her?"

Lieutenant Castigliano cleared his throat. "You wouldn't want to do that."

"Why not?"

"The car burned." Lieutenant Castigliano fitted the edge of his palm into the groove atop his Stetson then focused his eyes directly into mine. "She's unrecognizable."

Whosits wants to say goodnight. Now listen closely: 'Goo-nightie, Dada.' She sounds like me imitating Mickey Mouse, doesn't she? Or should I say 'Johnny Mouse?' Remember when we walked up to the old forge? I understand why you love your memories of this place, Pete. Honestly. But that boy no longer exists. He's been replaced by a fine man that I love as big as the universe times googolplex.

"I'm going anyway. She's all alone." Tears burned the back of my eyes and Rit's face swam.

Rising with me, he blocked my departure. His strong fingers clamped onto my biceps. "She's with God now," he said.

The professionally solemn mortuary men appeared to lift Libby's coffin as easily as balsawood. Two sets of wheels clicked down as it slid out of the hearse on rollers. A kind of tunnel vision of disbelief distorted Lakeview Cemetery, New Canaan's Victorian burial ground. Down a grassy slope awaited a neatly incised pit surrounded by garishly green Astroturf, above hung a leaden sky. Tom Dorsey and Libby's two big blond brothers, Erik and Lars, walked beside me as pallbearers, faces pinched by sorrow, hands atop the casket that bumped along on its gurney. My fingers tingled on the polished rosewood. At graveside, Libby's parents stood as immobile as funereal statues, a knot of our friends from the *Bulletin* behind them. My father was in Venezuela, negotiating oil exploration leases, but sent flowers, gladioli in multiple colors. They splayed conspicuously from a large brass pot. Libby had always disliked his Veblen-like showiness. But maybe some underling had made this selection. The Rev. Elway, whom I had called because I knew no other clergymen, officiated. I was obliging Libby's parents, who'd wanted a religious service. Since my boyhood, the clergyman's handsome face had collapsed. Wattle quivering under his chin, he read from the Episcopalian Book of Common Prayer in a stagey preaching voice.

In sure and certain hope of the resurrection to eternal life through our Lord Jesus Christ, we commend to Almighty God our sister Elizabeth Tanya...

He mispronounced it tan 'ya (like what happens after a sunburn) rather than the softer tahn-ya. At this, something registered on Mrs. Lindquist's rigid face, which was as pale as soap. Then the Pulitzer Prize winner whom Libby had so emulated started to shake and wail. Her sons stepped forward and held her up by her elbows.

And we commit her body to the ground; earth to earth, ashes to ashes, dust to dust.

Ashes of her blond hair.

In the days afterwards, I lay on the bed, ignoring the constantly ringing phone. What should I do with her clothes? Stuff them in trash bags for the Salvation Army? I picked up the receiver one evening to find Father Elway on the line. He invited me for counseling in his rectory office, a cinderblock-walled retreat below the church sanctuary, painted the color of wet sand, and filled with shelves of references, scholarly interpretations, and concordances. He suggested I read the Lamentations in the Psalms and, like David, curse the Lord in my bereavement, purge the anger from my system, so that His limitless love could fill the aching void within me. "Life is unfair," he intoned, "but God is good."

Rit also called—repeatedly, he told me later. We met on a stormy Saturday afternoon at a place called the Granary, a coffee bar and bakery in Norwalk. I fortified myself beforehand with a few Fosters. Rit told me I shouldn't blame myself. It was an accident, we cannot control events. He seemed to be reiterating the same argument, basically that shit happens. Rotating my thick coffee mug, I fixated on how shiny and heavy it was. I entertained the idea of heaving it through the shop window onto the rain swept sidewalk. As I watched, drops of water on the pane of glass merged and abruptly slid down in tiny rivulets, as if giving up a struggle to hang on.

"Rit, I can't concentrate. Can we talk about this some other time?"

"Sure, buddy, sure."

NCC sent me on a business trip to London as part of the PC product announcement. With the plane skimming a horizon of cotton ball clouds, I peered out at the bouncing gray wing—with its complex system of flaps, trim tabs, and vortex generators—and sincerely hoped it would fall off. I arrived without my Dopp kit and slept through a press briefing.

Within six months, NCC let me go. Tom had been right. Unbeknownst to most observers, the company was bloated and overstaffed, had lost its PC market share, and was in deep financial trouble. The result was a massive round of layoffs—especially among staff workers, otherwise known as "clerks and jerks." Based on my years of service, NCC gave me a termination check of $6,000 (before taxes), which I used to pay down some of the growing house debt.

I kept working on the place in order to sell it—re-glazing the four front windows and rehanging the sticking front door on its strap hinges, for instance. Yet I didn't put it on the market. It still felt like a project I had to finish for Libby. The Winnie-the-Pooh wallpaper we'd picked out was half up in the nursery, and I couldn't decide whether to finish the job or strip it off. What would she want? One weekend—my grief like a physical weight—I drove to Hoboken to visit the park high above the Hudson where the harsh brightness of a spring day had revealed two chickenpox scars on her forehead. I'd touched the tiny depressions with my forefinger.

"You just notice the holes in my head, buddyrolls?"

"Have I told you today how much I really, really love you?"

"No, tell me."

Once more I sat on a child's swing, its rubber strap squeezing my thighs, and twisted the thick chains toward the next swing, now empty. The Manhattan skyline across the Hudson towered like the Rockies, but I didn't notice. I kicked at the deep hole worn by children's feet.

At night I read books with titles like *When Bad Things Happen to Good People* and *A Grief Observed*. A spouse's death, I learned, is as much a part of marriage as the honeymoon. I'd sit with our wedding album in my lap, sipping Scotch, and study Libby's smile, which always lumped up her right cheek. She'd complained that it made her look like a squirrel storing nuts. I'd awaken with the album sliding to the floor, an ecstatic dream of her already disappearing.

I stayed away from people, went grocery shopping only when I had to, avoided solicitous neighbors, who finally stopped leaving casseroles at the door, and drank to blackout—but not every night.

Sometimes, when not too wasted, I visited Libby after dark, driving into the cemetery with my car lights off, following the road that circled mausoleums and meditation ponds, and climbing the hill into the new section, as yet without plantings, where she was buried. Sitting in the dew-soaked grass beside her white marble stone, I'd run the finger that I'd placed on her scarred forehead along the incised letters of her name.

"Forgive me, Lib."

BOOK TWO

*Off Balance,
June 1995*

CHAPTER EIGHT
Landing On My Feet

The doctor labeled my growing unsteadiness a "neuropathy," an "idiopathic" one, because he couldn't determine the cause. He had me walk a heel-to-toe straight line, like how cops test sobriety, but I swerved at the second step. "You have weak feet," observed my new neurologist. He next rotated my arm at the elbow. "No signs of pin wheeling," he noted. He instructed me to hold out my arms. "No tremor in the hands." Following that, he administered tests that involved sticking a needle-like cathode, connected to a machine with a paper-dispensing readout, into my calves. It hurt. Posted on the walls of the examination room were color-illustrated explanations of various nerve disorders. Multiple sclerosis's depiction showed nerve sheaths pulled back like a banana peel: an autoimmune disease in which the body attacks itself. A blast of existential dread surged through me.

The doctor had mottled skin and gray hair, sparse on top and trimmed short. He spoke with an orotund lip-smacking delivery. He appeared puzzled by the results. By this time, he said, he'd ruled out ALS, MS, and Parkinson's disease. It was likely that I had Charcot-Marie-Tooth disease, he postulated, but without great conviction. "Your nerve conduction velocity is quite slow," he said mysteriously. He tapped my skinny legs as further evidence: "Not everyone with legs like yours has CMT, but I've never seen a Charcot patient who didn't have a similar pair. Okay, you can put your pants back on now."

"What's Shark-O whatever?" I asked, swinging my legs off the paper-covered exam table. I'd come to him, via referral, because I found myself tripping over nothing—even when I hadn't been drinking.

"A genetic disorder of the peripheral nerves in the limbs; the good news is you won't wind up in a wheelchair in six months." He told me to take vitamin B-12 and come back in a year for another checkup. "You may want to try physical therapy," he added.

"So what's the long-term prognosis?"

"Don't worry until you have to," he suggested, sensing my alarm.

A breeze blew the diaphanous white window curtain in Kitsie Shoemacher's bedroom, where I also had my trousers off. When *would* I be in a wheelchair? Kitsie was an ambitious colleague from my new place of work, Amsys Corp, a systems integrator. The company sold business advice and "interoperability" among computer systems, not obsolescing hardware, like NCC. When the big layoffs came, many NCC scribes had drifted into agency work, free-lancing, or early retirement. With Libby gone, there was no reason to call Deke at the *Bulletin*. With the help of a headhunter, I'd landed a job as Amsys's director of corporate relations, with an office in midtown New York. I'd survived thirteen interviews, eight at its headquarters in Los Angeles, and five within its consulting unit at 29th and Madison, where I now had an office.

The sun was long up on that hot Saturday morning. Hollow clangs from a garbage truck emptying a dumpster rose from West 83rd Street. Kitsie rolled closer in her sleep, pressing her warm clammy flesh against my back. We'd consumed two bottles of wine the night before. The impetus had been all hers; she'd asked me out by putting her head around my office door and asking, "What are you doing tonight?"

"Spending time with you, I'd surmise."

"Good guess. How about we go to the Blue Note in the Village?"

Now I inched away and lay flat, hands behind my head. A large black fly banged against the screen and droned off into the hallway. I wiggled my toes, which worked just fine, and thought more about my unsettling conversation with Dr. Phineas Judson, M.D, PhD. In retrospect, I was beginning to suspect that his tentativeness as a diagnostician was a leading indicator of his being a horse doctor. His questions went all over the place:

"Ever play football?" The doctor asked.

"Yes."

"What position?"

"I was a running guard and linebacker."

"In other words, your job was butting heads."

"Well, yes…"

"Ever get any concussions?"

"Three when I was out cold, maybe more minor ones."

"Drink much alcohol?"

"Sometimes."

"Ever to blackout?"

"Occasionally," I admitted. "But I can go months without

touching a drop."

"Swearing off like that usually means you have an alcohol problem. Does it affect your work?"

"Not really."

"Do you have trouble stopping once you start a drinking episode?"

"Yes, frankly, but not always."

"I see," he said, with a tug at his chin. "You know, long-term excessive alcohol consumption can have deleterious effects on the nervous system. If I had to guess, I'd say you're probably a functioning alcoholic. That's the worst kind; you guys don't seek help."

That hurt in a different way. And why was he asking about my booze intake? What did that have to do with atrophied calves? I asked him.

"It can also compromise balance," he answered. "I'm just getting the full picture."

"I see," I said, though I didn't.

Kitsie grunted and gurgled in her sleep. Conducting my own impromptu nerve tests, I picked up my legs, tenting the sheets off her body, and rotated each foot at the ankle. Everything in order there.

"Don't do that!" growled Kitsie. "That's totally obnoxious." She yanked the covers back up to her head and harrumphed. For a moment longer, her lips quivered like a baby nursing. Perhaps she was dreaming of last night's tart wine or where her mouth had wound up.

Kitsie had grown up on Round Hill Road in Greenwich, a locale that made most of New Canaan look like Skid Row. Every bit a princess of privilege, Kitsie was also scary smart. She had the reputation of being able to bend spoons by force of intellect. She'd gone to Yale as an economics major, then the Harvard Business School, where she'd been top of her class as a Baker Scholar. Her typical attire was a well-tailored black suit with a lot of clunky bangles on her wrists. Sometimes, she expanded her fashionista statement with five-hundred dollar Gucci scarves. This morning she was naked. However, only her tussled auburn hair was exposed. Lord knows why she'd taken a shine to me. Lord knows why she'd joined Amsys's consulting arm called Matrix, a distant competitor to the global biggies like McKinsey, Boston Consulting Group, and Bain. But maybe, since Matrix was the inventor of a hot new consulting fad called "business rationalization," she thought she'd make partner, and the big bucks, sooner. If so, she'd been right.

Kitsie had this compulsion toward career coaching, me particularly, which matched her occupation as a business consultant. Ms. Analyze-It, I called her. There was always a "best practice" answer for any business problem. In consultant-speak, its discovery was called "cracking the case." She'd entered my office one morning to ask a very off-putting question: Why didn't Matrix have better PR, or "mind share," as she put it. Why weren't we featured in national pubs like *Fortune* and *Forbes?* I almost snickered. Answer: We were nonentities, well below the radar of their readership of CEOs, who could buy Matrix's million dollar consulting engagements. I told her this was because—in her language—our corporate parent, Amsys, had neither a well-expressed value proposition nor a rationalized organizational structure to deliver value. In English, we suffered an identity crisis.

As I pictured it to her, Amsys's overarching marketing strategy was to build a kind of carwash. Clients would enter in need of business advice from the renowned management consultants like Kitsie, receive help from a bewildering number of units with separate identities, and emerge thoroughly hosed. That was a little cynical, but there was also a flaw. Amsys's stubbornly independent entities didn't work in tandem. Picked up in dribs and drabs, the bricks hadn't been cemented together. They retained their original names and leadership. Worse than lacking synergy, they had separate profit and loss responsibilities, sometimes even competed with each other.

"I don't understand why they don't call the whole shebang Matrix," I said to Kitsie. "Aren't business results what we're selling? And doesn't this start with a business strategy from you guys? Who cares about the mere mortals, the pipe fitters and code writers?"

That appeared to intrigue her. Apparently, in that instant, she saw me for the first time as somebody intelligent—not a clod to be manipulated. An ally she could work with. "*Results,*" she repeated, savoring the word. "That's absolutely marvelous! Not reports in binders, but bucks a CEO can see on the bottom line."

"Maybe we even take stock in our clients as payment to show how confident we are of our ability to deliver those results. That'll grab the attention of the big bosses."

"Oh, Pete, I'm going to take this to Trevor Henshaw."

The flaw with my elegant positioning was that I'd been hired to promote the entire Amsys team as one-stop shopping. The implied messaging went something like this: Tell us where it hurts, Mr. CEO, and then let us swarm in our disorganized way all over your problems. That meant nothing, if not trouble. As a result I was failing in my job of making Amsys a household name. Hence, a hovering sense of job insecurity nagged at me.

Don't get me wrong about Kitsie's sudden romantic interest in me. Imperious and plump, she was pushing a selfish agenda. And, again, she had this obsession to improve me, or maybe anyone in her sphere, which drove me up the wall. After a night at home in Silvermine, during which I'd stripped the bathroom floor of linoleum and its underlying black glue, she'd told me the next morning never again to come to work with dirty fingernails. Nobody, she warned, would take me seriously. She meant it. But Kitsie also had a raging libido and made no emotional demands. Perhaps the carnal nature of our grapplings—during which she said a lot of dirty words that shocked me at first—allowed me the excuse that my behavior was just a matter of physical release, that I wasn't being unfair to her, or betraying Libby's memory. It was a kind of free sex pass. Yet I never sought Kitsie out. In fact, I tried to avoid her, and felt a bit sullied when "it" happened. Like this morning. Acting on that squeamishness, I slid out from under the covers and retrieved my clothes from various locations in the apartment. I left a note on her phone table:

Dear Sleeping Beauty,

I couldn't bear to wake you. What a lovely evening. I'm going to have jazz tunes playing in my head all day. So, 'Take Five' and snooze on.

PW

Too bad Kitsie was such a cold fish. I could have used a confidant. It had been a bad week. I was in the doghouse with my boss who, being located in the mother ship in Los Angeles, was distant in both meanings of the word. Also, my father had died, after writing me out of his will. He'd suffered a massive heart attack. My stepmother Lucille notified me of his passing by phone from their waterside compound in Siesta Key, a retirement ghetto for the rich in Sarasota. Libby and I had never visited them there, had never been invited. He was to be cremated, Lucille said, and told me there was no reason to come, since no religious service was planned. So, after almost six years of not seeing and barely talking with him, I didn't get to say goodbye in person. That would have suited him just fine.

"You look like your dog died," Kitsie observed, the day following this depressing news from Florida. Of course she was very apologetic after I set her straight. She was fascinated that my father had been CEO of Middle Atlantic Oil, which I'd never mentioned before. She asked me about him. Yes, I told her, he was famous in the oil industry, negotiated face-to-face with Arab princes and banana republic autocrats, expanded exploration to wild and remote sites, doubled revenues during his tenure, had even played a role in the development of offshore drilling technology. Not only from rigs, but using drill bits that could make sharp turns to tunnel off in any direction geologists recommended. I related all this in a flat voice, the barebones bio of a near stranger.

"Wow," Kitsie marveled. "He sounds like he was a force in his industry. What was he like?"

"He wasn't a very nice guy."

CHAPTER NINE

Master of the Mute Button

As I came over the grassy hill in my clattering Saab, I assured myself I'd just see what they had to say, as a form of job insurance. Ahead, plonked down in an old apple orchard, sprawled the familiar low building, glaring white in the June sun. Through inflamed eyes, it seemed to waver, as if under water. Libby had never been at the National Computing Company's headquarters, yet always pinpointed it as the location where I'd sold out. Bile and black coffee churned in my stomach at the thought, augmenting this morning's hangover.

Within the building's vast atrium grew the familiar stand of potted bamboo trees, a little taller and wider now. A splashing fountain added its note of gravitas like tuneless organ music. From behind a circular desk, an expressionless guard instructed me where to sign in and handed me an adhesive red visitor's badge. As always, Mel Brooks' dialogue obtruded: *Badges? We don't need no stinki'n' badges!* I pasted the thing on my suit lapel and took a seat on a leather sectional. Next to me another apparent supplicant was wordlessly moving his lips, as if rehearsing.

Soon, Freddy Pritchard arrived. With gray hair and an unhealthy flush, he looked like an elder brother of the man I'd known. How old was he now? If I was thirty-five, he had to be pushing fifty. His clothes were transformed, too. He wore the new business casual: ultramarine dress shirt, dark slacks, tassel loafers. In pinstripes and white button-down shirt, I hadn't kept up with the times. I stood and dropped a courtesy copy of the *Bulletin* back on the low glass table with regret. Tom Dorsey's latest exposé of corporate malfeasance had been getting interesting.

"Guess I didn't get the memo," I said, extending a shaking hand.

Freddy's grip was cold. "What's that, Pete?"

I touched my carefully selected tie, a yellow foulard. "I'm out of uniform."

His vision shifted to my neck and then back to my face. "What's with your eyes? They're like roadmaps."

"Allergies."

"You look like you tied one on last night." His frown softened as he remembered something. "By the way, I was sorry to hear about your wife. I should have sent a card back then. Auto accident, I heard. When was it again?"

"Almost five years ago."

"Must have been rough."

"Still is."

"Yes," he said, his brow moving with embarrassment, "I can only imagine. So anyway, let's not keep the big man waiting. And next time maybe use some Visine? So you don't look quite so much like a lush."

I never cared much for Freddy. Maybe it was because he'd once given me a stinging performance review. Maybe it was because he affected tinny corporate neologisms like "we solution the customer's problem." As he turned to lead the way, even his gait was irritating. Back straight, arms hanging, he moved like a marionette.

Jason Dinsmore, he of the "shocking computer" cover-up, was the man I really needed to impress that day. Freddy paused on the red carpet in the wide upper hallway for executives called mahogany row. His face was a mixture of concern and encouragement. "Leave your ego at the door," he advised.

Freddy had been cagey about his invitation. The PR function's new budget just might accommodate a few key hires, he said. Was I interested in chatting with the boss? I tried not to sound too eager. Dinsmore had no idea how much trouble I was in at Amsys. He still ruled a domain of language manipulators: advertising managers, media relations flacks, speechwriters, and various other hacks who produced press releases, manuals, pamphlets, annual reports, and internal magazines. Line executives responsible for generating revenue called this output "verbiage." The PR skills learned here I'd brought to my current job, but they were proving useless without the authority to impose them.

Dinsmore was a clean desk exec: no family pictures, no plants, no company awards, or plaques. New, though, were photos arranged along one wall of Dinsmore and NCC's first outside CEO, Ted Devlin, a corporate turnaround specialist. Dinsmore in the flesh glanced up and pointed toward a pair of cubist tan-leather armchairs facing each other across a red Heriz rug. "Have a seat yonder," he said. He studied some papers for half a minute, long enough to signal my insignificance, and then rose slowly. Dressed in an electric blue shirt and charcoal trousers, evidently NCC's updated uniform, he truly was a big man, and just as I remembered him: six-foot-six, with a deeply lined face, a large fleshy nose, and buzz-cut brown hair the texture of a doormat.

"Welcome back. Frederick tells me you're prospering at, what's it called again?"

"Amsys."

Perfunctory smile, but no handshake. "Never heard of them," he said. Then: "Know what got me thinking about you?"

That was a rhetorical question, so I shook my head and waited.

"Your friend Tom Dorsey."

"After that glowing write-up in the *Bulletin* last month he should be *your* friend, too, Jason. Did Freddy have anything to do with that big wet kiss?"

Dinsmore appeared annoyed. "I'm disappointed with Frederick. He failed to get me an advance copy before it was published."

His statement was puzzling. "The *Bulletin* doesn't let anybody review its articles," I reminded him.

He gave me a sharp look. "Let's get down to cases," he said. "I received an amusing letter from Deke Malloy in the aftermath of that story. You know him too, correct?"

"Correct, my hard-charging managing editor in days of yore."

"Good. I'd like your insight on how he'll react in a certain situation. Let's get Frederick in here to kick this around. Wait right here, I'll go round him up." He exited the room.

After a few moments, jittery nerves and an acid stomach drove me to my feet. I examined the grinning pair in the photos then headed to the window. Through its tinted glass, the lawn sloped away in a precisely cut cross-hatched pattern like a major league outfield. In the parking lot beyond, hundreds of cars baked in the heat. A foreshortened man strode purposefully toward the entrance swinging a briefcase, his shadow in the overhead summer sun was reduced to dark dabs at his feet. As I leaned forward to track him, cold air moved over my face from a whispering duct beneath the windowsill. My eyelids itched. Deja vu. My last session here involved *Bulletin* strategizing.

I turned when I saw Dinsmore's reflection in the glass. He waved me forward like a traffic cop and led me into an almost refrigerated conference room next door. Freddy marched in a moment later and passed around copies of Deke Malloy's letter:

The *Wall Street Bulletin*
44 Van Zandt Street
New York, NY 10019

June 15, 1995
Mr. Jason C. Dinsmore
Vice President of Corporate Communications
National Computer Company
110 Apple Farm Lane
Westminster, NY, 10509

Dear Jason,

It has not gone unnoticed by us that our reporters' phone calls and emails have not been answered since our Page One profile of Ted Devlin appeared more than two weeks ago.

If anything was done by us to offend you, or Mr. Devlin, I assure you it was inadvertent on our part.

Our continued coverage of NCC, and our past fine working relationship, must not be threatened by any misunderstanding—if, indeed, there is one. We cannot accurately inform our readers of the doings of the largest technology company in the world without your assistance.

Will you call me at your earliest convenience?

Sincerely,
Dillon 'Deke' Malloy / Managing Editor

Head down, Freddy pored over the copy like an English major deciphering Joyce's *Ulysses*. The Deke I'd known was a truculent braggart. Famous for clamping an olive-green grenade launcher to his office wall, he vowed to publish stories with "muzzle velocity." But with this note, Dynamite Deke had started off in passive voice and descended into active groveling. I read it three times.

Dinsmore emitted a rumble of mirth. "He wants to kiss and make up," he said, tapping the text with a forefinger.

Freddy and I exchanged glances.

"What was wrong with Tom's article?" I ventured. I'd read Tom's profile with interest and it seemed right down the middle.

"Mr. Devlin didn't like it."

"Really? As I recall, it was about as good as they get. It said he'd improved performance by kicking ass…"

"You can stop right there," Dinsmore broke in. "That language mortified Mr. Devlin's mother. Also, his Wingfoot golfing buddies have started calling him 'Kick-Ass Teddy.' Worst of all, Dorsey gratuitously described Ted as having all the personal warmth of Lurch in the *Addams Family*. Did you read that gratuitous shit?"

"But that was from an industry analyst. They use colorful language to get themselves quoted. You know that, Jason. It's called 'balance.'"

"It was a personal insult. As a result, we're no longer talking to the *Bulletin*."

Beneath the bluster, Dinsmore appeared a bit queasy, as if aware of how asinine the idea was. Freddy cleared his throat. "Jason, you should know that one of the press reps in Atlanta *did* take one of the *Bulletin*'s calls about a product question. It was Joe Larkin, yesterday. Did you hear about that?"

Dinsmore's low chuckle sounded very bad for Joe Larkin. "Yes, and he's been appropriately chastised." His big head rotated my way like a tank cannon. "How are your former colleagues going to react to this?"

"Does anybody recall a woman named Jan Metzger?"

"Vaguely," said Freddy.

"She used to head up PR at Waukegan Steel."

"What about her?" Dinsmore demanded.

I launched into a cautionary tale: Metzger hadn't liked a *Bulletin* piece, either. It was one I wrote. She'd imposed silence on us because of my "grossly unfair coverage"—an accusation the paper joyfully published. For her pains, we lampooned her for weeks. One headline mocked her as "Queen Mum." The crisis peaked when she didn't respond to questions about a quarterly earnings release. Confusion about a write-down caused the company's stock to tank. *Then* she wanted to talk. I remembered her scared, fluttering voice on the phone. A week later, her CEO fired her.

"What's that got to do with us?" Dinsmore wanted to know.

"Maybe it's the old rule that you shouldn't get in public tiffs with organizations that buy printers' ink by the barrel."

"We're not in any public tiff. We haven't said anything, have we? Am I missing something here?"

"No, Jason," said Freddy.

"But if you go silent, what leverage do you have? They're going to publish stories about you regardless—inaccurate ones, by definition."

Dinsmore's face was set like a slab.

But I'd gone too far to stop. "You *have* to talk to them, Jason. Malloy cannot *not* cover NCC. And if you clam up, what will they have to lose by making fun of you? It will be Waukegan Steel all over again."

"Should I care? We're still the biggest tech company on the planet! We can get our story out through other major media and the wire services. Meantime, maybe they'll catch on and replace Dorsey. Don't you agree?"

"No. They'll give him a raise." I felt a little giddy at his obtuseness. The man I'd known could have written a book on savvy media relations, not ordered up this passive-aggressive nonsense.

"So how do we get respectful coverage?"

"Mr. Devlin will just have to develop a thicker skin. You've got to admit that beneath a few irritants Tom's piece was almost entirely positive."

Jason Dinsmore folded Deke Malloy's letter in half and creased it several times with his thumbnail. His eyes bored into mine. "That's all you got?"

I stared right back. "Either that, or make an honest complaint to Tom and Deke about the tone. It might not do much good, but at least you won't be at war."

"Any chance we can get Dorsey fired?"

"No."

"Thanks for your input," he said.

"You're welcome." And right then I figured, flapping away on imaginary little white wings, went any job offer.

With a rattle of papers and an unconscious sigh, we stood.

Back in the corridor, I tried to warn Freddy. "You guys are going to look like morons if it gets out that you're giving the *Bulletin* the silent treatment. You've got to convince Dinsmore to play ball with Deke for his own good. Can't you see the headlines: 'NCC CEO Adopts Dumb Media Strategy?' How about 'Devlin Sulks in Silence Over Story?'"

He sighed. "Did you ever stop to think Jason's under direct orders from Mr. Devlin?"

"It's still insane, and he knows it."

Freddy gazed down the hallway as if recollecting something. "We'll get back to you. But I wouldn't get my hopes up. We're officially in a no-new-headcount posture." He brought his focus back to me. "Want a piece of advice?"

"Sure."

"Forget you were once this big-shit, fearless reporter at the *Bulletin*."

"But isn't that why you invited me here, because I was? What else was I supposed to say?"

"We actually hoped you'd help us serve Mr. Devlin's needs, not just naysay. I sincerely doubt there'll be a next time, but if there is, lay off the sauce, will you? You reek of it."

Outside in the parking lot, heat waves shimmied off the pavement. The little black convertible was like a furnace. Thanks to an oil leak, it smelled like one too. Nine years old and bought second hand, its odometer recorded that it had traveled the distance to the moon. I loosened my "lucky" tie and tried to understand what had just transpired: Starting out as the expert,

Plausible Deniability

I'd become the meeting's designated stupid guy, the one who asks questions that others are either afraid, or too smart, to pose. Well I had to admit I'd done it with vast aplomb.

Chapter Ten

Straw Boss

I arrived three hours late to my New York office with a premonition of disaster. Sure enough, awaiting me was a string of flamemail messages from my boss, Jim Phillips, Amsys's marketing vice president out in Los Angeles who, because of the time difference, should have been arriving at work just when I was.

Phillips had begun tapping away at his keyboard very early. He'd titled his six a.m. screed *REWRITE-ASAP!!!* Stacked above was evidence of his increasing frustration: *GET BACK TO ME PRONTO; PLEASE RESPOND SOONEST; WHERE THE HELL ARE YOU?*

Opening them in order, I read: "What are you smoking out there? See my comments." The attachment contained my draft of an important speech to the Wall Street analysts who covered our swooning stock. The talk was scheduled to be given in three weeks. I'd had the company's Los Angeles-based CEO, Willard "Jock" Connors, launch into it this way:

Charles Dickens began The Christmas Carol *with one of the greatest disclaimers in literary history. Nothing that followed in the story would be at all wonderful, Dickens wrote, unless it was thoroughly understood that Jacob Marley was dead. Dead, in fact, as a doornail.*

Likewise, nothing I say this morning will seem wonderful unless you all understand that the standalone personal computer is equally dead. What killed it is connectivity to enterprise networks.

WHAT THE HELL IS <u>THIS</u>? Angry red strikethroughs crossed out the text. *Jock will never say anything like that. You should know better. He likes to build logically, from lots of data. Start with sales figures for servers, or whatever fits our scenarios about the growth of local area networks. Fill his mouth with trends and numbers, not literary allusions. Jesus H. Christ! Get something crisp back to me by tomorrow, first thing.*

"I'm on the case," I emailed back. My NCC bravado had vanished and I was too chicken to call. He was completely right. I *should* have known better. Speechwriters are never supposed to be creative. We're more like sensitive recording devices. We listen and then divine a way to phrase the jumble of concepts we've just heard into sentences that—and this is the real skill—put them in the executive's own voice. When successful, the speaker thinks he wrote it himself. NCC scribos added a step called "dulling it up" designed to block metaphors like mine. Reason: they tend to irritate left-brain thinkers, most of whom consider speechwriters an entirely fungible commodity.

My challenge was to make Connors come off as a business genius for buying his collection of tech companies. In my little corner, by force of personality and perhaps prestidigitation, I was supposed to impose PR hegemony across this disparate horde, which had started out as a tech firm supporting California's tax department. I was roundly ignored. Since nobody reported to me, my failure as straw boss—someone with responsibility but no authority—was more structural than personal. Phillips had dropped me behind enemy lines with two injunctions: "Make sure everybody sings out of the same PR hymnbook, and don't go native out there." Kitsie, aware of all this, told me I needed to ignore Phillips and work just for Matrix, where the real marketing action was. It was my fond dream as well.

I began composing an email to Dataquest, an analyst firm that predicts technology trends. I needed factoids in a hurry to rebuild the speech.

"Working half days now?" I swiveled around to see Larry Lieberman, a corporate lawyer who also served as my office confessor. Larry's duties were drawing up bullet-proof project contracts with clients.

"Just between us girls, I was at a job interview," I replied.

Larry spoke with a glottal New Yawk accent and was just as disenchanted with Amsys as I was. "Wunnerful," he responded. "Maybe I can negotiate a package deal for the two of us."

"That's doubtful, I underwhelmed them."

We'd gotten to know each other during "onboarding" classes at corporate headquarters in Los Angeles. Like a reporter, Larry liked to gossip and speculate. Over drinks at a trendy bar, whose walls contained tropical fish languidly waving their tails in mammoth tanks, he and I had shared our skepticism about the organization's overlapping management structure, fiefdoms, and palace intrigues.

"That's too bad you flubbed it, because you might be in need of a job soon." He held up a Matrix press release. "Ever see this before?"

"Never laid eyes on it."

He handed it over. "You'd better read it."

The release was about a consulting engagement by Matrix

for a pharmaceutical company called Pharmacom. Written by Teddy deGruening, Matrix's book publicist and general-purpose writer, it was another turgid document sent out to the news media without my approval. It detailed how we'd help the firm refocus its business model—which was based on developing antibiotics—into selling heart-disease statins. Rationale: people took these pills for the rest of their lives, making such products far more lucrative. Antibiotics promptly cured you; end of revenue stream.

"Larry, you know Dick Marin's people generate these things without checking with me," I said. "I hold nobody's pay card. But this looks harmless enough."

Larry scratched a scalp that was covered in what looked like steel wool. "Oh you think so, huh?"

"Is there a problem?" I asked.

"You bet your sweet ass there is," he said. "I just got a call from Pharmacom's legal vice president. The guy was ballistic. Turns out we signed non-disclosure agreements out the wazoo, and here we are laying out their whole confidential acquisition strategy. Apparently, we've also instigated a panic about imminent layoffs. He said his researchers *are climbing the walls!*"

I could hear the man's outrage echoed in Larry's voice. "What does he want us to do?" I asked.

"His company's PR people are going into denial mode; they're saying they're only exploring options in a market adjacency. But this could get messy. I told him we would hew to that party line. You'd better get old Jimbo on the horn." He paused and studied me with concern. "You okay, Pete? Getting enough sleep? You look kind of bagged over."

"This is my third screw-up before lunch."

Larry departed with a sympathetic smile.

I took a deep breath before picking up the phone.

"Where were you this morning?" Jim Phillips demanded. "I was about to send out bloodhounds and Northwest Mounties to find you."

"I had car trouble," I lied.

"Next time have it on your own time. Meantime, Jock Connors threw up all over your speech. It's as dead to him as Marley's doornail. So get cracking on a new draft. I'm sending you some examples of his prior talks to get the tone. Can you do it overnight?"

"You can count on me."

"Good boy. I'll leave you to it."

"Hold on one more minute, Jim, we got some trouble out here." I gave a brief rundown on the Pharmacom debacle and waited for a violent outburst.

Phillips didn't say a word.

"Do I have your permission to confront Dick Marin, maybe go to his boss, Trevor Henshaw? Set up some formal ground rules with Henshaw for handling releases mandating that I sign off on them before they go out?" I thought of NCC's new CEO. "You know, kick ass."

The line hummed over the 3,000-mile distance.

"You there, Jim?"

"This is exactly what I've been waiting for," he said at last. "Hot damn!" He rang off.

Chapter Eleven
Delivering a Message

Next morning I sent Phillips a revised speech. I'd been up until midnight to finish it. At the very same moment his latest screaming email arrived in my inbox. They must have crossed paths in the ether over Chicago. His bore the title "HEAD-CHOPPING." It ordered me to terminate Teddy deGruening, the renegade author of the unauthorized press release. Phillips was also sending a threat to Dick Marin, Matrix's cocky and diminutive marketing executive: play ball or you'll get the heave-ho next.

"That shrimp Marin has got to keep you looped in," Phillips said in a follow-up phone call. "We spent good money to own those Matrix guys; they're supposed to work for us now. You have my full authority to give deGruening the ax. Tell me how Marin takes it. And don't worry about any fallout; it's all good, clean fun."

Manfully, I walked down to Marin's area for the showdown. He was outside his office making corrections to a document his admin, Nancy Donahue, was typing on a PC. In his mid-thirties and tightly wound, Marin had finely textured light-brown hair combed forward over a high brow. He stood barely five feet tall and initially didn't acknowledge my presence.

"I haven't got time for you," he said, reacting as if approached by a panhandler. "If you want to talk, schedule an appointment with Nancy here. And by the way, I don't appreciate you and Kitsie Schoemaker going behind my back to Henshaw with that new 'We Sell Results' slogan idea. It sucks. The tag line is, 'We deliver Business Solutions, on time and on budget.'"

"Believe me, Dick, I don't know marketing from Shinola; it was just an idea that excited Kitsie. You know her enthusiasms, she can't help herself."

He leaned toward Nancy and pointed at the screen. "Make that read 'granular view,'" he instructed. "It sounds more measured than 'down in the weeds.' I'm going to have to have another talk with Teddy about his vernacular word choices."

"This will only take a minute, Dick. I bear a brief message from L.A. Can we go in your office? It's private."

He spun to face me. "No, we cannot. What do our illustrious West Coast geniuses want now?"

I paused for an instant. "Net-net: Teddy deGruening has to go."

"Go?"

"Yes, 'go.' As in he's fired."

"*What*! Says who?"

"Jim Phillips."

Nancy paused in her work, pretending not to listen. She'd always given off vibes that she considered me a figure of fun.

Marin's jaw muscles jumped spasmodically. "That's a crock!" he exploded. "Teddy is the key to our whole publication thrust. We can't lose him without imperiling our book-launch engine."

"Translation?"

"He knows how to engineer bestsellers." He faced Nancy:

"You can print that out now, and thanks." He turned back to me. "So what's Jim's reason?"

"Teddy's a loose cannon; he's giving out all kinds of unapproved messages to the press."

Marin opened his mouth to protest.

"Hold it, Dick. I'm not just talking about yesterday's Pharmacom blunder, which I told your boss Trevor all about this morning. He said he hadn't seen the release, either. So Ted's out of control. Did you also see where he told *Consultant Digest* that we actually prefer working with one of our telecom competitors, called them 'the best in the business?' That's treason, isn't it?"

Nancy Donahue walked to the printer, which had begun to whine and disgorge pages.

"He's only stating an obvious fact: Our own techies are idiots. Look, Phillips doesn't know jack shit about Teddy's connections with book sellers. Nor do I work for him. Our future hinges on Trevor Henshaw's next book."

"What connections?"

Marin bit his lip. "I can't go into that."

"Your say-so isn't much of an argument, Dick."

Marin glared. Sunshine coming through the spun glass curtains lit his fine hair like electric filaments. "You sit in on our quarterly management meetings, Wendell. Christ, we're looking for ways to keep the lights on around here. We absolutely *need* Teddy."

"All I know is L.A. is not paying for Teddy's 'connections' anymore—or his flapping lips."

The little man fought to control himself. "You're a nobody," he said. "I'm going to make it my job to get *you* fired. I hope you leave real soon—and take your boozy stench with you. Did you sleep in that suit?"

Actually, to finish the speech, I *had* slept in my office.

He stalked off in the direction of Trevor Henshaw.

Nancy Donahue slid back into her ergonomic chair and gave me an insolent smile.

Black gum spots stippled the sidewalk as I headed up the Park Avenue ramp toward Grand Central that afternoon. I was meeting Teddy deGruening at the Oyster Bar to formally let him go. He'd selected the location, saying it was where he wanted to end his day. High in the sky, the bronze statue of Mercury, god of commerce, stood atop the crouching figures of Hercules and Minerva. Mercury's sword was turned inward as a symbol of mercy. Mid-stride, I confronted my reflection in a plate glass window. I looked worried.

I'd never entered the Oyster Bar, even though I passed it every day on the way to the train. Overhead were a series of massive domes lined in large white tiles. The effect was part shower room, part Gothic vaulted ceiling. Noises and conversation swirled around up there and bounced back in muffled dissonance. Dressed in a hounds tooth-check sports coat, the lumpish deGruening sat at the bar sipping a carrot-toned martini so massive it looked like a gasoline funnel. Rotating around on the leatherette-covered stool, he waved a chubby hand.

To give him his due, deGruening—an old hack in his late fifties—had pulled off some notable successes. One was a fulsome review by *Business Today* of the first book Marin had created for Henshaw, who was not only Matrix's president but—thanks to the prodigious efforts of Marin & Co.—had become a nationally recognized management guru. It was about replacing people with computer networks and had sold briskly. For a while, industry observers touted Henshaw as the father of a business revolution. Dick Marin strutted the corridors like a rooster. But management fads are fleeting. Trevor Henshaw's "Technology-Enabled Process Rationalization" mantra had become as outdated as fat ties. Worse, after going on a recruiting binge from the top business schools, Matrix's revenue had evaporated. The firm had to renege on its lucrative starting bonuses to top MBAs, a betrayal not soon forgotten in the halls of Wharton, Stanford, and the Harvard Business School.

"What'll you have?" deGruening asked, as I sat beside him.

I ordered a beer and then pulled the trigger. "As Dick no doubt told you, Amsys's corporate office has decided that your services are no longer needed. I'm sorry, but I'm sure he'll provide you with stellar references. You'll bounce back quickly. I have no doubt."

His response was surprisingly laconic. "Is that so? How much time does that give me?"

"Friday's your last day. But California's giving you three months' severance pay, free career-transition counseling for six months, and paid COBRA benefits for a full year."

I watched deGruening take this in without a qualm. In appearance, he affected a literary persona, complete with a paisley handkerchief drooping out of his sports coat's pocket and gelled hair that swept out in wings. "Well, that's certainly generous of them," he said, "but can you give me the rationale?"

"You know the drill. Matrix is supposed to tee up big honking engagements for the other units, not be an independent arbiter of the best IT providers out there. Amsys simply can't have schizophrenic messaging."

"Then why don't they have me report to you? I can spout any line you like. Why get rid of me?"

It was an excellent question. All I could say was: "Because that's the way it is, Ted."

For somebody who'd just been fired, the thickset man's equanimity was impressive. "Okay, but have a drink on me," he said.

"Sure."

"Actually, I have some news for you, too."

"Good news, I hope?"

"Excellent." He put a twenty-dollar bill on the teakwood bar and said, "You may want to switch to martinis. I hear you like to drink."

"I'll have a club soda," I told the arriving server, whose plastic name tag read Ivan.

"Very good, sir," said Ivan, who nodded and turned.

deGruening appeared as pleased as if laying down four aces. "Well," he said, drawing out the word. "You may be interested to hear that earlier today Dick Marin put me on a year's retainer at double what I was earning. In effect, I'm getting a hundred percent raise for my services and, thanks to California, that really sweet benefits package for getting fired."

"And how does Marin get away with *that*? Phillips is going to become unhinged."

"He got Amsys's CEO Jock Connors to personally agree to it."

"No shit, Marin did that? All before the end of the day?"

"No shit," deGruening agreed, "but Jim Phillips will."

My water arrived, but I didn't touch the glass. "Just out of curiosity, Ted, does Marin have dirty pictures of Jock Connors?"

He shook his head. "Blackmail is an intriguing idea," he said.

"But no. He just makes sure that Matrix sells a ton of books."
deGruening tilted back his glass. "Cheers," he said. Then he
pushed it forward along the polished bar to get Ivan's attention.
"Sure you don't want something stronger?"

"Some other time, I've got a train to catch."

The Metro-North commuter car rumbled hollowly as it crossed
the Mianus River Bridge in Cos Cob. I was on the 7:26 express
to New Canaan. Far below, in the wide inlet, floated millions
of dollars' worth of idle yachts. Trucks kept abreast with us
along the parallel I-95 bridge, a section of which had fallen into
the river one June night in 1983. With a loud bang, the view
vanished behind a train streaking the other way. Beside me, a
banker type wearing pink suspenders deftly opened and refolded
his *Bulletin* into quarter squares. I'd never been able to do that
without spreading my arms and watched closely to see how he
did it. Staring too long, I drew a hostile glance.

I'd gone back to the office to report Teddy's miraculous escape
to Jim Phillips. But his administrative assistant said Jim was in
a meeting. I gave her a truncated version of what had happened
and said I'd wait for his call. But after an hour, I heard nothing. I
sent Jim an email account of the events and departed once again
for Grand Central. Sucked into the echoing station like ants into
a mound, a swarm of commuters surrounded me as we marched
down into the station's dim underground. The sloping ramp
sparkled with tiny specs, an Aladdin's Cave of dinginess. Stepping
into the silver car, I heard electric motors cycling beneath me.

Now, in my swaying seat, I took another sip of the big Foster's
beer can I'd bought from the pushcart vendor at the head of the
platform and pondered an extraordinary deus ex machina. In

going back to send my last report to Los Angeles, I discovered an email from Freddy Pritchard at NCC. Jason Dinsmore wanted me to meet with the company's CEO, Ted Devlin. As the great philosopher Fats Waller once observed, "One never knows, do one?"

I turned back to *Great Expectations*. The yellowed paperback copy from college days lay open on my lap, broken along the spine. Rereading Dickens was a guilty middle-brow pleasure like listening to Tchaikovsky. I was near the beginning, where Pip stole food for the convict in the churchyard. The mature narrator meditates on the origins of his childish love for the simple blacksmith, Joe Gargery, whom he would deny but ultimately come to understand was his moral superior.

But I loved Joe—perhaps for no better reason in those early days than because the dear fellow let me love him...

A Dartmouth English instructor, generally scornful of Dickens' oeuvre, said this book—in which shame and self-delusion battle humility and honesty—was the exception to the author's treacly sentimentality. True, Joe was just another "holy fool" caricature of the kind that populated Victorian literature, but the story's almost modern theme was about loss, disillusionment, and acceptance. It contained the startlingly true insight that, "our worst weaknesses and meannesses are usually committed for the sake of the people whom we most despise." In my case, the Old Man?

The smear of passage flickered beyond streaked double panes of safety glass: flashing junk ailanthus trees, the flowing ribbon of brownstone retaining walls, abruptly ending and resuming, winking backs of houses and shops, the rhythmic rise and fall of the bowed catenary wire between high galvanized stanchions. I closed my eyes. I needed to figure out a better way to live. What would I do if I had my druthers? What would I become if I knew I couldn't fail? I didn't know. Maybe Pip's lesson applied. You can't attain contentment by acquiring more and more of what you don't really need.

BOOK THREE

Rit to the Rescue

CHAPTER TWELVE

Jogging a Memory

Something changed after deGruening mocked me inside the Oyster Bar. When I got home that night—full of resolve, anger, and not a little motivational beer—I dug out my running stuff. My sneakers were stiff from disuse, but I stamped my feet into them and double-knotted the laces. Screw Dick Marin and Dr. Judson. I'd adjust my attitude, and beat Charcot whatever, by regularly putting in miles. Dry out in the process. Health and contentment beckoned. Stepping outside, I pulled the rickety door shut and began a slow trot north, upstream and uphill. The evening light cast a lovely glow, every backlit leaf and branch distinct. If I kept this up for a few weeks I'd be feeling as great as Tony the Tiger.

But within a half mile, my face glowed like I'd stuck it inside a sweat lodge. A stitch gnawed my side. Laboring up Clapboard Hill, I became aware of my own rhythmic gasps. They acquired the tempo of Huey "Piano" Smith's *Don't You Just Know It*. "Ah, ha, ha, ha… ah, ha, ha, ha… day-ay-oh… gooba, gooba, gooba."

Irritated, I sprinted with a scuffling left sole—an irritating reminder of Dr. Judson—for the summit at Carter Street, an effort that pushed me into lightheadedness. I halted, bent over, blowing and spitting, near the large granite gravesite of Captain John Carter, a Revolutionary War veteran who left this world in January 1819. It was there that Rit DeMarco pulled up in his police cruiser.

"Hey, Hambone," he yelled. "Need a lift?"

"Up yours, Chooch."

We'd coined these nicknames as kids. His meant "jackass" in Italian. Mine derived from my unused first name, Hampton.

"I'm serious, you look ready to keel over."

"I'm just catching my breath."

Whereas I had been Given Every Advantage, Rit had grown up in a stubby brick bungalow in the Italian section. In high school, he wore the same clothes every day, but no one teased him. Nobody dared. He was big and powerful, and won so many sports letters kids called him Varsity Rit. In any game, the never-fail strategy was "give the ball to DeMarco."

The cruiser door opened and he sauntered over to stand in front of me, arms crossed like Mr. Clean over his massive chest. "What would Coach O'Malley say if he saw you sucking wind and looking like a salty bag of shit?"

"He'd say, at least Wendell doesn't drive his fat ass around in a cop car all day."

"Oh yeah? Well, I can kick *your* worthless butt anytime," which was certainly true.

I'd known Rit since my parents moved to town in the 1960s. His ancestors went back a century more, not so far as Captain Carter, but at least they were still around. Arriving as servants for the wealthy Brooklynites who built shingled summer manors out along the ridges, they'd prospered and multiplied. They became the townies. Over the generations, they'd quietly attained wealth in construction, real estate, and the trades. Maybe that's because their fathers brought them into the family businesses and trained them with care. The plumbers joked that they made more than the brain surgeons they'd started out as.

In high school, I blocked for Rit: the 43 play, fullback (number 4) through my left guard's 3-hole—a violent crash of plastic shoulder pads and helmets, four or five chopping steps to move my opponent, and Rit would be through. Sprawled on the turf in the aftermath, I'd watch Rit scamper away, juke stepping and stiff-arming, amid a mounting roar.

My football days didn't last; I was too heavy for Dartmouth's 150-pound team and too skinny for the varsity. Rit, though, was recruited by Syracuse, but either flunked or had been tossed out. I never heard which. For a while when I was at Dartmouth, and home for holidays, rumors came my way of his struggles with drugs and alcohol, which confirmed a memory of him in a drunken fistfight after a high school dance. I'd helped pull Rit off some unfortunate kid from Wilton, who'd stupidly called him a dumb Wop. It had taken three of us, all linemen.

"Only my *friends* call me Wop!" he'd shouted as his opponent ran away.

Twenty years later, I'd seen Rit out on the dusty lawn of Waveny Park, directing traffic for the town's Fourth of July fireworks celebration. I'd introduced him to Libby, who sat in my battered open convertible.

"Why do bad boys always become cops?" I said, stopping to greet him.

"Well, look who's here, the Hamster." Hand on the top of the windshield, he leaned in and treated Libby to one of his leonine grins. "Nice to meet you too, Libby. This guy gives you any trouble, you call me."

"Yeah, call him Choo Choo Chooch."

"Okay, Hammy baby, get moving, you're holding up traffic."

"He's handsome," she said, looking back as we parked in the grass near the water tower. "But why do you call each other that?"

By the time Rit and I met on Carter Street that evening, his thinning widow's peak was isolated from the rest of his curls. His athleticism remained, though limited now to golf, doubles tennis, and horseshoes.

"Speaking about Coach O'Malley, remember how he used to call you 'Stork Legs?'" Rit rested an elbow on the stone wall surrounding the cemetery. "Well, I totally see it now. Standing there you look exactly like a big bird. If possible, they've become even skinnier."

We both studied my dripping calves.

"Want a word to the wise?"

"Never knew you to have any."

"I was just going to suggest you stop keeping your own lonely company. You've been skulking around like a man with no friends since Libby passed away. Come and play some doubles with Joey and Mike and me at Mead Park on Saturdays. And why don't you call Vicky? She was asking me about you the other day."

"Vicky who?"

"Gingerella. You guys would get on great. She can be pain in the butt, but she has a good heart."

The thing I recalled most about Vicky was her resemblance to Annette Funicello, the chaste Disney Mouseketeer with the big chest, which jibed with my vague image of her being a bubbly cheerleader and opinionated overachiever. "Isn't she your cousin, or something?" I asked. "Aren't all you guys related up there on

Garibaldi Lane?"

"Yes she is, and no we're not. Some of us Guineas even married into the upper crust." Rit was referring to his wife, Gail Carrington, who'd maintained an infatuation for him since third grade. It had survived her separation at boarding school and college, to say nothing of the disapproval of her socialite parents. Rit and Gail now lived off of fashionable Michigan Road in a big colonial.

"So why don't you give Vicky a call? Go dancing. She'd like that," he said.

"With your 'pain-in-the-ass' cousin? Some endorsement. Forget it."

Rit let loose a flatulent bray from his lips. "Okay, *stunod*." He returned to his cruiser, settled his hulk behind the wheel, and yanked the shift lever into gear. He turned sideways to point at me. "But skip the cocktail hour tonight. Your face is all red and bloaty. You're beginning to look like a genuine alky."

"What does *stunod* mean?"

"Ask Vicky."

He rolled past, tires crunching, twin exhausts burbling. His brake lights flashed ahead as he slowed to disappear around a curve.

Alone in the deepening dusk, I resumed jogging. The respite had restored me. Lengthening my stride, I experienced a forgotten power, a joy in movement. I pictured myself running the entire night like this, effortlessly following the yellow line down the middle of the crowned road through the soft sibilance of surrounding trees. On the right, the oldest house in town, a 1724 red saltbox, came into view then fell behind me in the gloom. But after a minute or so, my left shoe began to scuff once again and I slowed the pace.

Where Stanton Road falls away toward the Silvermine River, I had to ease up even more. Running down its washboard slant—especially in the dark—invited a tumble. The road falls at nearly a twenty percent grade. Each stride jolted my knees, even though I was now trotting crossways. The old country lane bends right and left like a staircase with landings. Coming into view on the first level was an elderly man standing outside another town antique, a taupe-colored Cape with a pair of doghouse dormers. He was bent over, searching for something. I recognized Loring Davies, onetime Navy pilot, ex-Brown Brothers Harriman investment banker, and my former Boy Scout leader. A bag of groceries lay at his feet.

"What are you looking for, Mr. Davies?"

His head flew up. "Where the hell did *you* come from?"

"I'm Pete Wendell. I was out jogging. You were my scout master for Troop Five. Do you remember me?"

"No."

"Let me help you there. What are you looking for?"

Mirth crinkled the old man's face. "Now isn't this something? A helpful Boy Scout materializes out of the darkness."

We discovered what he was seeking—his missing key—stuck in the front door. I hauled the rest of his groceries, mostly canned goods, into his dim galley kitchen. There, two decades dropped away.

Home from Dartmouth for Christmas, I'd stood on the same spot, stirring Wassail and feeling intellectually intimidated by Lucy Davies' friends, a crowd of Harvard students and professors. Loring Davies' daughter was a Radcliffe pre-med who also liked to fool around. My nickname for her was Lucy Straps. Her guests' monumental self-assurance pushed all my inadequacy buttons.

At dinner, the conversation was about the silly essays sent by unqualified candidates seeking admission to the Harvard Medical School.

A middle-aged jerk named Terrance Grimley, a professor, tittered at the recollection of one especially pleading application. "This guy wrote that his grades were not indicative of his, and I quote, 'totally sincere desire to serve humanity.' He was from some half-baked school like Rutgers."

"Ha, ha," came the muffled laugh of an undergrad friend of Lucy's, his mouth stuffed with food.

"Can you imagine the sheer idiocy?" said Professor Grimley.

"Can you imagine the sheer hopelessness?" I muttered.

"What's that?"

"I was just putting myself in that guy's shoes. I'd never have a prayer of getting in, either."

Grimly passed the potatoes in silence, his expression matching his name.

After dinner, feeling conspicuous but ignored, I slipped into Mr. Davies' snug study. I pulled a copy of *A Tale of Two Cities* from the wall bookcase. In the same section stood a silver-framed photo of a young man beside a dark, bulky warplane with a huge white star on its fuselage. I sat in a leather club chair to reread the book's best-and-worst-of-times opening.

Loud groans and laughter erupted from the living room. I considered tip-toeing out the back door. A moment later, Lucy joined me bearing a glass of wine.

"Are you hiding in here?" she asked. "Here, have some more cheer."

"Just catching up on my reading. Sorry if I offended the prof." I took the drink and motioned with it at the photo. "That your dad?"

She pulled the image down and squatted beside me. "Yes, see? He's with his SB2C."

I took it from her hand to look more closely. "SB2C?"

"They were dive bombers. Dad named his 'The Flying Oil Leak.'"

"Where was this?"

"Pearl Harbor. Dad was training for the invasion of Okinawa." She stood to replace the picture and made a soft disapproving cluck with her tongue.

"Something amiss?"

"Somebody left the safe open." She reached in between a gap in the books and I heard a metallic click. "Come back in the living room, we need you for charades."

"No way, I'm all self-conscious now. Can't I just skip out the back?"

"Oh no you don't, you coward. You've got to help me suck up to Professor Grimley. I need his recommendation on my med school application." Her lips turned up in a salacious grin. "This could be worth some nookie to you."

Now, under his front door's portico as I left, Loring Davies shook my hand in bewildered gratitude. He remembered so little about me, I so much about him and his daughter who'd become an oncologist in Colorado, presumably with the help of the pompous Professor Grimley.

The stars had come out. I waved a farewell to the old man and started a half-jog down the dark hill, but my energy had vanished, and my left foot was dragging alarmingly. Trembling with weakness and breaking out in a cold sweat, I had to halt. Around me, cicadas ratcheted like asymmetric points of longing. In the pulsating gloom, I knelt down and vomited.

Chapter Thirteen
Regression to the Eighth Grade

Vicky Gingerella sat with her back to the millpond on the elevated wooden deck behind the Silvermine Tavern. Around us in the darkness, the trunks of maple trees poked through holes cut in the pressure-treated planking. A faint breeze stirred the tabletop candle's flame. From below came the liquid hiss of the waterfall. I'd first eaten here from the children's menu.

"I used to order something called The Squirrel when I was a kid," I said, clomping down memory lane. "It was a hamburger, but in my feverish little mind I really wanted it to be macerated squirrel meat."

"So what did you think they put into The Swan?"

"*You* ate here?"

Vicky gave me a sour squint. "Why do you sound so amazed? Do you think my family was too plebian?"

"No, of course not. The Swan was chicken, wasn't it?"

"Yes it was. And it sure beat pasta e fagioli."

"Oh? What's that?"

She pinched three fingers together and shook them at me. "It's an Italian dish made with lentils. *Capisce?*"

"Did I say something wrong?"

She was grinning now. "No, I'm just trying to shatter a stereotype."

I nodded, wondering how to respond. To the contrary, she seemed to be confirming one. "I think you've got the wrong idea that I'm some kind of snob," I said.

"Maybe you're just unaware of it."

Though familiar from childhood, I couldn't remember ever speaking to her before tonight. Yet, here she was kidding me like she had some right, shared some close history. Rit had hornswoggled me into this evening by telling me that he'd promised Vicky that I was going to ask her out. An eighth-grade blackmail strategy dependent on the victim's kindness, it still worked. This was a pity date, but maybe I was becoming the pitiful one. Vicky did in fact resemble Annette Funicello. Possessing the same wholesome air, she had penetrating brown eyes, big dimples, and short black hair that flared from a prominent cowlick at her hairline. She pushed it off her face as she bent forward to scan the menu. The errant lock flopped right back.

"So what looks good to you?" she asked.

"Anybody ever tell you that you have amazing hair?" I said. "Am I allowed to say that?"

"That's a polite way to say it's unruly," she said. "Rit called me Paint Brush Face when we were kids. Because it sticks up."

"I can relate. Kids called me Hayhead."

"I remember that. The other girls thought you were cute in a Huck Finn sort of way. Think the sirloin will be any good?"

"But you didn't?"

"Nope…I'm definitely going with the salmon. So why did you come back to New Canaan, Pete?"

"It's hard to put into words."

"Oh go on, give it a try. You're supposed to be the big word maven."

Her teasing and directness were disconcerting, midway between impertinent and intimate. I don't know why I'd brought Vicky to the tavern, except that it held other, more recent memories. Libby and I had celebrated an anniversary here. We'd made pregnant love upstairs in one of the guest rooms, with champagne in a silver wine cooler and the sashes thrown open to the clinks and murmurs of dinner guests eating and conversing on the deck below.

I swirled my half-empty drink with a swizzle stick, the alcohol beginning to caress my nerves, and wondered if it was too soon to order another. The tinkling ice went round and round. Why *had* I come back? Libby had asserted that it was about measuring up, which entailed wearing dark suits and living amid broad manicured lawns. To Vicky, I joked, "Maybe I'm returning to the scene of the crime."

"Not many people can afford to come back," Vicky observed.

"I'm not sure I can, either. I suppose it was partly because I remembered limitless possibilities here," I said, trying to solidify inchoate thoughts. "I was good at stuff: honor student, football player, swim champ, class officer. Afterward, my life kind of spun off like a bad golf slice. Maybe I'm trying to drop a Mulligan."

"A re-do?"

"Yeah, and I've never gotten over this sense that this is where I'm from. Memories are everywhere—skating at Mud Pond, pool parties out on Turtleback Road, touch football at Tim Eastman's family estate, coming-out balls and tobogganing at the country club. Even the quality of the light around here feels like home." I drank the rest of my gin-and-tonic at a gulp. "Not very articulate, am I? Want another wine?"

"I always thought nostalgia was a flabby emotion. Nor did I ever live in that version of New Canaan." She circled the top of her wineglass with a fingertip. "Want to know what I think?"

"That you can't go home again? I already know that."

"No. You rah-rah boys were set up to fail. You were all supposed to become company presidents like your dads, but you obviously couldn't. It still bothers you guys."

"Rah-rah boys?"

"Commuters' kids, heirs presumptive; downward mobility was your real destiny."

"I never thought of it that way."

"Hence the wistful regrets, the where-did-it-all-go-wrong musings." She gave me an almost defiant look. "Ever hear the saying, 'expectations are resentments waiting to happen?'"

"No I haven't, but I'm no 'heir.' My grandfather Janush was a Polish stockyard worker. Does that shatter *my* stereotype?"

"So where does 'Hampton Peter Wendell' come from?"

"The other grandfather was an English immigrant, a steamfitter; it was *his* handle." I selected a brown olive from among an assortment in a small pressed-glass bowl. "I'm a ne'er-do-well who arose from humble beginnings," I said, and popped it in my mouth.

The waitress returned. Wearing a man's white dress shirt and shiny black bowtie, she removed a scarlet leatherette pad from her back pocket to record our order. We made our choices, I asked for another drink, and she left.

"Sure you don't want pasta e fagioli?" I said. "It's not too late."

"Speaking about stereotypes, did you know my father is chair of the English Department at Norwalk Community College?"

"I always thought he ran Ginger's diner on Elm Street. That guy's hair stuck up exactly like yours."

"That was my Uncle Angelo. My dad is Vincenzo, but people call him Enzo. He teaches literature and Shakespeare."

"Ah yes." I held out my hands—thumbs touching, fingers raised—framing her face like a movie director. "'She walks in beauty like the night.'"

"Actually, that was George Gordon Lord Byron."

"Oops." I drained my glass and beckoned to the waitress for another. "Oh well, 'correction is affection,' as somebody always used to tell me."

"Somebody? Somebody who?"

A short, bitter laugh and then: "My late wife, actually."

"Oh, I'm so sorry, Pete. Rit told me that her name was Libby."

"Yes, her name was Libby." I tried to will Vicky not to ask the next question, but she did.

"What was she like? You must miss her terribly."

My face froze. "I don't talk about her," I muttered.

Vicky rearranged her place setting amid a brittle silence.

"So, how come you never left New Canaan?" I said, breaking the uncomfortable moment.

"I did. I'm in Norwalk. You picked me up there tonight, remember?"

"Right, of course. Then fill me on the past twenty years. What do you do now?"

"You really want to hear?"

"Absolutely, one plebian to another."

Her story came out: She'd become a professional flutist after going to Boston's Berklee College of Music. She played with symphony orchestras in cities across the state—from the Hartford

Symphony to New London's—and taught music at a fancy prep school in Stamford.

"I'm impressed," I said. "Can I hear you play someday? And is it flutist or flautist?"

"Flutist and that can be arranged. But I'm curious, why did you leave journalism? Rit said you once worked at the *Wall Street Bulletin*."

I glanced up at the audibly moving leaves above her head. Vicky was getting on my nerves. "I got disillusioned," I answered, "cynical."

She wore a black sleeveless dress that displayed her muscular arms. Through the open glass doors behind her shoulder, I could see the Tavern's collection of antique implements. Rakes, eel forks, draw knives, block planes, apple corers, unknowable nineteenth-century tools festooned the walls, along with flat primitive portraits of unsmiling New Englanders. Some were as familiar as ancestors. One yellow-haired man displaying a stoic grimace reminded me of myself.

"Can you tell me why? It seems like a high-minded profession. I mean, you did help people, didn't you?"

I held up my glass and the waitress nodded back as she delivered our entrees. "You want the truth about why I left?"

Vicky nodded.

"I wanted bucks. I was making 600 dollars a week—big money in that newsroom. But it was a treadmill to nowhere. Mostly I wrote earnings stories and recycled press releases for the ticker. My wife was pregnant and I wanted to own a nice house, be able to send my kid to a good school, live in a place like this. And if that meant writing corporate dreck about new computers and speeches for fat cats, so what? There isn't anything dishonest about it. Or at least it didn't start that way."

Vicky wouldn't let go. "But you don't need a ton of money if you don't spend a lot. Six hundred a week sounds like a heck of a lot to me. As they say, 'enough is plenty.'"

I fought an urge to get up and leave. "So did you and Rit live next door growing up?"

"No," she said, "down the street. Am I bugging you?"

"I'm not used to being interrogated. It's usually the other way around."

"Sorry."

The waitress arrived with my third drink. I relented and tried harder to explain: "Okay, so leaving journalism was like giving up heroin. I really enjoyed making guys like my Old Man uncomfortable."

Her brow furrowed.

"But there was another factor. One day I looked around the newsroom and didn't see many gray hairs. It's called the Peter Pan profession for a reason. They'd all been forced out. I was thirty years old and I decided it was time for self-preservation. Conveniently, that's when PR came calling."

"Have you ever thought about teaching?" She bent forward toward me.

"No, never. Why do you ask that?"

"You'd be great. You really ought to consider it."

By now Vicky had gone into gauzy focus. In the candle light, her face glowed with conviction.

"Rit mentioned you had a really nasty divorce," I said. Good grief, did that just come out of my mouth?

Vicky sat back in her chair. "You *are* a pushy reporter, aren't you?"

"Insensitivity was a big plus in my line of work."

"If you must know, Danny divorced *me*."

The story involved one Daniel R. Reardon, star Boston College baseball player with a 93-mile-an-hour fastball. Full of promise, he played the game not quite well enough and for too long. As she spoke, her face revealing hurt and frustration, Vicky became less of an abstraction, less of a background character in my own narrative. Unlike me, she was revealing herself.

"So I stayed with him for years in tank towns in the minors like Elizabethton, Tennessee. We argued constantly. He got very huffy. I failed to understand the meaning of his existence, don't you see? He claimed I was always trying to control him."

"It's tough to give up a dream," I said. "Or have it taken away."

"I was only trying to assert reality. And of course we couldn't plan a family bouncing all over the country. It was all so futile. He kept playing games that only mattered as statistics to get into the Big Leagues."

"And that's when you gave up on him?"

"No. I came home to finish my music studies, and he found a bimbo in Florida to share his fantasy." Vicky snorted. "That's all men want isn't it, a fawning dumb broad to puff up your egos?"

"I don't know, beyond sex, I think most of us want two things: emotional generosity and honesty."

She jabbed apart some pink salmon flakes with her fork. "So do women."

Unbidden, the waitress arrived with another drink. I handed her my empty glass and held up the new one to Vicky. "Cheers."

"Is that your fourth?"

"So what happened to Danny boy? Still pitching erratic heat?"

"He's divorced again and works in construction. He calls me

up when he has a snootful, says he wants to get back together; claims we're not divorced in the eyes of the church, that only death will separate us."

The waterfall seemed to get louder, as if someone had turned up the volume. The tavern had been a turning mill in the early 1800s. How many bobbins, spools, and balusters had it created? How much water had spilled over the dam since Libby died? How many maple leaves had fallen in the mill pond and been carried out to sea? I understood snootfuls. I thought about Elizabeth Lindquist, from some dinky town in Michigan's Upper Peninsula; her mother asking me at the funeral if I believed in God's Will, extorting a lie. Two years had passed since I'd called out there, Sven assuring me that they were both just fine, son. He still sent me birthday cards ostensibly signed by both, but in his handwriting only.

Vicky was staring at me. "Where did you go just then?"

"I was remembering you when we were kids," I lied. "Weren't you voted Most Outgoing or something?"

"No, Biggest Pain in the Butt, according to Ritinsky."

We laughed and finished the meal trading reminiscences of high school. I ordered a brandy and, linen napkins splayed over the cleared-away table, we glided back into memories of teachers and classes and personalities. She reminded me that we'd been in the same biology class, which I had no memory of, and recalled how she could always recognize me on the football field by my "dancer's legs." I told her that her exuberant cartwheels had been incredible. But I wanted to know something in the here and now: What had Rit meant when he called me *stunod* out on Carter Street?

Vicky's dimples deepened. "It means a stupid person," she

said.

"Just as I thought."

We departed through the gatehouse on the lower level, but not before I'd stumbled on the steep carpeted stairs.

"Do you want me to drive, Pete? You've had a lot to drink."

"Nah, I've been having trouble with my balance lately. My neurologist says I've got to lift my feet."

"What's wrong?"

"The technical term is clumsiness; it'll go away."

The evening was warm. I put down the Saab's cracked top and drove slowly along the Norwalk side of the river. The passing trees left a trail of whispers in the mild night air. I didn't want the evening to end. "Hey, Paint Brush Face, did you ever go to the trampolines at Calf Pasture when you were a kid?"

A passing street lamp revealed her delight. "Did I ever! I used to do flips."

I downshifted and drove with purpose. But the bouncing pits were no more. Nevertheless, the parking lot at Norwalk's public beach was jammed. A smell of caramel and popcorn was in the air. Some kind of clam festival was under way. I led Vicky away from the neon glare, from parents buying soft ice cream for their kids, who capered and called to each other among a deeply shadowed grove of Norway maples. Instead, we approached the black waters of Long Island Sound. Off shore, Peck Ledge lighthouse stroked the water with a rotating beam: red, pause, white, pause, red again. Behind us, an amplified guitar blared and died; then a drum rattled and began a monotonous four-four beat. A band was warming up. Halogen lights on poles gave our shadows long curving legs on the sand. We took off our shoes and waded into the gently lapping water. I searched for stones and began to skip them. After a while, we heard the rhythmic thump of loud rock music, a classic, the singer badly off key: "Well shake it up baby now"—

Vicky held out her left arm, palm upwards. "Want to dance, Hayhead?"

"I don't know, Vicky, those guys are unusually rotten."

"Who the heck cares?" She grabbed my hands, and began yanking my arms back and forth like connecting rods. "C'mon, c'mon, c'mon, c'mon, baby, now," she sang while prancing on her toes. She had a pleasant voice.

The music shifted to a slow-dance number. Frankie Valli. This time the band wasn't too bad: "You're too good to be true…" It wasn't my kind of music, but its innocent sweetness affected me. "Can't take my eyes off of you…" I took Vicky in my arms and we circled slowly at the edge of the water. As it ended, I dipped her backwards and lost my balance. I took a splashing step to keep from dropping her.

"You're a good dancer," she said. "Sorry I'm so heavy."

Driving home to her condo in West Norwalk, radio turned up on an oldies station, I stomped on the turbo and the old car leaped ahead with a roar.

"The heap still has some punch," I shouted.

Vicky threw her head back and laughed, her wild forelock fluttering like a broken wing. On the concrete stoop of her condo unit, we enacted a pantomime of trying to shake hands. Mine rose and fell, then hers. Arms at our sides, we stood face to face, unsure what to do.

"This is awkward," I said. "I feel about sixteen years old."

"More like fourteen." Her eyes were in deep shadow from the porch light, but I could see her watching me intently.

She rose on her toes as I drew her toward me. Her lips felt soft and yielding, but her broad back was a surprise. Libby had been a tiny woman.

Chapter Fourteen
Reduced to Protoplasm

Someone was pulling me out of unconsciousness by my armpits. Whirling red and blue lights shadowed a man's face as he hoisted me off the ground. "Upsy daisy," he muttered.

We staggered together in the stroboscopic glare.

"Have a seat."

He eased me down on a cool narrow surface covered with sharp objects. Bolting upright, I saw rows of gravestones blinking pinkly in the night and recognized Lakeview Cemetery. I'd sat on remembrance rocks, a Jewish custom I'd adopted when yellow roses turned brown too quickly. I brushed the pebbles off and sat back down on Libby's head marker.

"He's down here!" the man yelled up the hill. His profile showed against the flashing lights.

"Rit?" I was full of wonder. "Whah *you* doing here?" My tongue was two inches thick.

"Better question: What're *you* doing here? I thought you'd gone out with Vicky."

"Mmmmaaahh, visit'n Libby."

"At 2 a.m.?"

"Talk'n to her." I started to fall forward and Rit grabbed my shirt. I'd really dosed myself. Even seated I was reeling.

"How much have you had to drink?"

I took some deep breaths and tried to concentrate. After dropping Vicky off I'd stopped at a package store and bought a twelve-pack. There was no particular reason, except I still didn't want to go home. I'd driven around aimlessly, the car's engine whining through the gears, wind buffeting my ears, the occasional moth flashing in the headlights and then vanishing into the black vacuum behind. At one point I passed the driveway to my father's former shingle pile, where I heaved out an empty can.

"Don't remember."

"Well, my friend, it's against the law to sleep in the cemetery."

"Thought *everyone* was sleeping here, har, har."

Rit's face contorted. "Cut the crap. You're in trouble. The neighbors called the police station. You left your convertible up in the circle with the radio blaring oldies. They thought somebody was having a party down here."

"Jess l'il ol' me."

"I got a suggestion: Conduct further nocturnal conversations with Libby in your living room." He stooped to grab an empty beer can. "I should arrest you for littering, too. Here's the evidence."

"Sorry, Rit."

"Why do you *always* reduce yourself to protoplasm?" he asked, dropping the empty. He had every right to make this observation. He'd first seen me in this condition in high school, where another of his nicknames for me was Peter Potted.

"Won't happen again. I can quit anytime I want." (What I really said sounded more like, Wownhap nagin. Kin kwit any timewahhnt.)

"Like I should believe that? Denial is not a river in Egypt, pal." He withdrew his supporting arm and stepped back. "So what were you talking to Libby about?"

"Was pologizing."

"For what?"

"For killing her."

"We've been all over that. It was a drunk driver. You were just back from California, remember?"

"I was supposed to be driving her to the doctor's. I'd been drinking, instead." My voice cracked. "Too late…she'd said she was ashamed of me. Told me right to my big fat WASP face. Become an ass kisser. Hadda leggo of my banana or she was going to file for divorce… 'very regretfully,' of course."

"What are you talking about? What banana?"

"Greed. Need to impress. Hand in the box."

"You're shit-faced, not talking straight."

"*You* know, Father Elway's morality tale."

"No I don't know. You been talking to that old guy some more? What'd he say?"

"Coulda been a *great* journalist like her wonderful boyfriend, the estimable and crusading Tommy Dorsey. Wait, wasn't that a saxophone player? *He* enforces accountability on power. *I* became a smarmy flack." I coughed and spat up a big hocking lunger on the grass. "Little Petey in his Brooks Brothers suit. She had my number."

"Take it easy, Pete. That's just the booze talking."

"Slippery yes-man. Or should I say yes-person? Ever hear the word 'oleaginous'? Means oily, greasy."

"Hey, stunod, knock it off!" He squeezed my slack cheeks with a big paw. "You wanted to provide for her and the kid coming along, thought this was the best place. Nothing wrong with that; hell, *I* live here and I'm not a phony."

"Why couldn't *I* die instead? I was supposed to be in that car." My chest heaved like a coming sneeze. Then I let go and sobbed like I'd never stop.

"Breathe, breathe. And by the way," Rit said, arms akimbo, "you're wasting the theatrics. Who are you feeling sorry for most, yourself or Libby?"

I rubbed tears from my eyes and licked mucus from beneath my nose.

"You need to grow up."

"Wha?"

"Think Libby would be real proud of you crawling around on all fours like a baby and crying in your beer?"

"Fuck you."

"Think she'd want you to destroy yourself like this? Think she'd like seeing you dead drunk and a menace for vehicular homicide, yourself?"

"Oh, God."

"Know what? I think she'd call you a pussy. I can hear her: 'Pussy Petey.' That's a really good name for you, the self-obsessed crybaby. You ain't much, but you're all you think about, right?"

"Lemme alone."

"Isn't that right, Pussy Petey?"

I staggered up and threw a wild punch. He pushed me forward and the ground rushed up with a thump. The grass smelled the same as when I'd thrown a block and watched Rit's bongo drum-shaped calves pumping down the sideline. But there was no jubilant crowd, no big red numbers flashing on the scoreboard, only the clacking of police lights revolving atop the squad car in the driveway above.

Rit picked me up and leaned me back against her stone. "Got that out of your system, Hammy?"

"Yeah."

"Bottom line, she loved you, in spite of your douchebag tendencies. My advice to you: *Stop* listening to your feelings, they lie. Get off the pity pot. Get some help. Go see a shrink or what's-his-face, the old Episcopal guy. Better yet, join AA. Meantime, what am I supposed to do with you tonight?"

"Can I just drive home?"

"No way, they'd arrest *me*."

"Then lemme sit here."

"No can do."

I began to gag. Rit stepped back as I threw up.

When I was through, he grabbed a handful of grass clippings and roughly wiped my chin. "Why do I always twelve-step the wet drunks?" I heard him mumble. "Yuck." Turning uphill, he yelled, "Hey Billy! You know how to drive a stick?"

From the swirling lights above came a confident reply. "No problem, lieutenant,"

"Good boy. Let's pile Stork Legs into his back seat."

The arriving voice was disbelieving. "You mean you're not going to run him in? I just checked his record, and he already has one DUI with a suspended sentence."

"We didn't find him behind the wheel, did we?"

"But the guy's totally snockered." Billy eyed me with deep disdain as I plucked blades of grass from my mouth. "He'd melt the breathalyzer. Look at him, for Pete's sake."

"Yes," I said and giggled, "*I'm* Pete."

Billy ignored me. "Jail time would do this guy a lot of good."

"Let's just get him home." Rit stepped forward and put one of my arms over his shoulder. We tottered and he motioned to Billy.

"You sure about this?" Billy asked. "I know he's your pal, but his next visit here might be in a box."

"Help me."

Putting his face close to mine to lift, Billy recoiled. "Whew, this guy stinks. How much have you been drinking?"

"'Nuff to turn me into protoplasm," I said. "Ain't that right Rit?" And then my forehead seemed to slide down over my eyes.

The horseshoe knocker awakened me. I was lying on the camelback couch with a cushion wedged under my head. The house was quiet except for the stream's burble out back. Car doors slammed. A moment later headlight beams swept across the low ceiling. My ears buzzed and the room spun. I had to urinate urgently but a blanket was wrapped tightly around me. Pulling my arms free, a flat object slid off my chest and hit the floor. Splayed on the wide old boards was a book. The grainy darkness made it hard to make out the title. I picked it up and brought it close to my face. Along the binding it read: *Alcoholics Anonymous*.

Chapter Fifteen

Becoming Henshaw's Ghost

The skin around Dick Marin's eyes wrinkled with suspicion. "I don't understand your pitch," he said. "Trevor doesn't need any more writing talent. That's Teddy's job. Is this another maneuver to get rid of him?" Wary of my motives, he didn't realize I was running up the white flag.

I'd spent my post-cemetery Sunday groaning, napping, sipping black coffee, and vowing never to drink again, not ever. I couldn't touch food. But sometime during that vale of torture a survival plan had floated up from the muck. Monday rolled around and I'd marched into the little man's office to try it out.

"You're too Machiavellian," I said. "Your turf's as secure as Fort Knox. But my question to you is this: Can deGruening get Henshaw a management column at the *Bulletin*?"

"Can anybody?"

"I think *I* can. I've known the top editors there for years."

Marin rubbed his brow as his mind soared. "Say, that's not a bad idea," he said. "Maybe I'll vote to keep you around after all." Then he frowned. "Wait a minute, has L.A. blessed this? You're kind of wandering off the reservation, aren't you?"

That was true enough but Jim Phillips, who paid my salary,

quickly came to understand my rationale: Matrix's president, Trevor Henshaw, was the closest thing that the stodgy Amsys Corp.—whose main claim to fame was stitching together back-office systems—had to being a rock star. He'd published one huge management bestseller and gave speeches costing forty grand each to overflowing audiences of technology-spooked senior line executives. It was the beginning of the era of the Information Superhighway, and he was the company's only prominent rainmaker, futurist, and name brand guru—and he lapped up publicity. Also, once installed as his wordsmith, I might be able to keep his marketeers from gratuitously insulting the rest of Amsys. Maybe even make it appear we were working as one. Most importantly, keep Marin from stabbing me in the back. It all made sense to Phillips, who had a further rationale: "You need a powerful rabbi like Henshaw to protect you out there."

"Okay," Marin assented. "But remember I'm running marketing around here, and don't you, or Phillips, or Kitsie forget it."

Henshaw, himself, wasn't so sure. "How many typewritten pages *is* 800 words?" he asked. "Won't producing monthly columns rather swamp us?" We were riding up in the elevator, where I'd accosted him as he'd arrived for work. "They'll have to be jolly good. Where will we get the ideas?"

"About three pages, double spaced, and leave the last to me," I said.

"I suppose it's worth a go, and of course we'll benefit from their imprimatur. But you'll have to mimic my voice convincingly." He tapped my chest with the backs of his fingers. "Can you manage that, old fellow?"

"You bet; you'll come across as empathetic and super

knowledgeable."

"Hear, hear." The doors slid open to the reception area, where we stood talking under the firm's chrome logo, which looked something like a math equation.

"I'll work up a couple of drafts," I said. "You'll approve them in advance, of course."

"Right you are."

Turning toward my office, the edge of my sole caught on the plush carpet.

"Pick up your feet, man," Henshaw said.

We dubbed Henshaw's column *Executive Decision*. It took a few weeks to convince Deke Malloy. But I sealed the deal after submitting three sample columns that were not the standard here-are-the-four-strategies-you-must-adopt-to-make-pots-of-money-business-school-publication drivel. The columns would be about difficult choices—like when to sell off an aging cash cow, or manage the exit of a failing executive—and would run in the special new weekly management slot the *Bulletin* had introduced in its Second Section, where Libby would have worked had she lived.

"You send me anything remotely fluffy, and I'll print it in agate type on the funny pages," Malloy blustered, "and you know we don't run comics." Though burning with curiosity, I didn't ask him about NCC's refusal to answer *Bulletin* phone calls or emails. But the snit seemed to be ongoing.

Kitsie Schoemacher was the first to congratulate me on the *Bulletin* placement. "This is just super," she said, when I found her seated in my office on the morning it was published. She was wearing a gold silk blouse and the paper lay open on her lap. "Keep up this kind of sharp promotion and you'll be running marketing around here. Watch out, Dick Marin!"

"Jeez, don't go spreading that around. That's the last thing I want. The guy already has me in his sights."

"It's gonna happen, you just wait. People around here are noticing your influence on Trevor."

The inaugural column that Kitsie liked so much began this way:

> Advice for the modern CEO: "You don't have to see the whole staircase; just take the first step." Who said that? Jack Welch? Management thinker Peter Drucker? Actually, it was Martin Luther King, Jr.
>
> Today's business leaders operate in a fog of ambiguity. They have to straddle multiple, even opposing tracks in fast-emerging markets and technology, making hard choices with inadequate information. Which way is onward and upward? Risk can never be avoided. But the answer to paralyzing uncertainty lies in knowing the destination, not the precise route, to the top and staying flexible. In the software industry, they call this "build a little, test a little." And it's both constant and self-correcting. Take the case of Ralph Shaw, president of...

We were off and running. Nevertheless, as Henshaw anticipated, finding grist soon proved a challenge. Sometimes, as deadlines approached, I resorted to divining his point of view, creating some kind of dramatic choice for an unnamed CEO, sprinkling it with dilemmas from the business press, and then running it by Henshaw. After a while, he trusted me implicitly.

For a while, I built these columns from kernels I'd heard him say during his speeches, which he winged from a standard set of themes designed to sell consulting engagements. Henshaw could come off as vacuous, but he was nobody's fool. He captivated senior managers with aphorisms that, from his lips, sounded like revealed wisdom. They had to. A single appearance was worth a third of my annual salary. Sometimes he contradicted himself. For instance, he'd counsel CEOs never to cut back on R&D, *especially* in bad times. Why? Because you never knew who was working on the next big idea in a garage somewhere. Then he'd turn right around in another talk and proclaim that major players should always be "fast followers," not leaders in risky innovation.

Even the blindingly obvious would get heads nodding. For instance: "Strategy means making decisions about where to participate and how to win," he told a packed conference. "The target is hitting full economic potential."

The problem with such irreducible pearls of wisdom was that they were just that, scattered axioms. Taking copious notes was entirely unnecessary. Reviewing what I'd jotted down, I'd get the feeling I'd just chomped down on cotton candy. The only hard granule of advice was to spend scarce money on technology instead of people. I grew facile at expanding Henshaw's rhetoric into narratives that delivered a moral. For instance: Kodak's failure to exploit digital photography, which it had invented in 1975, for fear of cannibalizing its own film business.

I also became adept at capturing Henshaw's Britishisms, such as the use of "turnover" for gross earnings, instead of the American "revenue," or the occasional "good show" or "bollocks" for emphasis. The *Bulletin* left these in. It was interesting, creative work in which I was crafting a management expert's voice from behind a thick curtain of anonymity.

The day after I convinced Deke Malloy to take the column, I received two outside emails. One was from Vicky:

Dear Hampton,

I remembered that "Amsys" is where you work and, being the PR bigshot, found your email address online. I want you to know that I enjoyed dinner with you last week immensely. It's always gratifying to converse with another low-born plebian. I'd like to reciprocate. How about a nice pasta e fagioli dinner at my place? Just kidding. I'll cook whatever you like, along with helpings of "honesty and emotional generosity." By the way, you should get an answering machine for your home phone, or are you avoiding bill collectors?

The other was from Freddy Pritchard at NCC:

Peter,

Can you be on deck next Thursday at 9 a.m.? After your recent meeting with Dinsmore, the pressure from the Bulletin *has been building. He'd like you to personally brief our CEO, Ted Devlin, on the personalities of Dorsey and Malloy. Maybe you can bring along a formal presentation with illustrative clippings, a little "who's who" background, and perhaps an organization chart? You know the routine from the old days, right? The Big Picture Book. Jason would like to review it by Tuesday EOD.*

Fred

I sent an affirmative to Freddy though, surprisingly, I felt reluctant. Presenting to Ted Devlin would be terrifying. Nor, for that matter, was I as desperate to jump ship anymore. Henshaw's happiness had placated Phillips. Meantime, I accepted Vicky's invitation. Maybe there'd be more kissy-face.

Chapter Sixteen

Senior Flaco's

Besides writing his blather, I started scheduling meetings for Henshaw with features editors and reporters. The idea was to position him as *the* source for quotes and industry background in management consulting pieces. Unfortunately, he was less impressive with ink-stained wretches than before executives. Henshaw shied away from negativity or controversy, the definition of newsworthiness. His desire not to offend made him evasive under questioning and at odds with his written persona.

His first backgrounder was with Tom Dorsey and it quickly flew off the rails. Pitched as an off-the-record get-together, the purpose was to promote Henshaw's second book and give Tom an advance copy to review. Soon to be published—and rigorously researched at real companies, Dick Marin assured me—the tome was called *Pulling the Right Tech Levers*. The overall premise was a kind of "know thyself" argument about understanding your strategic focus in order to invest technology dollars for best effect. The subtheme urged readers to measure themselves on customer satisfaction, not stock price.

The schlocky Mexican joint along 11th Avenue that Tom selected for the meeting set the tone. Henshaw elevated his nose as he stepped out of the taxi outside Senor Flaco's Genuine Juarez Eats—a name, I'd mistakenly assumed, for a trendy eatery. Tom had apparently come from the gym. He wore sweat pants and a stained New York Athletic Club T-shirt. He waved from a back table in the empty place. Recorded Mariachi music buffeted the garish hacienda atmosphere. The place resembled a movie set. Tom offhandedly greeted Henshaw, who leaned forward to hear better.

"Can you turn down that music?" Henshaw asked a passing waiter, who sported a Zapata mustache and sombrero. A moment later, the horn shouts stopped mid-blast. Tom's steel-rimmed glasses gave him a studious appearance that belied his intensity. He would have made a good prosecutor.

"I read your last book," he began. "The theory didn't have legs, did it?"

"I beg your pardon?"

"Hasn't the wholesale downsizing you advocated simply hollowed out American industries?"

Henshaw turned to me questioningly as Tom gave me a conspiratorial wink.

"Be nice, Tom," I said.

"So you're the high priest of 'business-process rationalization.' Is this more of the same?"

"Oh, I wouldn't say 'high priest,' old man. Maybe an 'acolyte' of the kind of in-depth research we do at Matrix," said Henshaw. "In fact, some interesting new data of ours point to the fact that most modern corporations usually can't even define the kind of businesses they're in. Did you know that there are basically just four distinct types? We're releasing a book about our findings next month."

I was impressed by Henshaw's parry and thrust, but Tom was having none of it.

"It doesn't matter how you define a business if you've cut it to the bone," he said.

"You misunderstand me, my dear fellow," said Henshaw, "you need to select which bones to pack the muscle on. Don't you see?"

The waiter, whose lopsided handlebar mustache appeared pasted on, returned to take our drink order. The conversation ceased. Tom asked for a Dos Equis and Henshaw wanted a vodka tonic. I ordered a club soda with lemon.

"Club soda?" Tom asked. "What's with that?"

"I'm in training"

"In training for what?"

"I'm going to run a marathon," I said. Where those words came from I had no idea. But I'd been struggling to stay on the wagon since my cemetery exploits with Rit. It was proving to be a torment: obsessive running punctuated by long nights without shape, my skin crawling with craving, and oblivion reached only though sleeping pills.

"I'll believe you'll be in a marathon when I see it," Tom said. "So Trevor, the whole point of your last book was to do more work with fewer people, wasn't it?"

"No, it was about doing work more efficiently, so that businesses could grow and *hire* more people." Looking put out, Henshaw tried to explain that he was there to discuss right business definitions, the new theory, not rightsizing.

"Sounds like another con, let's stick with your *last* book. That was about machines replacing workers, was it not?

"Alright, let's *do* talk about staffing," said Henshaw,

"particularly the way it relates to information flows. In the old corporate paradigm, middle managers served as information carriers, sort of like a data bus in a computer. They transmitted directions downward from senior line managers to workers, and then carried messages and numbers back upwards from the factory floor or sales office. They oscillated back and forth with critical data, but without a lot of added value."

"And now these middle managers get thrown under the bus?"

"No, now they're empowered to make decisions. They're *driving* the bus." Henshaw hadn't touched his drink. "Can we talk about my *new* book now?"

"I've got a proof copy here," I said, holding it out to Tom. "Maybe you'd like to do a review of it? You have first dibs."

Tom took it, scanned the cover, and slid it back across the table. "Oh, I'm sure you'll send me a nice press release." Tom lifted his wrist to examine an oversize sports watch. "Hey, would you look at that. I've just got time to change and get back to the office. Nice meeting you, Trevor, old bean. Can I have a word with you outside, Pete?"

Back on 11th Avenue, Tom informed me that Trevor Henshaw "spoke Pablum fluently." He added that Henshaw's new management theory was a tautology:

"Good companies are good companies because they're good at what they do. Some insight. Reviewers are going to crucify him. I feel bad for you Pete. When are you going to quit this kind of work and rejoin the resistance of the downtrodden masses?"

"Before I do, can you at least take a look at the book?" I again handed him the review copy. "It's very well researched if not exactly scintillating. You'd be doing me a favor if I could say you at least took it. I'm afraid my days may be becoming numbered at Matrix."

"That might actually be a very good reason to refuse. How many times do I have to tell you to walk away?"

"Believe me, I'm trying to figure that out. Meantime I've got to eat."

"Okay, okay." He snatched the paperback from my hands. "I just hope the print doesn't come off on my ass." He strode away waggling the book with a cheery wave.

"What a loathsome man," said Henshaw, after he emerged on the sidewalk. "He's impervious to logic; it was as if he arrived with his own theory about consulting. And you say that's the chap we're forced to deal with at the *Bulletin*?"

"He's the one."

"If I had my way, I'd never speak to that beastly fellow again."

"Welcome to public relations, Trevor. I'm sorry to tell you this, but you *have* to talk to skeptical reporters. If we don't define our company and industry for him, our competitors will."

After Henshaw hailed a cab and rode off, a shouting street vendor wearing a bulging Rastafarian tam drew my attention. He was selling knock-off TAG Heuer, Rolex, and other ersatz high-end watches from a tray. I picked up a rubber running watch. Since I'd impulsively committed myself to entering a marathon, I'd probably need to own one. Depressing buttons around the bezel produced a tiny stick figure, whose audibly clicking pace could be adjusted. I pushed the button again and got the little guy jogging. Once more and his limbs were flailing in a sprint: a tiny Pete Wendell, going nowhere fast.

Keeping an eye on me, the vendor was busy chatting up an intrigued professional woman, who was fingering a convincing copy of a Cartier tank watch. He bowed my way. "You buy that

watch, mon, you'll be doing four-minute miles in no time flat."
To the woman he said, "That's an exact duplicate in every way.
You can't tell it from what they sell at Tiffany's."

I laughed. "Tiffany's watch is mechanical, isn't it? The second
hand sweeps around; that one clicks."

"Someone getting *that* close to the watch is trying to steal it,
mon. Nobody will notice."

I held up the sports watch. "How much is this one?"

"Know how I can sell that for ten dollars?" he asked me, while
picking up another watch for the woman's comparison.

"Because it's fake?"

"No." Waving his free arm upward, he said, "Because I have
sky-high overhead."

It made no sense, but the woman burst into laughter as I
handed over my ten spot.

CHAPTER SEVENTEEN

Abrupt Men

My fateful meeting with Ted Devlin, CEO of the National Computing Company—and one of the highest-paid executives in the country—lasted all of five minutes. I should have anticipated such brevity in a company that fetishized decisiveness.

"I hear you used to work for those scumbags at the *Bulletin*," Devlin said, using a word that no doubt would have offended his sensitive mother. "You made the right decision to leave."

"Yes, sir."

We were in the same icy conference room next to Jason Dinsmore's office. We had not been introduced, and he either didn't know, or didn't choose, to use my name. I was simply "you." Even seated, Devlin was intimidating. My binder of information was in front of him. He snapped it open, scanned a page, and then shut it.

"I read your deck and concur. We've got to resume contact. Refresh my memory, Jason. What did friend Dorsey say in his last voicemail?"

"'Vee haf vays of magging you tawk,'" Dinsmore replied, "in a German accent—the wise ass."

Devlin's gaze was like a death ray. "I don't normally respond to threats, but do you think I can talk to him off the record without getting lampooned?"

"We'll have to formally establish the ground rules," I replied, "but if he agrees, he'll abide by them. He's honest," I added, needlessly.

NCC's chief executive received this information without comment. He'd once been the youngest partner in the history of the worldwide management consulting firm of Hyde & Co. Since leaving, he'd returned to profitability a slew of distressed companies in industries ranging from the oil patch to consumer goods. As the current savior of NCC, (and thanks to NCC's massive share buybacks that ballooned the price of his stock options) his compensation was something like $25 million a year. He struck me as a human industrial monument. Compared to the magazine-cover images I'd seen of him, his face was more jowly and florid, his eyes even more intense.

"Was Aubrey Wendell your father?"

"Yes, he was," I said.

"I knew him from the U.S. Oil & Gas Association. He had a penetrating business mind."

"Yes he did." A shiver rippled across my back. Why did they keep this place so cold? One theory: nobody could possibly nod off in this meat locker.

Devlin swung his leaden glance to Dinsmore. "Okay, have our guest here set it up like he suggests—an insider first look at our new strategy, a scoop." He pronounced the word as if it were funny. "I just hope you're right about this," Devlin added to me. "I don't want to be made a fool of."

He rose and left the room.

—

I went back to see my neurologist when it began to feel like the chestnut plank floors at home had turned into a funhouse tilting ride. I'd come around the corner into the bedroom and have to take a step backward to regain my equilibrium. Standing on one leg to put on my trousers had also become impossible. Strange, how I hadn't paid much attention to my increasing stumblebum imitation until it became inescapable.

I'd taken time off the same day I'd briefed laughing boy Devlin to demonstrate this all-new dance routine for Dr. Judson. He put me through more coordination tests. "Run up my hallway," the doctor ordered. I did. "Now turn around and run back." Again I complied, as he watched with arms folded. "I think I'm beginning to see what's wrong," he said.

"What's that?" I replied. "Do I have flat feet?" I was jesting again in the face of trouble.

"You're not swinging your left arm properly, but let's look at some other things." He'd already noticed that my left hand was not steady. "Tap your forefinger and thumb together fast, like so." He imitated playing castanets. "Now the other hand. Good. Faster! Faster! Really try!" He held up a hand for me to stop. "Now move your feet, like this." He tapped the floor with the tip of his shoe like a drummer stomping on a bass-drum mechanism. My right foot worked fine, but my left's movement was tenuous. After several tries, it didn't work at all. Next, we both discovered that I couldn't walk on my heels; couldn't even lift my toes off the floor.

I was back up on the paper-covered exam table as he peered into my face from about ten inches away. "Hmmm," he said. I could smell cigarettes on his breath.

"What do you see?"

"You don't blink much and I'm seeing some mild hypomimia."

"Excuse me, I was an English major, what's 'hypomimia?'"

"It's a medical term for poker face. It's a symptom."

"Of what?" This was getting unbearable. "Poker face disease?"

"One last thing, count backward from one hundred by threes."

"Ah, let's see. Ninety-seven, ninety-four, ninety-one; is it eighty-nine? No, eighty-eight."

"That's enough."

"So what's the verdict?"

"It looks like you're in the early stages of Parkinson's disease."

"What happened to my tooth disease?" I pointed into my open mouth in another pathetic funny.

The doctor did not smile. "Your Parkinsonism hadn't present-ed itself fully before. The fact that you're not swinging your left arm when you walk is the real tipoff."

I was more numbed than devastated. Wasn't it an old per-son's disease? I remembered someone's dad had it. He'd been in a wheelchair, all twisted and squirming uncontrollably. All I could think was, this isn't possible. I'm not even forty. Now what?

Dr. Judson read my mind. "Parkinson's is not fatal. You die with it, not of it," he said. "You have the early-onset version. I'm going to put you on Sinemet, it's an artificial dopamine. You'll feel like a new man for a while, but it won't help your balance much."

"For a while? How long is that?"

"The average PD patient has about ten years before symptoms reach the point that significant movement and cognitive difficul-ties arise. But well before then, you might be a candidate for a surgical intervention."

"What's dopamine got to do with all this? What, in fact, is

dopamine? Why is staring a symptom?"

"The muscles in your face are stiffening, It's also known as 'facial masking.'" The doctor then gave me a flurry of definitions that, in my shocked state, didn't stick: a key neurotransmitter, death of neuron-making capabilities in the substantia nigra, folded alpha synuclein buildup in the brain, something about the basel ganglia and facilitating smooth muscle control. The cause of the disease was unknown; scientists thought it had something to do with genetics and maybe exposure to toxins, like pesticides. It was degenerative, progressive, and there was no cure. He gave me a pamphlet and suggested I also read a book for new patients. He wrote its name and a pharmaceutical prescription on separate slips. He'd see me again in three months and shook my hand. Diagnose, adios, as the expression goes.

Just to make sure, I got a second confirming diagnosis as soon as I could. And then I tried to forget the whole thing. Acceptance was not then in my vocabulary.

Chapter Eighteen
Down the Drain

Amsys President Jock Connors was clearly nervous in front of the eight securities analysts scattered the following week amid the mostly empty chairs in Matrix's frigid and darkened conference room. It struck me that I'd been spending a lot of time in artificially cold business chambers. The stakes for him were high. Our stock was tanking, and short sellers were betting it would go even lower. I was tense, as well. Connors might hold me responsible if his revised talk didn't stabilize the share price.

Securities analysts create a market for trading a company's shares. In effect, they also control the size of the stock-based performance bonuses chief executives can pay themselves. Our analysts appeared crashingly bored. They shifted in their seats as Connors' slides flashed up on a big screen behind him. I was overseeing the synching of the visuals with the speech. I'd labored over half a dozen versions since my "Jacob Marley" draft, but this one seemed entirely new. Connors had to tread lightly in hyping our future results. Speaking in stupefying detail, he was employing a purposeful vagueness.

Here's why: the stock's price was still going down based on a new report citing our poor organizational integration written by an influential First Cambridge stock watcher. There that day, Pierre Montrachet, was a sartorial dandy in a livid peacock-blue suit, who had a long supercilious Gallic face.

Connors droned on in the standard three-part business speech structure: let me tell you about what I'm going to tell you, let me tell you about it in some detail, let me summarize what I just told you. He set the stage with some forward-looking public data.

"Before I review our encouraging recent results, I want to speak this afternoon about the marked uptick in corporate purchases of local area networks and servers," he intoned in his flat Iowa accent, "and what this trend means for enterprise-wide service providers over the next fiscal quarter, and for the fiscal year in its entirety. Dataquest forecasts that between now and 1996…"

From the back of the room, I followed along making sure the audio visual guy matched the right slides with his text. Connors couldn't stand using a hand-held device.

As Connors labored on, Kitsie Schoemacher, the Matrix partner overseeing the presentation's venue and mechanics, slipped into the seat next to me. She'd angled for the assignment in order to raise her profile out in Los Angeles. She lowered her voice and leaned forward. "Hey, handsome, I think you need to see this." She held out a pink phone slip. "It could be important. It might even impress these dudes." She tilted her head toward the analysts.

"Jason Dinsmore of NCC called," the message read. It was marked "Joint Announcement, Extremely Urgent."

"Don't they supply us with mainframes?" Kitsie wanted to know. "Are we doing a press release with them on some big outsourcing deal? It might be something financially material that we'd want to slip to Connors. You'd better go find out. I'll fill in for you."

"Jock's talking right here," I said. I pointed to the spot on the script and handed it to her. "Just make sure what's-his-face behind us stays on track." She took the sheaf of paper. I tried to ease out as unobtrusively as possible, but a ray of light from opening the conference room door caught Connors' attention. He scowled fiercely.

In my office, I punched in Dinsmore's number.

"Well that was quick," he said. "They said you were at an all-day meeting. Where are you?"

"We're laying out our wares for the investment community," I explained. "So what's this big-deal joint announcement that's so urgent?"

"That was a little subterfuge to get your attention. What I really wanted to say is, 'Congratulations.' Our illustrious CEO wants to hire you. We need you on board before our earnings report next week to smooth the way with Dorsey. Freddy will brief you on our messaging structure. By the way, I think he's a little jealous of you for getting all that face time with Devlin. I am too. Ted said if you're half the man your father was, you'll have a great future here. Why didn't you ever tell me about your dad?"

Once I'd almost prayed for this, but one word instantly rose to mind: No. Work for Dinsmore? Quake in my boots in front of "Lurch" Devlin? Would the Count of Monte Cristo return to the Château d'If? Not likely. Things were just fine where I was.

"You have no idea how flattering that is," I said, "but I'm going to pass."

"Hold it, you can't turn this down. Is it money? We haven't talked about that yet."

"No, Jason. It's just that I don't want to disappoint Libby again."

"Who's that?"

"My late wife."

"Pete, you're talking nonsense."

"Sorry, my mind's made up. So long Jason."

As I reentered the conference room, Connors was glowering at a questioner. "No," he barked, "I wouldn't agree that we overpaid for our new software acquisition. Not when you factor in the synergy we anticipate with our consulting and systems integration units."

"What's Connors so pissed off about?" I whispered to Kitsie.

"We couldn't get the clicky thing to reverse when Jock wanted to return to a point."

"Eeew, boy."

"But Trevor recovered beautifully for Jock."

"How'd he do that?"

"While the AV guy was fiddling with the gizmo, Trevor stood up and said, 'Sometimes it's hard for us to find the right words to tell you how much we appreciate your coverage.' Everybody laughed, even Jock."

"Nice."

"So what did NCC want that was so urgent?"

"Nothing that's important here."

Connors now faced off against Pierre Montrachet, the dapper First Cambridge analyst. "So what about those synergies you touted, Jock?" the stock watcher demanded. "You've got duplication all over the place. And you're still adding bits and pieces. When are we going to see any of this hit the bottom line?"

"I think you'll see some changes this quarter from consolidations," Connors said. "But I'm not going to preannounce anything special." His homey Midwestern diction made his last word come out like he'd said "spatial."

"Will their effect be material?"

Connors ran his tongue over his upper lip as he weighed an answer. "Maybe a couple dollars a share."

"That's quite a savings. Are you contemplating layoffs?"

Connors had messed up. He'd just promised a change that would be hard to deliver. His statement would surely lift the stock price in anticipation, but it would fall back like a boulder if the company failed in its apparent promise to eliminate a great deal of operating expenses. The fingers of his left hand began to tap a tattoo against his pant seam. The atmosphere came alive with follow-on questions, but Connors ducked them with promises of full details at a later date. When the Q&A finally petered out, he left without the usual individual analyst chit-chats.

That evening, I stayed on in the office until nearly nine o'clock to make a deadline for Henshaw's next *Bulletin* column. Its putative author was also working late. On my way to the washroom, I saw lights burning behind the curtained glass wall of Henshaw's office. Slipping past, I heard Connors' booming voice: "Ke-rist, do I need to remind you of where our stock closed this afternoon? Up three points on heavy volume on the expectation of massive efficiencies."

"Well at least you've stopped the downward drift," said Henshaw.

"Not for long, unless you can dig up at least two million dollars in cost reductions out here, and pronto."

I felt bad for Connors. Inside the men's room I closed the stall door and pulled a folded copy of Henshaw's draft column out of my back pocket. One final read invariably uncovered some error or typo, and I still preferred to edit paper. Errors are harder to spot on a screen. I saw a needed change and reached for the pencil behind my ear, but bobbled it. Ticking rapidly, it rolled out into the middle of the tiled floor, right over a chrome drain. As it came to a stop, the door opened and a pair of voices entered in mid-conversation.

"Why did I ever say that malarkey?" Connors said with a wheezing sigh. "I can't stop thinking about it. Sometimes I think this is the only place in Amsys where I really know what I'm doing. Ahhh," he added, accompanied by sounds of noisy urination.

"Not to worry, Jock" said Henshaw, adding his splash. "We can pull projected earnings forward. And I'll identify all the personnel cuts you'll need. After all, right-sizing is what I do for a living."

"What was that bastard's name again?"

"Who?"

"That First Cambridge clown with the zoot suit."

"Pierre something."

"That's right, the dehydrated Frenchman."

"Must make it hard for him to go oui, oui."

They both laughed.

I grinned. It was amusing. They were joking like teenage boys.

"Speaking about dicks," said Connors, "is that guy Wendell adding any value for you out here?"

My smile froze.

"He had only one job today: keep my slides straight. Where was he? Worse than that, he was no help at all on my speech. I had to have Dick Marin write the damn thing; now there's a sharp guy. Marin's been keeping me informed about Wendell. Says he sits around the office hung over and disappears for hours at lunch time. Says he's actually staggering sometimes."

The roar of flushing signaled they were through. Water gurgled in sinks, followed by the thunks and rips of paper towels being dispensed.

"Well, Wendell has his uses to me," Henshaw said.

"Like what?"

"He ghostwrites my management columns."

"So what? How much business do we get from those articles, Trevor? Can you cite a single case when one triggered a client inquiry?" I could hear them wiping their hands on the stiff paper.

"Not directly, but they're super collateral when we make a sales pitch."

"It's the books we write that bring in the calls, they drive the business. So when is your next bestseller coming out again?"

"One week. We've got a big rollout plan in place."

"Good, and designed like always by Marin, right?"

"Yes, of course."

"Good. You like Wendell so much, put him on your payroll. After today's fiasco, I told Phillips to get rid of him. His drag on my corporate marketing cost center is something like a hundred and fifty grand, fully loaded."

"He's not that valuable to me," Henshaw answered.

There was a crumple of paper towels.

"You work it out. But get me those operational savings. Do I have your commitment?"

"Bloody hell, do I have a choice?"

"Not if you want your bonus. And if you need a pencil to do your figuring," Connors said, "there's one right out there in the middle of the floor."

I raised my legs out of sight.

"I don't usually fetch things off the floors of loos, Jock—unless they happen to be made of platinum."

"We should be so lucky."

Shoes scraped on tiles and the door opener wheezed. A loud click plunged me into darkness. One of them—perhaps Henshaw in his first austerity move—had switched off the lights.

Before heading to Grand Central, I agonized before I left a contrite message on Jason's voicemail. Gist: On second thought, I'd be glad to take the job. That evening I had three Foster's on the bar car to keep up my spirits.

Chapter Nineteen

Spec Piece

"We moved on without you," said Dinsmore, when I finally got through to him late the next day.

I'd spent the proceeding night activating my usual response to career setbacks—getting a bag on. My temples pounded and my eyes felt gritty. "Moved on?"

"Yes, moved on," he repeated. "The job offer is off the table. I told Devlin you'd turned us down flat. But we could do our own make-nice routine. Like you suggested, we'll give Tommy boy an exclusive interview on our new services-based strategy two days before we issue the earnings report. The old one-two punch. Messaging being: We're now 'The solutions company.' We don't care where you buy your hardware and software. Our value-add will be linking all your systems—new and legacy—efficiently to capture and analyze data that yields business insight."

"That's Matrix's positioning, too," I said, having the disorienting sense that I was listening to Kitsie Shoemacher's new tag line: "'Objectivity, Technology, and Business Results.'"

"Hey, 'great minds,'" Dinsmore said. "Ciao, baby." He chuckled and rang off.

The future began to slide around in an alarming fashion. But after a few minutes I clutched at a straw. How about trying to deliver Trevor Henshaw's impossible dream: to author an op-ed article in the *New York Transcript*, the nation's sober paper of record? On the face of it, the idea was ludicrous. Landing one is a million-to-one possibility, a walk-off World Series winning homerun, a buzzer shot for the Final Four championship, all clichés the editors would never allow. Moreover, authors who appear are either already famous or brilliantly insightful on Big Important Issues. Mostly, these notables write about national policy, foreign affairs, and politics, never business management trends. I had a hunch Henry Kissinger would get solicitous treatment if he lobbed one in. For the hoy polloi, there was nada encouragement. The only means of gauging the editors' interest was contained in the instructions for sending a full-blown electronic draft. As the text informs hopefuls, if three days go by and you haven't heard anything, you can safely assume that you've been rejected. Hundreds still try.

The trick in op-ed placements is to link the point of view to a current news story or trend. This is called "the hook." I found one in a strike that was paralyzing plane travel. One of the major airlines, no client of ours, was in the midst of a bitter labor dispute with its baggage handlers. The pilots' union had followed them out in solidarity. The impasse was in its third week. Bleeding money, the airline's management nevertheless refused to negotiate. It had to get rid of redundant unionized workers, its owners maintained, to stay in business. Meantime, passengers of cancelled flights fumed and flew on other carriers.

I put on my Henshaw hat and in about ninety minutes I'd written a 600-word draft. Its thesis was that if airlines were half so focused on customer service as they were on bottom line cost cutting they wouldn't have profitability problems, or picket lines. Nor would they have to threaten their own bankruptcies in an attempt to wring wage concessions from employees. Take the problem of customers flying faster than the speed of luggage, a line I knew I had to lose. The answer was the application of innovative technology that would save jobs, build passenger loyalty, and boost profits. Done right, the article would make Henshaw come off as both a defender of workers and a management genius. It also meshed with his new book's exhortation to measure customer satisfaction as the primary metric that drives profits and stock price.

I went online to check what the strike was really about. Beyond money, a major issue was antiquated work rules. The company had put stopwatches on their workers' activity and had discovered numerous ways to eliminate time. For instance, they'd redesigned conveyor belts to be at waist level and lowered the seats in the electric carts, so that baggage handlers could shave extra seconds in getting into them. All of which was only marginally helpful, I had Henshaw observe.

Instead, why not eliminate the entire rigmarole of check-ins and weighing, which irritated customers anyway? Have passengers carry luggage directly to the jetway for bar-coding there. They do this already if their carry-on bags are too big. Combine that with the snazzy technology of unmanned carts on tracks, waiting on arrival, each equipped with the ability to sort tagged bags. As for the unionized workers, they'd be retrained to operate the new systems and make design suggestions that only their valuable hands-on experience could reveal. Attrition and retirements would do the rest. Presto: happier passengers, willing workers, declining costs, and a competitive advantage. I recognized a major weakness: more than being a facile remedy, the piece was blatantly self-serving.

Henshaw glanced through the draft, knitted his brow, and then reread it carefully. I expected his veto. This wasn't his standard format. He was giving advice to a real company in real trouble, not hypothesizing based on some defunct or disguised company that had screwed up. Did the argument hold up? Was it too critical of a potential client? He opened his mouth, closed it, and searched through the first typewritten page until he found what he wanted. "Drop this line about 'flying faster than luggage.' It lacks seriousness."

"Sorry."

"The rest reads like my voice. Where'd you get the examples?"

"WebCrawler."

"Do you seriously think this is the *Transcript*'s dish of tea?"

"We'll know soon enough."

Henshaw passed back the pages and grew pensive. "You've been doing a good job for me, Pete," he said. "So it pains me to say I might be forced to let you go. You're on Jock Connors' shit list."

"I know."

"He blames you for the cock up with his speech. And you're being undermined by others around here, whose names I needn't mention. I'm trying to keep you on, but I wouldn't be candid if I didn't tell you it's time for you to look around."

"I appreciate your support."

"Think nothing of it. Maybe if all else fails we can work out a free-lance arrangement. We'll talk more when I get back from Nantucket for a long weekend. Marianne will give you my number there if you need me there on this *Transcript* thing before

Monday," he added, "but I'm not holding my breath."

"Me either; on either matter."

I returned to my office, tinkered some more with the language, and came to four conclusions.

One: There was no way the *Transcript* would take the piece.

Two: I needed to learn how to apply for unemployment benefits.

Three: I wasn't going to drink alcohol anymore; last night was just an understandable slip—but never again.

Four: With Henshaw gone, I'd be able to squeeze in a jog around Central Park Lake before catching an early train home.

Kitsie Schoemacher showed up. "Knock, knock," she said. "Want to get that drink this evening? I'm buying. And then there's later."

"Sorry, I'm crushed by work," I lied. "Which is too bad because 'later' sounds extremely interesting. Maybe next week, okay?"

"Give me a day and a time."

"Next Friday, six-ish. I'll meet you at the Trio."

"You got a date."

She left. Touching the computer's keyboard, I launched my doomed bid into the void. I logged off, and sneaked up the stairwell to the company's small, rarely used workout area. Its changing room comprised a narrow carpeted space with a pair of benches and a wall of louvered lockers. Within mine was a new pair of Nikes with bulky unused cushioning.

I met Marin in front of the elevator in my shorts. "Is this the new business casual?" he asked.

"A little bird told me you're bad-mouthing me to Connors," I replied. "Behind my back. Besides being sneaky, it'll blow up in your face. Who'll write Henshaw's columns?"

"The same guy who writes Jock Connors' speeches—me—or maybe Teddy. Either way, there's not much skill needed. Have a nice run. Maybe you shouldn't bother to come back."

Outside in my shorts, I received a couple of curious glances until I crossed over Fifth Avenue and entered the Central Park at 59th Street. Cerulean high-pressure skies offered a preview of New York's pleasant early autumn weather. I fell in behind a group of hollow-eyed runners mechanically pounding along the wide dirt path. The first half mile I shuffled along, logy and spent from the prior night's spree, and seething about Marin. More than that, I was now super aware of my gait, which was way off kilter. My left arm wasn't pumping at all normally. I made an effort to swing it higher. The effect probably resembled a wooden soldier on fast forward. Don't worry until you have to, old Doctor Schmocter had said—i.e., never underestimate the power of denial. So I shifted my attention to the people around me and their costumes: a T-shirt reading "Run Spelled Backward is Nur," neon yellow mesh singlets, the alternatingly stretching nylon fabric on moving butts, the jerky pendulum swings of a woman's ponytail. Our sneakers pattered on the earth like soft rain. Glancing over at slack profiles, I passed the pack near the South Gate House. I began to feel stronger. Fence pickets flickered in my peripheral vision like a silent movie. The metronomic thudding created a growing sense of timelessness and peace—the runner's high.

My phone's red light was blinking when I returned from the locker room. A woman named Caroline Jones of the *New York Transcript* had left a voice message. "We're accepting Mr. Henshaw's piece, but it needs major revisions. Call me as soon as possible. I want to run it tomorrow"—which would be a Saturday. She provided a phone number. Immediate elation turned to a sense of foreboding.

"This has potential," said Ms. Jones when I reached her. "He's really attacking management hubris and arrogance. Showing how workers always pay for their strategic blunders. Intellectually, they're like the French generals who killed off a generation of soldiers in World War One, am I right?"

"I don't think he's saying that."

"I want to sharpen this and send it back for his approval within the hour. May I talk with him?"

"He's not here."

"Do you have power of attorney to approve my edits?

"I suppose I do."

"Is that a yes or a no?"

Chapter Twenty
Ethics Lesson

The small Silvermine River valley was settling into dusk. Through the wavy window panes over the kitchen sink, the last rays of daylight angled across the cupped surface of an antique linen press. Inside was a bottle of retsina, a housewarming gift from some neighbor. Untouched since the unpleasant discovery of its pine tar taste, it was the only intoxicant in the house. I massaged my forehead and replayed my decision. Ms. Jones's rewrite had resulted in a powerful op-ed. It had simultaneously created a dilemma. Henshaw's piece was now a polemic. Companies with union problems richly deserved them, or words to that effect. Was it good to go? I tried to play for time. She flatly refused. No way could she hold it until Monday. The piece might become stale, the strike settled. I hemmed and hawed, negotiated a few edits to tone it down, and said I'd call her back with a final decision.

"The clock's ticking," she warned.

I couldn't raise Henshaw at his vacation home. Could he live with this worker manifesto? More than its stridency, the thing was based on no first-hand knowledge. What if I'd misinterpreted some source I'd cribbed from? The immutable newsroom rule is ironclad: When in doubt, leave it out. The only sensible thing to do was to kill the thing.

Ms. Jones didn't wait long for my call. Within a minute she was back on the line. "Do I have your permission to run the piece as it now reads?" She sounded pressured, exasperated.

I said nothing, thinking hard about all that could go horribly wrong, measured against the possibility that the placement might keep me employed by Henshaw.

"What's the answer, Mr. Wendell?"

"Yes."

"You're saying that you have full authority from Mr. Henshaw to approve the draft that I just sent to you."

"That's what I'm saying."

Now, I stared at the plane marks on the board-and-batten door. Crackled ox blood paint attested to its early nineteenth century origins. The wooden lozenge holding it shut had created a circular wear pattern over the years. I twisted the opener and tugged at the cabinet's big mushroom pull. The clear bottle inside was labeled Kourtaki, its contents the color of urine. I shuddered and reached for it.

The phone rang. For a crazy instant I thought it was Ms. Jones. I let go of the retsina to snatch up the receiver. "Hello?"

"My God, is that really you, Pete?" said Vicky. "Did you know I've been trying for days to set up a time for you to come over for dinner?"

I made some excuse about work.

"I know, I know. We're all busy, but how about tomorrow night?"

"Sure, see you then. Seven o'clock okay? No, wait a minute." I desperately needed to unload. "Ah, this is a little embarrassing,

I've got a problem. Do you have a few minutes to talk?"

"Of course, Pete, what's the matter?"

There was a brash quality about Vicky that reminded me of Libby. She'd never bullshit me. "I think I've made a terrible business decision," I said.

"Have you eaten? I've got some leftover beef stew I can warm up."

"Be there in a flash."

My Saab keys were on the kitchen countertop in front of me. So was a statement from my bank. My mortgage payment was a month overdue. I'd have to go in and talk with the bankers for an extension.

Vicky gave me a quick kiss on the mouth outside her door. "Come on in, Gloomy Gus, and tell me all about it."

"This is very kind of you," I began, and then stumbled on the doorstep.

She caught me by the arm.

"I wonder if tripping over your welcome mat is a bad sign."

She released me. "Are you okay?"

"Too much running, I think. So, willing to hear my sorry tale?"

"Of course. You said it had something to do with your work?"

It all came out. After I concluded, she placed a basket of hot garlic bread on the table and delivered her opinion: "Maybe you'll get away with it." Her eyes met mine. "But why did you take such a chance? You're endangering your company's reputation and most importantly your own. And for what?" Her baffled glance was painful. I'd obviously fallen in her estimation.

"I really can't explain it. It started out like an interesting story assignment, an exercise in what I used to do. More important, it might save my job. The words sort of wrote themselves, but then this Ms. Jones person got ahold of it. I should have spiked the thing, but I was thinking, what an incredible win. Even though Trevor Henshaw has never been near an airport baggage operation, the recommendations seemed pretty ingenious, if I do say so myself. He sounds brainy and humane. For once, a consultant doesn't come off like he's advising a company to squeeze more money out of its human assets. I have just two regrets. The first is for him. He could become the laughingstock of consulting. His only defense would be: 'I didn't write that horseshit, my ghost-writer did.' Some excuse."

"But they are squeezing labor, aren't they?"

"Sure, but now the piece is aimed at a general audience. It doesn't have the required empathy for barons of industry, the 'I feel your pain Mr. CEO' tone. He's angling for new business, not votes. What if he gets an irate call from the head of the airline?"

"What's the other regret?"

"This particular human asset will get the boot."

"Maybe that wouldn't be such a bad thing. Did you consider that?"

"People keep telling me that, but how would I live?"

The stove timer dinged. Vicky brought a white enameled pot with a red handle over to the oak kitchen table, part of a set of pressed-back chairs with cane seats. I placed a piece of bread on my plate and she ladled stew next to it. Her gaze turned inward. I was afraid she would tell me to leave as soon as I ate.

"I'm sorry to dump my heinous problem on you. You must take me for a slime ball."

"You came here for total honesty, correct?"

"Correct," I said. "And some warmed-over stew."

I got a wan smile. "My take is that you're human. You caved under pressure. Happens all the time, even to the best of people."

"I beg to differ. Nobody held a gun to my head. This was idiot boy's own brilliant idea."

"At some level you were under heavy stress, which makes people stupid. But I know you'll make it right."

"How do you know that? And what is the right thing? Should I demand a retraction of my own work?"

"It's telling the truth if this thing comes to light and letting the chips fall where they may. You've really learned a valuable lesson."

"Maybe I've re-learned a lesson: Smart flacks don't lie, as they say at NCC. Main reason: they get caught."

"You've learned something bigger than that, Pete," Vicky said. "And I have one other piece of free advice: Think seriously about a career where you put your integrity on the line for people you don't respect."

"Okay, one new career coming up. But what is it? I can't go back to journalism, I've burned that bridge."

"Like I said at the Tavern, have you ever thought about teaching? You'd be fabulous."

"That's ridiculous. I'm thirty-five years old and devoid of any teaching experience. But you're actually the second person in my life who suggested that. Remember Mr. Keating?"

"Sure, the English teacher, him too?"

"Yeah, he said I had a gift for it."

"Alright then. What could it hurt to talk to my dad about it?" She put the pot back on the stove and picked up the kitchen wall phone's receiver.

"You mean right now?"

"Why not?" Vicky punched in the number.

"What am I supposed to say?"

"I'll do the talking." She turned her back to me. "Hey there, Poppa, it's your little cucciolo. You busy? Good, I've got a favor to lay on you. Can you advise a friend of mine about a career in teaching?"

I listened to her side of the conversation:

"Oh, please, Poppa, do it for me. Tomorrow morning. It's kind of urgent. You're free and I just know you will." Her affected girlish voice told me she got away with murder with the old guy.

"Mumble, mumble, mumble," replied a deep baritone.

"So what's the big deal? Tell Momma she can visit Aunt Theresa later."

More mumbles, followed by a longish wait.

She cupped the mouthpiece. "He calls me his cucciolo," she explained. "It means puppy."

"A pet name, in other words."

"He's talking to Mom." The mumbles started again and she signaled a thumbs-up. "You two can talk sports, too," she informed her father. "He played football with Rit."

Mumble, mumble.

"Yes, he's the one I told you about. Right, that guy... the special one." Her hand returned to cover the phone. "You weren't supposed to hear that." Then it came off. "He's very bright, an English major at Dartmouth. You'll have a lot to talk about. Yes, yes. I love you too. Tell Momma I'll be over next week sometime. Of course I'll call her before then. Bye."

I was booked for ten the next morning, she informed me. She wrote out the address on a pad of paper, ripped off the sheet, and stuffed it in my shirt pocket. She tapped the fabric twice. It was time to leave.

"You make a lot of snap decisions don't you?"

"Uh huh."

"I just hope he doesn't give me a test in English Lit."

"Don't worry about that, you and Father are going to get along famously. And hold your horses for a second." Vicky came over and sat on my lap. The old oak chair creaked as she twisted around to nibble my ear. "I hope we get along, too," she breathed.

I pulled back to confront her shining eyes. "Aren't you forgetting what a contemptible liar I am?"

"Yup, I sure am."

"And the disgraceful fact that I don't return calls?"

"Forgot that, too."

"Well in that case…"

My departure was delayed by an oddly chaste make-out session. It brought back memories of virginal love—that almost out-of-body experience of lingering kisses, where the top of your skull seems to lift off. Vicky nibbled and munched my lips; she couldn't help smiling, such that I was sometimes kissing her slick teeth. We moved to a couch where she allowed me some fully clothed liberties, but closed her legs when my hand moved there. It was frustrating but incredibly sweet, the return of an almost rapturous innocence.

"You'd better go home, Pete," she said, breaking away with a wanton expression.

"Why don't I just spend the night? We're both adults, almost middle-aged, in fact."

"Believe me, there's nothing I'd like more." She got to her feet, smoothed her blouse, and took a couple of useless swipes at her flopping forelock. "You make it extremely hard for me to follow the teachings of my church."

"See? I told you I was untrustworthy."

"It's me I don't trust."

She followed me out to the car in bare feet and leaned in through the window. Our lips brushed. "I'm just so happy you're going to talk with Dad," she said. "Don't forget to call afterward. Do you promise?"

"Scouts honor."

"Cross your heart and hope to die?"

"Want to cross pinkies?"

Vicky whirled and, hair flying, sprinted hard for her condo; I watched, afraid she'd step on a stone or piece of glass in the parking lot. She reached the door and waved.

CHAPTER TWENTY-ONE
Welcoming a Heathen

Amid a deafening squeal, Deke Malloy removed the olive green grenade launcher from his office wall and aimed it squarely at me. "You are the scum of the earth," he shouted over the din. "I'm doing this for Libby." He pulled the long stamped steel trigger. Nothing happened. "Now get back to your desk and don't make any more trouble!" But I couldn't remember where my desk was, or what I was supposed to do. Besides, the light was too bright. The glare made my eyes flutter. I couldn't keep them open. The piercing screech intensified. I was on a ferryboat crashing into a wooden pier. That was the source of the earsplitting noise. People began to run. One woman stepped onto a rail. She jumped, skirt flying upwards, into the churning brown water way, way down below. "Aaaahhhhhhh!" she shrieked.

I slapped the alarm clock and the racket ceased.

Sunshine seeped through the bedroom blinds. My heart was racing. On the floor, the maroon tribal carpet was divided by glowing bars of light. Libby had picked it out to keep her feet warm on the way to the bathroom. I pictured her mincing steps over the frigid planks before we'd bought it, complaining of her "popsicle toes." She had a mania for creature comforts, forever adjusting thermostats and tossing our bed comforter off and on. I yanked up the blinds with a clatter and the nightmare receded back into the dark.

From close outside came the shouts of bicyclists. It was eight o'clock Saturday morning. "If we hang a left up ahead," one was bellowing, "the road drops down into Norwalk." The whir of sprockets, chains, and tires increased and diminished in a Doppler Effect of passing proximity. From farther away came a response: "What the hell's in Norwalk?"

For one thing, it contained Norwalk Community College, where Enzo Gingerella taught English. I showered, shaved, and put on pressed khakis, blue blazer, and my yellow foulard. A waste of time was coming up, but might as well dress for success. The Saab's engine rattled like ice cubes tossed into a pan and then settled into its irregular thrum. My route took me up Silvermine Road to 123, and then headed right and upward toward the town's "Italian section." In all my years in New Canaan, I'd never been up Garibaldi Road, seen its modest houses. Someone had told me they were going for serious bucks these days. The road twisted back on itself before I spied No 35.

I hadn't anticipated its exterior: copper gutters, cedar roof shingles, beaded clapboards and thick-mullioned, twelve-over-twelve sashes. Beside it stood a reproduction barn painted soldier blue. The Gingerella residence could have been in a *Colonial Homes* magazine spread.

"Yes, we like it," said Mrs. Gingerella, a matronly version of her daughter. I stood on her flagstone stoop, admiring the door surround's fluted pilasters. "Our son Vito dressed the old place up this way. He's rich as Croesus, you know. From putting up all those mansions on the hill across from East School?"

"Yes, I've seen them," I assured her. "That would make him a pretty big-time builder."

"Oh, yes, rich as Croesus. Our little house is his hobby. Vito says it's one of the few places left in town that's still in the proper scale, not gargantuan. Come in, come in."

"I live in a little home in Silvermine."

"Oh yes? Vito's awfully busy these days. But maybe I can put in a good word."

"I'm sure I couldn't pay his prices."

"Pretty soon he won't have to work at all, maybe you can call him then."

"That's the Protestant work ethic, you know," I said. "You kill yourself to make so much money that you don't have to work."

Mrs. Gingerella gave me a quizzical look. "I don't think anyone would mistake my Vito for a Protestant," she said.

She ushered me into the living room and offered me coffee and biscotti from gold-rimmed china on a butler's table. A skillful oil painting of a girlish Vicky in a white dress hung on the wall. Following my eyes, Mrs. Gingerella said it dated from when Vicky was confirmed into the church. She apologized. Her husband would be on the phone for a few more minutes. I'd have to put up with her for a while, hoped I didn't mind. As she bent to pour, she asked me something few people knew.

"Didn't your mother go to St. Mary's for a while?" The flutter of falling liquid ceased and she glanced up at me. "Grace, wasn't it?

"Yes. Her real name was Gracja. Did you know her?"

"Only briefly."

"It must have been very brief. Mom only went there for a few months. It was after Dad divorced her and she was living in her apartment on Park Street. Then she moved back to Chicago, where she died."

"Do you know what Grace confessed to me, once?"

"I have no idea, Mrs. Gingerella."

"Dear Grace told me she was glad to get back to her Catholic roots. Did she ever mention that?"

"No she didn't. She was always seeking some kind of spiritual connection. I don't think she ever found it."

"Did you ever join her there?"

"At St. Mary's? No, I was in college back then," I said.

"But you do go to *some* church, don't you?"

"I don't believe in God." Too late, I knew it was a stupid thing to admit.

Mrs. Gingerella put the pot down very slowly and gave me a level gaze. "What *do* you believe in, if I may ask?"

"I'm not proud of that," I said, thinking of a dead wife and unborn child, "but the only way my life makes sense is if *nothing* makes sense."

"Not one thing?" she asked. "Did you ever discuss this with Vicky?"

"It's never come up."

"I see."

Behind her, the den door opened. "Well, well," said Enzo Gingerella, striding into the room, "the great NCHS running guard. My nephew Ritaldo has told me all about you."

With the same forward hook of hair as his daughter, the professor was of medium height, powerfully built, and very handsome in late middle age. He walked on the balls of his feet, betraying the family athleticism. Taking his huge mitt felt like shaking hands with a boxing glove. Its immensity triggered an irrational thought: I'd hate to be hit by that thing.

"I wasn't great at all," I said. "I just acted as Rit's human shield. If I didn't move quick he'd run right over me too."

"You're too modest. You were All-State, right?"

"Definitely not. They called me Stork Legs."

Enzo sat in a leather club chair. "Hmm," he mused, "a man of brutal honesty. Vicky tells me you might be interested in teaching." He looked over his shoulder at his wife. "Concetta, can you see we're not disturbed?" Mrs. Gingerella reminded him that they had to be at Aunt Theresa's house at noon.

He nodded and turned back. "May I ask why this sudden interest, Pete?"

"That was kind of Vicky's inspiration, but I guess it's because I was complaining to her about my current job. What I do is not particularly ennobling, Mr. Gingerella. I'm a PR guy."

"Yes, I talked with Vicky about you this morning. But why teaching, specifically?"

"It's not a burning desire, nor one I've ever even imagined before." I confessed. "I'm just exploring Plan Bs." I related how my high school English teacher, John Keating, had said I'd make an outstanding teacher. He'd written a gag sentiment in my yearbook. I knew it from memory: *Who wooda thunk youse wooda comeup wit da highest grade in all da classes I ever taut?* It was one of the reasons I drifted into English as a major in college.

"So let me get this straight," Enzo responded. "Because of some humorous note this Mr. Keating wrote nearly a quarter century ago—and my daughter's spur-of-the-moment suggestion—you're thinking about chucking your career?"

I felt silly. "Maybe you should talk me out of this. After all, PR does pay a lot of money."

"But you just said it's not rewarding, not 'ennobling.' And yet you've made it your vocation. Let me just ask you: What's it worth to want to get up and go to work in the morning?" Enzo poured himself some coffee and waited.

"Good question. Maybe my self-respect?"

"You'll have to decide what kind of sacrifice you're willing to make for that. But teaching isn't an easy escape hatch from, what, your moral uneasiness?"

"That's a good way to put it."

"It requires a devotion that few other callings do, and it can be political and nasty at the department level. I happen to love it, because every now and then—very rarely with the kind of students who struggle to go to a community college—I can change a life. And that really is worth getting out of bed for. Most of the time, though, it's a grind like any other job; kids don't think they can learn anything from great literature. They think they're wasting their time, earning a required credit to graduate, and do the minimum to get by. And starting such a career at your age, believe me, you'll never teach at Dartmouth. It's too late for you at the college level. Still interested?"

"Theoretically."

"Let's list your options." He held up his massive hand. Thumb erect, he said one choice was to quit my job and pursue a master's degree, fulltime. It might take two years and cost $20,000. He raised his forefinger: Or I could go evenings to a place like Norwalk CC, which would take many more years. He gripped his middle finger and said maybe I could get an entry-level job in a private school, without any teaching degree, see if I liked it, though even that meant stepping off in blind faith. His pinky, as big as a hot dog, represented the final alternative—substitute teaching in a public school.

"The only problem with the last," Enzo summed up, "is penury. Substitute teachers make something like forty-five bucks a day. If you worked five days a week, every week with summer vacation off, you'd still make less than twelve grand a year. And that's before taxes."

"What about working at a private school?"

"Vicky doesn't like to admit this, but she's slightly above the poverty line with her salary from the Dewitt School. She makes up the deficit by giving flute lessons and playing with the symphonies."

"If I may be so bold, what does a full professor at a community college pull down?"

"I'm in the mid-forties," Enzo said, "and that's pretty good for a state school. The average is the mid- to upper-thirties."

"Any possibility of teaching journalism, which might give me an advantage?"

"You'd have to talk with that department up at Storrs, and I think Quinnipiac grants a master's degree in it as well. But you'd still have the same long struggle for eventual low pay."

"Yeah, and I'm afraid those numbers don't add up for me."

"Why not? You must have saved a bundle from that fat job."

"I'm house-poor with a big mortgage. I live from paycheck to paycheck."

"Got any equity in the place?"

"Not enough to tap. People always say you can't go wrong with New Canaan real estate, but I did."

"Help from your father?"

"He's dead and I was disinherited."

"I'm sorry to hear that. But if it's to be, you'll find a way. As my Concetta likes to say, 'God doesn't reward success, He rewards effort.'"

"That's not what New Canaan teaches," I said.

Enzo Gingerella pressed his lips into a tight smile. "No, I guess not. Still any interest?"

"I'm not sure I can swing it. Talk about irony. I need a pile of dough in order to be able to make less money. But thank you for your time, Mr. Gingerella. I appreciate your wisdom."

He proffered his gigantic hand and I took it. "Call me Enzo. To be candid, I seem to have acquired a stake in your future. My daughter thinks a great deal of you. This all seems very sudden to her mother and me, but Vicky is impulsive and tenderhearted; she gives affection a little too trustingly, if you get my drift."

"Yes sir," I said, "ah, Enzo."

"Good. I expect you to treat her right."

Mrs. Gingerella entered from the kitchen to announce that it was time to leave for Aunt Theresa's house. She offered to show me out. Her frostiness made it obvious she considered me no catch for her daughter. Smith Ridge WASPs, at least my kind, were the wrong sort.

After she closed the door, curiosity made me turn back to examine the leaded-glass transom. As I suspected, it was a true antique, with bubbled lavender panes. Standing there, I couldn't help but overhear the conversation inside.

"He's not such a bad guy," Enzo said. "He just forgot to grow up."

"He's a heathen," said Concetta Gingerella.

Chapter Twenty-Two
Break-In

It's the first drink that gets you drunk. Not the fourth, the eighth, or the tenth. Alcoholics have two things working against them: a built in forgetter (i.e. no alcoholic consciously starts out to crash his car or get arrested like last time). And they have a physical craving (i.e. they metabolize it differently, have a more pleasurable reaction, and can't stop). Rit explained this progression to me much later, along with the phrase, "I didn't always get in trouble when I drank, but every time I was in trouble I'd been drinking."

After leaving Vicky's parents, I bought a six-pack. It was innocent enough. On my training agenda for that afternoon was a lengthy sprint-and-jog fartlek sequence. I'd read that drinking a beer after a grueling run was a good way to replace electrolytes.

I decided to explore the Wilton side of the river. Running well, and thrilled that I was experiencing no Parkinson's symptoms (had it gone away?), I headed up Route 106 to Belden Hill Road and turned left past a series of large nineteenth century Federal homes. Their spacious grounds were paeans to gracious living. They were the kind of places I'd always assumed I'd own myself one day. How was never seriously considered. I made a left to descend Old Huckleberry Road, another paved cow path. Where it crossed over a slice of the Wilton reservoir, I stopped to watch cumulous clouds drift over the mirror-calm water. At the far end of the lake, the puffy shapes and their reflections merged and disappeared over the dam like laundry running through a wringer. Sweat falling from my cheeks, I watched this phenomenon for a long while, feeling in synch with existence.

Picking up the pace again, interval sprints had me pounding past leafy estates and then slowing to trot beside a horse farm with a high three-board fence. Speeding up to run full tilt, I re-emerged on Route 106 not far from the old Quaker Meeting Hall, just visible through a thick stand of hemlocks up a dirt road. I checked my new runner's watch. I'd been clocking seven-minute miles. Not bad.

Back home, the river bubbled merrily beyond the porch. I stripped off my running shirt and leaned back in an aluminum-and-mesh deck chair. A deep sense of accomplishment filled me. The sun heated my upturned face. Closing my eyes, floaters wavered and sank on an orange-red background. The can of Foster's went down fast. Without thinking about it, I went back for another. When I returned, the sunlight was streaking lower through the trees. The scene had softened and diffused, yet my vision seemed to have gained heightened sensitivity to light and color. I was in a transcendent green and golden bower. My hearing too had acquired greater acuity, picking out the chuckling water, buzzing insects, and the hollow machinegun tock of a woodpecker off on the left someplace. A mockingbird landed with a rattle of gray and white wings on the porch rail close by. It jerked its tail up and down, regarding me in profile with one glittering black eye. My contentment widened to encompass birdbrain over there. My chest expanded with a long sigh of well-being. How very much I had to be grateful for.

After four more quick beers, my mood shifted. The ancient limbic part of my brain, the one that spurns inhibitions, had gained the upper hand. I emptied the last can and felt restless, like I was missing fun somewhere. In the bedroom I pulled on jeans and a navy polo shirt. Like the bicyclists I'd heard that morning, I decided to head toward Norwalk. I craved excitement and the kind of sexual thrills I couldn't get with Vicky.

With her rhinestone-covered bra hooked back on, the skinny teenager's shape appeared more normal. A short-haired blonde, she was awkwardly descending the stage steps in tremendous stiletto heels. Moments before, as she'd swung around the brass pole, her large immovable breasts had given her an odd totemic appearance. Yet she was obviously proud of them: She kept arching her back and smiling at me. Domed as Bundt cakes, they were absurdly false. Poor kid must have gone to Jiffy Boob. I smiled at my own joke.

The music started up again and her replacement, a sullen redhead, started to gyrate. I motioned for another beer and critiqued the new girl's routine, which was grimly robotic. Eyes fixed on the ceiling, she began a repetitive forward and backward step. She seemed utterly uninterested. And at that instant, I wanted to be someplace else too. Once the novelty quickly wore off, watching adolescent girls prance around undressed was not just a letdown. The place called Centerfolds was vaguely embarrassing, as if I'd opened a bathroom door on somebody's naked little sister. It took all the air out of the balloon of anticipation. My second Budweiser would be the last.

"What were you smiling at, sweetie?" The prior dancer's rubbery mounds now appeared at eye level. A moment before I'd been alone with my thoughts. Strange, how thumping rock music and dim light can make one feel invisible. I looked up at a pimpled face, thickly coated with pancake makeup. Eyebrows lifted, she bore a look of expectation.

"Smiling?"

"Yeah, you liked what you saw, didn't you?" She had some kind of Eastern European accent.

Her bold approach laid bare vulnerabilities beyond her nakedness—rejection and ridicule. No, I was laughing at your appearance, I almost said. But my instinctive reaction was pity; which presented a ticklish issue: How to dump this skank without hurting her feelings. Simple manners forbade the truth: *You're right. You've made yourself comically grotesque. But that's not funny at all. Somebody should have protected you.* Yet boozy sympathy pulled me toward intimacy, even confession, one detestably maudlin: *You see, my wife died, and I just wanted to ogle a woman's body without any involvement whatsoever. But now you've broken through my barroom anonymity and I'd really rather be alone. So, see you around, kiddo.* This unmade speech exemplified the oxymoronic axiom that an alcoholic isolates because he's lonely.

"I was having a good time," I fibbed.

The girl waved a hand before her thrusting bosom. "I saw you checking me out. Specially my generous endowments. Was that part of your 'good time?'"

"Indubital…" *Whoa, getting a little greased.* "Without a doubt."

She extended the same hand toward me, fingers drooping downward like a countess would extend her hand to be kissed. "My name is Wanda Lust. What's yours?"

"No kidding?" Her hand was small and calloused. "My name is Vasco da Gama. I like to get around, too."

"Mind if I sit beside you, honey?"

My word play had sailed past her like a Spanish galleon over the horizon. Maybe she never listened to men's names, or rightly figured most men here were liars. I saw her glance at my wedding ring and that was another lie, a false one. I understood the rules: Identity was sham, tawdry fantasy the reality.

The girl slid onto a stool next to mine. Pushing her stiff breasts into my shoulder, she confided, "See? I don't bite."

"I think you're putting the bite on me right now, Ms. Lust."

"You want to go in the back room and have some fun?"

"What kind of fun?"

"A lap dance; it cost you twenty dollars. I make you real happy."

At that instant, three of me sat within the joint's swirling smoke: One was determined to walk away from this crass negotiation. Another liked jerking Wanda's chain. A third wanted to be talked into it.

"So what do I get for a lap dance?" I asked.

"You know, I get you excited."

"Actually, I don't know. Tell me how."

"You've never been here before?"

"Nope."

"I sit on you and move my butt. You get, you know, aroused?" She lowered her eyes with surprising delicacy. Then her painted face grew serious. "But they no allow you to grope me."

"I'm not up for that—no pun intended."

"Sometimes I break the rules," she confided, "for a special handsome man."

I gulped down the last of my beer and put a tip on the bar. "Thanks all the same, Ms. Lust, but I don't think so."

She placed her last bargaining chip: "I'll give you the first dance free. Then you decide."

"Sorry, gotta shove off."

"Please help me, mister." Her sophisticated façade dissolved, revealing the scared girl that she really was. "Nobody has danced with me all night. I have to pay a lot of money to work here." She touched her sequined bra. "Do you think my breasts look strange? They cost me three thousand dollars. I just had them done and some men have been very cruel…"

"You're the prettiest girl here tonight," I said. Like all effectively evasive PR, this was both true yet dishonest. The others were even less attractive.

"So you'll dance with me?"

"I'd feel like a dirty old man. How about I just give you twenty bucks?"

"Just one, that's all I'm asking."

"Oh, alright, just one. Then I split."

Relief relaxed her face. "I'll make you *real* happy, sweetie!"

"Call me Vasco."

The young black woman behind the counter was apprehensive when I entered the coffee shop. I couldn't blame her. For one thing, it was past one o'clock in the morning and she was alone. For another, I was doing a box step to maintain my balance.

Somebody had optimistically named the place "The Baker's Dozen," as if to celebrate abundance. But its grease-streaked interior was harshly barren in the neon lighting. The walls were covered by buckling green-plastic panels, each held in place by corroding chrome-plated strips. Under a heavily scratched glass counter, the icing atop some stale vanilla doughnuts had acquired the dull sheen of old sink porcelain.

Local promoters called the surrounding area SoNo, but this section had escaped gentrification. The raucous strip club thumped through the wall. No doubt the wary young woman had seen plenty of ex-patrons similarly worse for wear. Perhaps her most pressing concern at the moment was that I wasn't capable of answering a simple question, even though I'd just tried. So she asked it again: "Want cream and sugar?"

My mind was saying yes, but my mouth was anesthetized. I bobbed my head up and down.

She held a foam cup beneath a stainless-steel dispenser and rattled its metal lever several times. Dropping in three tablespoons of sugar, she poured coffee from a Pyrex carafe with an orange plastic handle. I hadn't wanted decaf, but was incapable of telling her that.

"For here or to go?" She posed the question with deliberate enunciation, as if as I was dull-witted in the bargain.

I jerked my thumb over my shoulder like a hitchhiker.

From the evidence of her cautious behavior, I was very intoxicated. But I didn't feel that way. My mind was working like a well-oiled machine. I'd been staring up at a dusty light fixture resembling a carriage wheel. I was reasoning thusly: My deep respect for Vicky had led me to this place. It was a case of philosophical right ratiocination: Nice Catholic girls came with strings. Pole dancers only wore G-strings. Ha, ha. Which were a lot less entangling. Oh good one! The overhead light grew less mesmerizing as my line of logic began to feel as circular as its shape. Where was I going with that thought? Oh yes. Ergo, twenty dollars wouldn't get Vicky's bra off, but the lie she wanted me to say would do it for free.

Wanda had been a bore. She actually wanted to become an accountant. Maybe that was why I was reasoning now in terms of cash payments. Did I think that was a good idea? Did I know any accountants? I wound up paying for four dances, though even the first didn't do a thing for me. After that, we just talked and I drank. Relieved of her mission, she sat hunched over, with her elbows on her knees, as if her new breasts weighed her down. She came from Poland, like my mother, but I didn't tell her that. Her real name was Agata. She wanted to know what I did for a living, what my hobbies were, did I follow baseball, was I a Yankee fan, did I like Mustang cars, and other topics to keep me in my seat. I told her I worked for a company that made bowling balls, followed Olympic curling closely, and drove a Honda Civic. There was nothing sexy about her. What was that phrase? The tyranny of the needy? Something like that.

"You're not into this are you?" she said, finally. "Is your marriage very unhappy, Vasco?"

"Sadly, it's over, and so is this evening, Agata." I had a hard time struggling out of my chair. "Accounting is a good career," I said, "cause accountants never lose their jobs—they just lose their balance."

She gave me a questioning look.

"Like me." I walked out unsteadily, stomping down a couple of times on my left foot, which seemed to have fallen asleep.

"Hey, mister," said the coffee shop waitress, "that's going to be eighty-five cents."

I could read her name tag: "Vanessa." Slowly, I grasped the

words' intent: I had to pay for the coffee. Of course I did, you always have to pay. I pulled a wad of bills from my pocket. What were they doing there? Oh yeah, for tipping dancers prior to meeting the disfigured Ms. Lust. I peeled one off and handed it to Vanessa, who extended the cup. Taking it without bobbling, I felt a sense of mastery. Coach Declan O'Malley never allowed me to touch the football. I tucked the cup close to my chest and zigzagged toward the exit.

The parking lot was surrounded by a high chain-link fence with concertina wire on top. Lit only by a waxing almost full moon, it was a good place to get rolled. I put the cup on the Saab's canvas top and fumbled for the slender key. The coffee slopped as I swung the heavy door open. It took several tries to push the key into the ignition, placed with Swedish inexplicability between the bucket seats. I ground the gears, and then drove with straining eyes under a low railroad overpass and through the empty city streets. There was a tiny portion of me that was still mindful. Take it easy on the speed Hammy; don't get picked up for another DUI. And why the hell did I keep poisoning myself with alcohol?

A symphony played softly on the radio. Miles passed without notice. A cackle broke through my stupor. It was mine. Something had just struck me as hilarious. What was it? Oh yes, the expression on Henshaw's face when informed that his long-desired *New York Transcript* column had been unmasked as bogus. "Bogus!" I shouted at the glowing green dashboard. He'd be the butt of jokes, his reputation vaporized, and I'd be unemployable even in PR. So why was I chortling like the Riddler? I took a long breath. Get a grip on yourself. Ahead, a traffic light grew larger. It was where the Merritt Parkway exited onto 123. Lifting my leg to downshift caused the Styrofoam cup to flex between my knees.

Consider the bright side: Getting canned might be a good thing, a fortunate turn of events. That's what everybody wants for me. With time on my hands, I could go back to school. Take some courses from Enzo. Read Great Books. Get right with the world. Money was the only glitch. Where would I come up with twenty-thousand bucks to get a teacher's degree, to say nothing of an income to live on for a couple of years? Needed was a better plan. What? Hit up my stepmother Lucille for a loan? Fat chance.

I turned right onto the heavily treed upward slope of Carter Street. Moon shadows scuttled over the hood like giant spiders. The road's yellow center line began to diverge into two. I shut an eye and the left stripe disappeared. After a little while, the eye watered and twitched. I clapped a hand over the other one. The tires sang. A warm fatigue enveloped me. My chin dropped to my chest.

Bouncing violently, I awoke amid a loud snapping and scraping of branches. With a final jolt, the car halted. The motor bucked and stalled. I'd come to rest inches from a stone wall. My lap was soaked with coffee. Trembling with adrenaline, I rubbed my neck and tried to get my bearings. Symphonic music continued playing on the radio. I recognized the questing passages of Schubert's *Unfinished Symphony*. Wherever I was, I needed to get the hell out of there. To my astonishment, the car restarted and, with more crackling and metallic screeches, I backed out onto Carter Street. I wasn't too far from home. To stay awake, I licked my fingertips and rubbed them over my eyelids. Stanton Road came into view and I downshifted to second. The gears gave off a mounting whine as I descended.

Loring Davies' darkened home appeared on the left. I realized for the first time that its tiny flat-roofed portico exactly resembled the one on my little place. Wasn't that truly remarkable? Why hadn't I ever noticed that before? Could the same builder, a nineteenth century Vito, have fashioned both? Slowing to make a mental comparison, I stopped altogether and left the car idling on the side of the road to take a closer look. Approaching the low overhang, I reached up to touch the simple cornice to take measurements. From extended pinky to thumb I counted seven and a half lengths. It took a while to compute the length. What was that, eight inches each? Let's see, seven times eight is fifty-six and four makes sixty. That was Libby's height: five feet. I'd go home and check out my own portico. Seven and a half, seven and a half, seven and a half: she would have been fascinated by this coincidence. "Wouldn't you Libby?" I said out loud.

A gray fog descended. I heard a creaking and was aware I was inside the narrow hallway. From beneath my feet, came the click and hum of a pump starting up in the basement. To my right, the old high clock ticked sonorously onward from within the parlor. Tempus fugit. It was where Lucy's self-assured college friends had played charades. A dog-like panting caught my attention. I closed my mouth with a plop. I took a step toward the paneled library. Some memory was pulling me forward. The safe in the library. Money for my degree? I took another step, but the floor seemed crazily humped and canted. My balance was atrocious. I put my hand on the wall and groped onward. My fingertips trailed a faint scratching over the wallpaper; upstairs the ghostly memory of Lucy, the wild abandon.

Footfalls creaked overhead. "Who's down there?" shouted Loring Davies. He sounded scared.

I bolted toward the front door, a moonlit oblong ahead, but something tripped me. Glass shattered, cutting my palm. The old man came thundering down the stairs. "You!" he bellowed, pointing a long boney finger at me. "Stop right there!"

CHAPTER TWENTY-THREE

Hangover

I lay atop the sun-warmed coverlet, groggy and dry mouthed. My clothes stank of stale cigarette smoke. The glowing clock numbers read 12:13 in the afternoon. I moaned and shuffled to the bathroom where, head cocked above the bubbling drain, I slurped water straight from the tap. The mirror on the medicine cabinet revealed raw eyes, greasy pale skin, and an upswept wing of hair. I stuck out a white coated tongue and studied my reflection. "You look like a morgue photo," I croaked.

It wouldn't have helped much to know that such self-loathing and remorse sprang as much from biochemical antecedents as guilt. In a kind of trickle-down action, drinking causes the judging portion of the brain, the neocortex, to get anesthetized first. That lifts constraints on the party-loving, impulsive primitive brain. The good times roll. Sobering up reverses the process; now the neocortex rules without any counterbalance. From no inhibitions, your mind swings to no mercy.

The phone rang. I spat toothpaste and guided myself, hands gripping furniture, toward my rendezvous with justice. A Band-Aid was on my palm.

"You're not very good at remembering things, are you, Wendell?" It was Vicky.

"Remembering?"

"You were supposed to call me right after you talked with Poppa yesterday morning. Does that ring a bell?"

"Oh that," I said, touching my throbbing forehead with trembling fingers. "I forgot."

"So what did he say?"

"He said school teachers are underpaid." The effort to synthesize this thought was immense.

"And?"

"I don't think he likes me."

"What're you talking about? Dad was *terribly* impressed by your sincerity."

"I know your mother hates me for sure."

"No she doesn't."

"I thought she was going to crown me with a teapot."

I'd found the camelback couch by this time. Laying my pounding head on a padded arm, I held the receiver to my ear and closed my eyes. Green and blue blotches shimmied in a dark haze.

Vicky laughed, apparently at something I just said. "She wouldn't dare, it's Meissen," she said, bringing me out of a mini doze. "Pete, I'm so glad you met my folks. I really want them to like you."

I rubbed my tender eyes. "Why? What have you told your parents about me?"

"That you're kind of growing on me."

"Really? It felt like the Twelve Trials of Hercules for a prospective son-in-law. Trial by religion, trial by income, trial by character..."

"Don't flatter yourself, Hay Head."

An urgent thought blocked out everything else: I had to go back to Davies' house. "Can I call you back, Vick?" The phone was in the cradle before she could reply.

Last night's low point came back: me lurching wildly through the door to clamber into the convertible. My manic accelerator-to-the-floor escape causing such violent torque steer that I'd almost rammed an embankment. I must have scared the old man half to death. Why hadn't I stood and talked to him? Instead, I'd run like a criminal.

I drove straight back in my rancid clothes, but there was no police cruiser, no yellow crime-scene tape. I pulled the convertible onto the patch of gravel out front. Knocking on the door produced no response. I peered through one of the glass panes beside the entrance. A metal dustpan lay next to a whisk broom on the floor. It contained the curved shards of an oil lamp's chimney. There was a little table next to it.

Should I call the police and give myself up? Billy the cop's low opinion of me in the graveyard was proving accurate. Jail time *would* do me a lot of good. I decided to wait for Davies and got back into the convertible. Sitting on the hot leather seat with the top down, I imagined iron bars clanging. Captivity would certainly dry me out. Closing my eyes, I became aware of the hum of insects and the rustle of leaves. I listened intently, gauging distances and direction. What would I say when the old man came home? My head dropped to my chest.

Dreaming that I hadn't studied for the big test, nor even found the classroom, I awoke to a snorkeling noise coming from my throat. Another urgent thought gripped me: I had to go see Rit. I knew where to find him, at Mead Park. He played doubles there every Sunday at this hour with his buddies. And that's exactly where he was.

With a manly brush of chest hairs protruding from his tennis shirt, Rit was zipping the cover over his racket. As I walked up the grassy slope toward him, he gave me a critical once-over. He'd just finished playing on one of six clay courts on the knoll above the town's duck pond. His partners passed by me, congratulating each other, and joking that I was just in time not to get beat.

"Your eyes look all bloodshot," Rit greeted me.

"I've done something terrible," I blurted. "I need your help."

"I already know what you're going to say."

"You do?"

"Yup, my aunt Connie thinks you're a horse's ass."

A choking laugh burst from me. "It's much worse than that. I think you're going to have to put me in jail."

"How's that?"

"Honestly, I'm not kidding."

We sat on a park bench about ten yards back from the courts. There, as best as I could recall, I told him what had happened just hours before with Davies, how I'd broken into his house in a drunken stupor. "I came to my senses inside his place," I said. "It was weird. He heard me moving around and came down to investigate. He shouted at me to stop."

The next doubles group yelled and pounded around the green clay as I talked.

"And you ran away?"

"Like a goosed rabbit."

"Jesus, Pete, why did you that? Don't you know that guy from the old days?"

"Because I'm a scumbag. I feel just awful."

"Hold on. Let me see if I can find out where Davies is, and how he's doing." He reached beneath the bench into his gym bag and pulled out a stumpy police radio with a rubber-coated antenna. Atop the black instrument, a tiny red light blinked. "Worst case for you is burglary. That's five years."

"I guess I deserve it."

"But you say you didn't take anything?"

"Yes."

"It might not be that bad."

He made inquiries of the dispatcher's records. He watched me as he listened, revealing nothing, then put the radio back into the nylon bag. "Mr. Davies hasn't reported any B&E to the New Canaan Police Department—yet," he said. "But you're not out of the woods. It all depends on whether he recognized you and presses charges."

A shout from the players made me turn. One of them was waving his racket in triumph.

"From what you've told me, it sounds like you knocked over a lamp after going through an unlocked door. That's trespass. The minimum offense carries a $500 fine. That's if Davies only wants you punished lightly. Davies knows the law. He used to be police commissioner, you know. Or, he could press for criminal trespass with intent of burglary, a class-A misdemeanor. That'll get you up to a year."

"Oh, Lord."

"The difference is in the perpetrator's intent. So I have to ask you, Pete: What were you going in there for?"

"I really don't know. His daughter once told me he had a safe in the library's book shelves. I think that's what I was after, or at least once I was inside. It was money for an 'honest' new life as an underpaid teacher. Pretty crazy huh?"

"Crazy's not the word. What were you *thinking*?"

"You sound just like my father. As I used to tell him, I wasn't thinking. I was staggering drunk and walking in a dream. I barely remember stopping the car to study his portico, which seemed like a splendid idea."

"His *what*?"

"The little porch outside his front door. It's just like mine."

Rit rolled his eyes.

"I'm interested in architectural details, what can I say?"

"Okay, but you can't get arrested for something you didn't do. And who knows in your state? Maybe all you really wanted to do was talk to Davies about his interesting portico and were so absorbed you weren't aware of the time of night."

"You're starting to sound like a shyster lawyer. I'm guilty as hell, aren't I? You just told me I could get years for this. I believe you."

"What I sound like is a guy who's trying to prevent you from self-destructing," Rit said. "You're no burglar, Pete. You're an alcoholic. Normal people don't pass out drunk at two a.m. in Lakeview Cemetery, enter homes in a boozy dream state. Just how much more convincing do you need? Listen, learn."

He spoke loudly, with the zeal of the reformed. The essence of his argument was that drunks are actually seeking a spiritual experience with ardent spirits, an encounter with some force outside themselves. The terms for alcohol and the highest religious experience derive from the same Latin root word: *spiritum*. This was according to Carl Jung, the great psychiatrist, by the way.

"Can you explain this AA orthodoxy some other time? I can't focus." My eyes kept straying to what was going on out in the court. The foursome was changing sides after winning one set apiece. They were excellent players and ripped shots in long, exciting rallies.

The lecture continued: Drunks are childish, overly sensitive people with grandiose illusions that we can never attain. We drink to escape the terrible pain of failure. The answer is acceptance to the fact that we're powerless over alcohol; that we have to surrender our life and will to a God of our understanding.

I replied that I had a problem with that, i.e., if people exist by chance and suffer horrible random fates, where was this so-called Higher Power? Life felt controlled more by a Lower Power.

He told me I was overthinking the issue. The only thing a numbnuts like me needed to understand was that there *is* a God and He wasn't me. He made this global statement: "God is like light. You can't see it, but it reveals everything else."

"Did you just make that up?"

"I heard it at a meeting," Rit said. "I haven't had an original thought about how to live since I joined AA fifteen years ago."

Dusk was descending and the players had left. The bench slats were growing damp. Below us, the street lights came on along the road skirting the duck pond.

"Come to a meeting tonight," Rit urged. He picked up his police radio and waved the antenna in my face for emphasis. "It beats waiting around for the sky to fall in. There's one at the Whale Church in Stamford at eight. I'll pick you up at seven-fifteen."

"No thanks," I said. "I gotta go see Davies. Maybe I'll go to one someday. But for now, you've given me a lot to think about."

"Think about this: Alcoholism wants you dead. Meantime, you want me to go over to old man Davies' house with you?"

"No. I'm going to face the music alone."

"Okay, making amends is our Ninth Step, but it's more than saying you're sorry. You have to change your behavior by entirely changing who you are. It's that simple and that hard."

Chapter Twenty-Four

Testosterone Surge

Loring Davies still wasn't home when I stopped by the second time, but I was when Vicky tapped the horseshoe knocker about an hour later. Under the porch lamp, she looked unbelievably ripe. Yellow linen shorts and a white sleeveless blouse set off her caramel tan and shining black hair. A heavy wicker basket hung from her crossed forearms.

"You look like a million bucks," I said. "What a nice surprise."

"I brought my homemade baked lasagna," she announced with a pleased smile. "All we have to do is heat and eat. Rit told me he met you at Mead Park, but wouldn't say any more. Did you play tennis with him?"

"No," I said, stepping back to let her in. "We talked about leading a spiritual life."

"Oh, really?"

"Yeah. He says I have to make amends to people I've wronged. So I'll start with you. I'm sorry I didn't call you back." My vision kept drifting six inches below her chin.

"You ought to be. I have to rely on my cousin to keep me informed about you."

I took her bag and put it down on a ladder-back chair inside the living room. Then she was in my arms and my tongue was in her mouth.

"That's a good start on apologizing," she said breathlessly, "but let's not overdo it." Breaking free and scooping up the warmer, she took an unsteady step. "Where's the kitchen in this place?"

"It's to the left. You're heading for the bedroom."

Vicky pivoted and I followed her toward the stove, where she turned to face me with a haunted look.

There's another residue of heavy drinking: A man's testosterone production shuts off when he's drunk; to compensate, it floods back twice as strong when he sobers up. I was boiling with lust. Looking me over, Vicky sensed it.

Dinner never made it out of its container. She let out a faint squeal as I kissed her hard and cupped a breast. We stumbled toward the bedroom, joined at the lips, struggling to remove her blouse and my stinking shirt.

"Hold it, hold it," she said as we fell onto the rumpled bed. "No need to rip this." Vicky undid the last button and tossed the garment on the dresser. Then she reached back and shrugged off her bra. I started pulling at her shorts, but she stopped me and held up my palm to kiss it. Her eyes held a plea. "Please go slowly," she said, "and fuck me like you love me." She removed the rest of her clothes and closed her eyes, ready.

Vicky's voice afterward in the dark: "You awake?"

"Yeah, your paintbrush hair keeps going up my nostrils."

"Did I shock you?"

"Kind of. I'm just wondering if I followed your instructions to the letter."

"Oh yes! You *cannot* believe how wonderful that was." Vicky whacked my sternum with the flat of her hand. She did it again and then once more. "Love attack," she explained with a wild laugh, and began rubbing away the hurt with a fierce circular motion.

"Ouch, you're pulling out my chest hair."

"Sorry, I just can't help myself." She tugged me up and down by the shoulders, making my head bounce on the pillow. "Yi, yi, yi, yi, yi!" Unlike Libby's post-coital comas, sex seemed to rev Vicky up.

"Want more?" I asked. "Or is this just violent affection?"

"No, no, I couldn't. But we've got to change position." She scooched away from me.

"What's the problem?"

"I was sleeping in a big puddle."

Sheets rustled as I slid after her to the edge of the mattress, where she again nestled her head on my shoulder. Her warm breath tickled the skin along my collar bone. "Want to know a secret?"

"What?"

"I had this gigundo crush on you in high school, but you never saw me."

"Sorry, I was pretty dull boy back then."

"You were worth the wait," she said in a husky voice. "Thank you for making me feel so loved."

"You *deserve* to be loved," I said, feeling swinish.

Chapter Twenty-Five

Consequences

I waited on tenterhooks for the *New York Transcript* op-ed to explode, but nothing happened.

No comment came back from readers that Monday, or ever. It was as if the piece had never been published, or dropped down a memory hole. Evidently, nobody cared what Trevor Henshaw opined about an airline strike. That's not exactly true. Henshaw was elated over the placement. I, on the other hand, was disappointed. Like Dostoevsky's Raskolnikov, I wanted to be punished.

Smiling broadly, Henshaw strolled into my office, holding a framed copy of the op-ed. "Dick Marin says this is quite a coup," he announced, brandishing the trophy that somebody must have made up Sunday, complete with a little brass plate. "I'm chuffed. The headline's brilliant." He read: "'When Management Forgets its First Duty.'"

"I'm glad you're pleased. I was a little worried it got too bellicose in the editing."

"Not at all. That's what made it so effective. But we need another one ASAP. My new book has only just come out and it's already a best seller. Dick says we need to align op-ed marketing messages with those in *Pulling the Right Tech Levers* to boost sales even more. Meaning, we have to educate that editor. Send her a follow-up."

Dick Marin's understanding of media relations—and by extension Henshaw's—was laughable. You can't dictate messages. With his *Bulletin* columns and this win, we'd had a nice run of favorable press. That was as good as it got. It also meant that the next time a major publication paid attention to a gnat like us the news would have to be bad. Otherwise, it wouldn't be news. I attempted to explain this oscillation to Henshaw. "Nonsense," he responded, "we're the hottest story in consulting."

Kitsie Schoemacher showed up in my office like a heat-seeking missile. "You're on your way now," she crowed. "See you Friday after work, and bring your balls."

Later that morning, an email arrived from Vicky.

Pete,

About last night… maybe what happened was inevitable. I mean, who was I kidding going over there like that? I dread my next confession to Father McIlinden, but I'm still overjoyed. I discovered how tender and genuinely caring you are, despite your efforts to hide it. You're also masterful at you know what. (I'm blushing.)

I can't write about this in an email. Can we talk tonight?

Victoria

P.S. I have a royal first name that's fancier than yours, so there!

I reread Vicky's note and tried to analyze all the pinpricks of conscience it stirred. Tender and caring was I? Maybe for a brave and lonely woman with the hots. But in another corner of my mind I was wondering when I could get her back in bed. Kitsie now Vicky, I was becoming as big a pig as my father.

The killing suspense surrounding my Davies caper lasted only until that night. Coming home from the train station, I saw lights burning in his house and his Audi outside. I'd rehearsed a speech and was as tense as an actor on opening night.

"Hello there," he said when the door opened. Despite the balmy evening, he was wearing a wool hunting shirt over an ancient white button-down.

"How are you, Mr. Davies?

He peered without recognition through his smudged horn rimmed glasses. "I'm fine. Are you a new neighbor?"

"No, I'm Peter Wendell. You were my scoutmaster for Troop Five, twenty-five years ago. I dated your daughter Lucy."

"Back here for a visit?"

"In a sense." My quavering voice sounded like somebody else's. "I wondered if I could talk to you for a few minutes."

Inside, I sat in a leather wingchair in the exposed-beam parlor. He eased himself into a Boston rocker by the broad granite fireplace and gazed at me expectantly. A wood fire glowed brightly behind a fire screen. In the corner, the stately figured-maple tall clock, with its trio of brass finials, rang the half-hour with a clear high note. As I talked, his eyes widened.

I told him how well I remembered this room from boyhood, especially the little Currier & Ives print hanging over the fireplace. It showed an old fashioned three-tined fork, beneath which cartoon human figures bent themselves into the capital letters W, U, O. The W was to the left of a shiny top hat. Decoded for me by Lucy one night, it read, "Fork over what you owe," an apt sentiment for a banker.

"Well, I'll be darned."

"Mr. Davies I think I owe *you* something," I said. The script I'd practiced went like this: I am a problem drinker. I stopped by after a heavy drinking bout to examine your portico early Sunday morning. It's a lot like mine. Under some bizarre impulse, I came inside without permission. When I heard you coming down the stairs, I ran away, which was despicable. I know that was trespassing at the very least and I'm ready to take the consequences. I've already talked this over with a friend on the town's police force. He's ready to arrest me if you want to press charges. I've also brought along a checkbook to make financial restitution for any broken property. How would you like to handle this?

Davies was bemused. "Well, my boy, I'm proud of you for owning up like that. So *you* were responsible for that ruckus the other night, eh? What was your name again?"

"Peter Wendell."

"Peter, that's right. Well Peter, thanks for manning up to this. And yes, as a matter of fact, I think I *will* charge you. First with attempted burglary, then drunk driving. Maybe leaving the scene of a crime. Sorry, but you need a strong lesson that you'll never forget. Booze is bad stuff. My wife was killed by a drunk driver. Did you know that?"

"No, I didn't." What was the likelihood of such a coincidence? Would he believe me if I told him about Libby's death? What would that accomplish except more confusion on his part? Overwhelmed by the thought of what lay ahead for me, all I could say was, "I'm so very sorry for your loss, Mr. Davies."

"Yes, it was in Colorado. Ten years ago. She was visiting Lucy out there. *That* guy was sorry, too." Staring trancelike over my head, he seemed to drift off. After a long pause, he said, "The other thing you can do for me, Peter, is buy tickets to the next policemen's ball. I used to be the Police Commissioner around here, you know. Make sure you buy them from my friend, Carm Triola. Poor bastard needs all the help he can get."

Chief Triola was long in his grave, but I promised to do as the old man wanted.

"So what's next?" I asked. "Will you call the police?"

"Yeah, you'll be hearing from them."

"There's one more thing I have to mention," I began and paused. "Actually, it's a question: Do you have a safe in the bookcase in your den?"

The old man's vacant smile was hard to interpret. "Now why would you ask that?"

"In full disclosure…" My voice cracked. "Years ago, Lucy told me you had one there; in my drunken daze I think I may have been planning to rob it."

His unchanging expression made me think he'd lost the conversational thread. At length he said, "She was pulling your leg. But better not mention that to anybody else. You'll live through this and be better for the experience."

He rose and offered a warm dry grip. "You say you were in Troop Five?"

"Yes."

"That's amazing. I suffer from CRS, you know." He led me to the door.

"CRS?"

"Can't remember shit." He grinned.

I turned to leave.

"Wait a second! Was your father Aubrey Wendell?"

"Yes, sir."

"I knew him at the Episcopal Church. The most arrogant man I ever met. He'd only been there a month when he tried to take over the building committee for the new church and the whole project. Said he'd built oil derricks around the world. What a conceited blowhard."

My immediate reaction startled me. I was breathless with fury. "He was a good man," I managed to get out. ""I never knew him to tell a lie."

Davies didn't notice my distress. "Well then, I guess the apple didn't fall far from the tree. You're honest too." He put a forefinger alongside his nose and then pointed it at me. "Did anyone ever tell you that you look just like him? Now that I remember it, I thought it was Aubrey, himself, driving off like a lunatic the other night. But I knew that was just plain crazy."

"Goodbye, Mr. Davies."

"Goodbye, son. But help me out, will you? There was some decision I just made concerning you. What was it again?"

"Filing charges for…

"Right, right. I'll call Carm tomorrow."

"Why don't you talk with Lieutenant Ritaldo DeMarco? He knows all about what happened."

"Thanks. I will. Can you write that name down for me?" He reached for a small pad of ringed paper and gold pen in his thick shirt pocket. "I have to carry these around," he explained. "Beats string. And what's the number?"

I called Rit with a full report when I got home. His opinion: The old banker's befuddlement might yet save me. "We can't act without hearing from him," he said. "Maybe he'll forget and it'll all go away."

"But shouldn't I turn myself in? It's his wish."

"Hell, no! Just sit tight and see how things play out. "

Sitting tight wasn't easy. Even the state of the silent little house filled me with reproach. In Libby's absence, it had grown tidier. Her newspapers and magazines no longer littered the wide floorboards in the small parlor. Libby used to read them on the braided rug, head propped on an arm, a tea mug atop a pile of clippings waiting to be filed, piles that could *not* be touched. I used to complain about the carefully sorted clutter. To me, her tear sheets were like ignored homework, evidence of intellectual laziness, reminders of my lack of interest in her deepest passion. Finally, I'd tossed the whole collection into the recycle bin.

I was never in love with news the way she was, with the fourth estate that A.J. Liebling called "the weak slat under the bed of democracy;" that disturbing record of venalities, violence, and bloated egos that Libby's mother had taught her to venerate. I knew first-hand that newspaper stories were riddled with errors and confirmation bias, and secretly agreed with Thoreau's opinion that news is "gossip, and they who edit and read it, are old women over their tea." All these stories about little guys getting screwed, what good did they do? The powerless still continued to get it in the neck. Libby recoiled when she learned the extent of my cynicism; she couldn't understand how I could work for years as a reporter feeling that disenchanted. Which was exactly why I wanted out so badly, I told her. Libby reminded me that, besides my truck tire piece, my stories had exposed insider trading and predatory lending. Wasn't that worthwhile? She kept a framed quote given to her by her mother and attributed to

George Orwell: *Journalism is printing what someone else does not want printed; everything else is public relations.* It was still on the kitchen wall. It represented the polar opposite of something my father once said: "Why would any businessman in his right mind talk to a reporter?"

Why, indeed? And why had I felt the need to defend dad's honesty? Davies hadn't impeached that, just his high-handedness. It was my veracity that was open to question. I was the one who'd written Henshaw's fiction that had morphed into the truer *When Management Forgets its First Duty*. And what is that first duty, anyway, taking care of workers or enriching shareholders, who are mostly traders and fat cats? Fear and greed moved markets, and managers were judged as human beings by high P/E ratios and ROI. It all was so deterministic, immutable economic forces at work that ultimately produced empty rustbelt factories where the wind whistled through broken windows. It was an inexorable process that economists call "creative destruction"—like forest fires allowing new growth. Was this evil? Libby had been right, I really didn't care.

I tried calling Vicky, but she wasn't home and I didn't leave a message. Not knowing what else to do, I dropped to the floor and did pushups until my arms shook. And then, putting temptation out of reach, I poured the bottle of yellow retsina down the toilet and flushed it. I'd had it with booze. It was killing me. I made a promise to myself to call Rit tomorrow and go to an AA meeting. I'd quit public relations, sell the house, rent an apartment, and try for a job at a local rag, maybe a weekly where I'd cover interminable zoning board meetings once more. These were good clean decisions, vows I knew I could keep. Libby would be pleased.

Fifteen minutes later, I was on my way to the package store.

BOOK FOUR

The Scandal Monger

CHAPTER TWENTY-SIX
Allegations

Nursing another blinding hangover, I sat at my desk chewing on a lemon bar from the Korean deli around the corner on Park Avenue. My gaze rested on the brick office building across Madison Avenue, but I was thinking about Vicky. I had a problem. Actions precede feelings, as someone wise once noted, and making tender love to her, as she'd begged, had produced a genuine regard. Beyond fondness, I wanted to spend time with her, confide my hopes and fears, gain her support in facing a wasting disease. Trouble was I didn't love Vicky the way I'd loved Libby. My affection took the form of wanting to protect her from my worthlessness. And that meant exit stage left. Didn't it? So I'd asked her to lunch tomorrow in New Canaan to do the right thing.

The phone's ringing brought me back from wrestling with noble motives.

"I know all about your book scam," Tom Dorsey said in a barely audible voice.

"About my *what*?"

"What frosts my butt is that we're friends. Hype is one thing. To enlist me in a fraud is another."

"Hey, what are you talking about?"

"Remember when you begged me to do that exclusive review of Henshaw's new book? At Senior Flaco's? Implied that you'd get shit-canned if I didn't do one? So I did, even pulled my punches, gave it a C-plus."

"Well, thanks."

"But I had to yank it."

"I'm sorry to hear that."

"Don't play dumb. Somehow you guys figured a way to game the *New York Transcript*'s bestseller list. You think that piece of crap went to the top based on its insights? Matrix employees bought piles of copies at the right bookstores. But of course you already know that. What you don't know is that we've got credit card receipts from all over the country to prove it. Your little scam was too clever by half. It might count as a criminal conspiracy."

"Criminal conspiracy?" None of this added up. "Can we go over this from the beginning?"

"We're running the story Monday after I get a few more quotes. We need a statement from you knuckleheads; I want to talk with Henshaw. Jesus, Pete, how could you sell out like this? You used to be one of us."

"Would you repeat all that?" I said. "What was Henshaw supposed to have done?"

"Spare me the fake innocent act. You're a lousy liar. What would Libby have made of this betrayal?"

"I didn't betray anybody. I'd swear that on her grave. So can you please make yourself clear?"

I took notes as Tom expounded. His voice's low volume was a measure of his disappointment in me. The scheme was something like stealing an election by counting nonexistent people. We'd allegedly purloined the list of bookstores that fed into the

Transcript's bestseller list. Whether we'd bribed somebody, or hacked some computer file, wasn't the point. The real intent was to ensure that Henshaw's new book was a *New York Transcript* blockbuster, or appeared to be one. In other words, the exercise was about convincing CEOs that our ideas were leading edge. That, in turn, would generate multimillion-dollar consulting engagements. It would have worked but for a pair of reasons:

First, we bought too many books in individual stores, sometimes a hundred at a clip, which raised red flags. "What's worse," said Tom, his voice filled with scorn, "you guys used your own corporate Amex cards to make the purchases. Pretty stupid, 'cause that left a paper trail a mile wide."

"How did you hear about this?"

"None of your business."

"What is the *Transcript* saying?

"I haven't talked to them yet, the poor slobs."

My mind sought answers. The immediate question was who stood to benefit from such an exposé? We were too insignificant for competitors to much care. Could it have been some whistleblower inside Matrix? Or somebody in the book industry?

"Can I ask one favor? Can you sit on the story until Tuesday so I have time to get answers?"

"You mean for old time's sake?"

"You want to print the truth don't you?"

"Okay, I'll see what Deke says, but you'd better come through."

I'd hardly put down the telephone when it sounded once more. It was Jim Phillips in Los Angeles: He was very sorry, and this wasn't his decision, he'd tried to go to the mat for me, thrown his body across the railroad tracks metaphorically, no kidding, because I was a really valuable contributor as far as he was con-

cerned, but because of budgetary reasons the company was going to have to let me go, which was unfair, he knew, yet he was
certain I could work out a free-lance arrangement with Henshaw
and that he, Phillips, would write me a great reference, so he had
no worries that I wouldn't bounce right back, and, oh by the way,
I had two weeks.

"Okay, message delivered," I said. "But the budget isn't the
real reason, is it? Marin got to Connors and told him I had a
drinking problem, didn't he?"

"Yeah, you're right. The midget did just that," Phillips admitted, "but everybody out there has seen you tripping and stumbling in the halls. It's been pretty obvious. I can't protect you
anymore. You ought to get to a rehab if you're in trouble. I'd like
to help. Maybe I can get our HR people to pay for one of those
twenty-eight day treatment programs. Would you like that?"

"That's very decent of you Jim," I replied, "but before I start
cleaning out my desk and heading for the drunk farm, let me tell
you about a little situation that just popped up out here."

Trevor Henshaw did not take a good photograph. On the cover
of Matrix's new recruiting brochure he wore an over-animated
smile beneath a lacquered prow of reddish-brown hair. The impression was TV game show host, not adviser to titans of industry. I wished someone could take Henshaw's picture now. Jaw
clenched, he was giving me a glimpse of the real person, a former
working-class Brit who'd escaped the Thames River dockyards by
winning a scholarship to the London School of Economics and
changing his accent, a kind of Dickensian Charley Hexam.

"That's rubbish," he responded after my briefing. "Find out
who's peddling this swill to Dorsey."

"Yes," Phillips' voice agreed, "find out the source. Then debunk it."

"Guys, he's not going to reveal his sources. I already asked. But shouldn't we find out if what he's alleging is true? The first rule in a PR crisis is to get out all the facts, pronto."

"There's *nothing* to it," Henshaw said. "We buy books in bulk for completely legitimate reasons: client meetings, mass mailings. What's dodgy about that?"

"Yeah, what's dodgy?" Phillips echoed. "It's what we've always done with Trevor's books. Go tell that to Dorsey. Make him go away."

"We may need an audit to get to the bottom of this…"

Henshaw made a slicing motion under his chin. "Jim," he said into the speaker, "why don't we let Pete handle this in his own fashion?"

"I'm all for *that*, Trevor." Phillips sounded relieved. "In fact, that's exactly why we hired Pete in the first place, to deal with the major media. Logistically, it's also best: He can manage directly from out there, avoid time differences with tight deadlines."

"Those were my thoughts exactly, old fellow. What do you say, Pete?"

"Fine by me—except do I still work here?"

Henshaw looked amused as Phillips improvised an answer: "Right now Pete, you are the most important person in the entire corporation. Nobody's going to fire you as long as I'm here. And if they do, I'll threaten to quit. So we're all agreed then. You take point on this thing. E-mail your strategy to me as soon as possible. Any previews on how you're going to handle it?"

I told him I'd cobble together a statement about buying books in volume for client purposes and gather favorable book review quotes to buttress the case that the book sold on its own merits. Maybe I'd also get some kind of official denial from the publisher. Another thought came to me: "I suppose I should also talk to the company attorney out here, Larry Lieberman."

Henshaw's face darkened.

"But maybe not yet," I amended.

"Keep me posted," said Phillips.

Once he left the line, Henshaw's jaw went slack. "This could ruin us," he said in a soft voice. "The consequences boggle the mind. We're a $300 million company that sells a very ephemeral commodity, which is advice. Ever hear of the 'Tinkerbell Principle?'"

"The what?"

"It's something that exists only because of believers' faith. And that's what keeps Matrix in business. Our only asset is our good reputation. You must understand that the research that went into that book was first-rate. We gathered data from over a hundred companies. Then we gave away a king's ransom to charitable causes to get CEOs to discuss the findings with us. And now..." His voice tailed off. "The fallout could be catastrophic."

"It's bad alright." I glanced down at my notes. "Dorsey mentioned that somebody might go to jail."

"Yes, it's *very* bad!" His strangled tone brought my head up to confront a pair of glittering eyes. "Now tell me how you're going to prevent that."

"You just heard me brief Phillips."

"That won't do, boyo. You've got to smother this thing before it's published."

"That'd take a miracle," I said. "The facts will emerge however we spin it. If nothing actually happened we'll get past this just fine. So I guess I should ask: *Did* we game the *Transcript's* best-seller list?"

"You think we just strolled in there and snaffled their secrets?" A flicker of amusement appeared. "We're not that bloody smart." He broke eye contact and resumed his somber tone. "Do this right and you can work for me forever—even if I have to pay you out of my own pocket."

Back in my office, my thoughts got me nowhere. Who could I call before the end of the day? Wispy cirrus clouds stretched above the Empire State Building like streaks of finger paint. What if I went for a run in Central Park and never came back? I didn't trust Henshaw. His statement sounded too...what? Hollow? On the other hand, could such chicanery even be done? Wouldn't alarm bells go off in the *Transcript's* elaborate tallying system? The walls were closing in on me. I wrote a Q&A and talking points for Jim to show to Connors. Then I did the only other thing I could think of. I spun my rolodex to the letter J.

Caroline Jones didn't match my mental image. The woman who'd put a razor edge on Henshaw's op-ed wasn't chubby and moon-faced. She was tall, elegant, and had a habit of tossing a sheaf of prematurely gray hair off her face. At her suggestion, we met at Junior's, a venerable deli serving cheesecake and pastrami sandwiches in Transcript Square.

"So what's this big crisis?" she wanted to know. A waitress placed a battered cup full of hot water on the counter in front of her. She dunked a tea bag up and down in it. I thought of Libby doing the same thing years ago at the PATH station. Ms. Jones and I were half-turned toward each other on adjacent stools. The physical positioning reminded me of when I'd tried to fire Ted deGruening. Outside, tourists ambled along the Great White Way, gawking at billboards and storefronts stuffed with electronic gadgets and tacky souvenirs.

"As I said on the phone, a friend of mine at the *Wall Street Bulletin* is planning to run a very damaging story for the *Transcript.*"

Ms. Jones eyed me warily. "So you mentioned."

"The thrust is that the *Transcript's* bestseller list has been infiltrated," I said, "that its ratings can be manipulated. I figured you guys needed to be warned."

"What's that got to do with *me*? I don't work on the *Book Review* section." She lowered the tea bag into a spoon and squeezed out the liquid with its string. Her curtain of hair slid forward, hiding her rather protuberant brown eyes.

"I called because you're the only person I know at the *Transcript*. The story targets the guy whose op-ed you rewrote, Trevor Henshaw."

She looped her hair behind her ear to regard me coldly. "You used to work on the *Bulletin*. I hear you were pretty good. How'd you wind up doing this kind of gig?"

"Look, it's not just Henshaw's reputation that's at stake. It's your paper's as well. My question is this: Is it *even possible* to con the bestseller list? Aren't there precautions? Accountants running around with chained briefcases? Tamper-proof redundancies? Something like that? I think it's worth your while to check this out before the story hits."

"I will."

"Thanks a lot." I reached for the check. "Let me get this."

She snatched it up. "That's against the *Transcript's* ethics policy," she said. Ms. Jones stood up, left five dollars on the counter, and walked out.

A half-hour later, she called with a terse message: "They say it can't be done. It's impossible. Our managing editor is calling the *Bulletin* to get the story killed." The line went dead.

I went to tell Henshaw, who clapped me on the shoulder with a hearty, "Good show!"

Tom Dorsey was furious. "Yeah, Deke just chewed out my ass because of your spilling the story to them. You're full of cute tricks aren't you?"

"They would have said the same thing to you," I pointed out. "Or would you rather have had your story retracted?"

Chapter Twenty-Seven
The Love of Money

The next day I walked down New Canaan's crowded main drag and realized there was nobody around from the old days. That should have been no big surprise, even on a blazing Saturday with Elm Street packed with shoppers. Statistically, the population turns over by ten percent every year, and I'd been away for twenty. Jobs supporting luxurious lifestyles are precarious. Even wildly intelligent people replete with cunning and acumen get fired, transferred, go out of business, or retire to less-expensive places.

Of course a few townie friends were still around if I sought them out. But financial pressure—like a neutron bomb—had cleared away all the people once inside my youthful landmarks. The same buildings now bore the omnipresent names of upscale retail chains. The bookstore was a branch of Ralph Lauren, the barber shop—where old Jake wielded something like pinking shears to thin my bushy hair—had metamorphosed into a Starbucks. The old savings and loan was now a Citibank, where I'd just had a discouraging discussion about refinancing my crippling mortgage to get a lower payment. Even Ginger's Diner, the locus of my junior high school social life, had long ago fallen victim to rising rents. It had become a chic eatery.

Vicky was waiting on a banquette inside what was now called Chez Jean-Claude's. She'd been visiting her parents and driven over separately. Like the New York restaurants it mimicked, the noise level was deafening inside Chez Jean-Claude's tangerine-colored dining room. Why was that? Clanks, clinks, laughter all blended and echoed amid waves of conversation that rose and fell like surf. I slid into the chair across from her and made a dumb show of greeting.

"This is horrible," she called out. "What a din!"

"Sorry," I roared back. "I thought you'd be curious about what happened to your uncle's old place."

"I've already seen enough!"

The leather-covered menu was entirely a la carte, confirmation of the spare-no-expense tab to come. Vicky put hers down with a grimace.

In a low-level bellow, I attempted to make conversation. "So, you're performing tonight?"

"Yes!"

"Where?"

She cupped her mouth: "New London!"

A waiter arrived. For some reason his sibilant voice carried beautifully. He said he wanted to tell us what Jean-Claude personally recommended: "May I suggest starting out with his very civilized dirty martinis? Then for our appetizers..."

"What do you have in the way of milkshakes?" Vicky interrupted.

"Nothing, I'm afraid." The waiter's expression was blank, a butler's face.

"This place has sure gone downhill since it was Ginger's," she said. "Don't you think so, Pete?"

"Yeah, what gives? Ginger's was famous for milkshakes."

"This is not Ginger's, sir," the waiter informed us, still deadpan.

Vicky darted her index finger back and forth toward the door.

I pushed back my chair and stood up. "Our mistake, we thought this place was more upscale."

Offended, but hiding it well, he collected our menus and pressed them to his chest. "Will there be anything else, sir?"

His reflexive stoicism pricked my conscience. Putdowns from rich assholes must have been an ongoing part of his job. "Sorry to bust your chops, buddy," I said. "This used to be a luncheonette where we came as kids. We were foolishly trying to recapture the past."

Understanding flashed in the man's eyes. "That's always hard to do," he said. "Have a pleasant day."

Nearing the exit, Vicky pulled down on my arm to put her mouth to my ear: "You were really kind to that snooty waiter; tenderheartedness is another winning trait I like about you."

"No big deal," I said, holding the door. "I just understand being treated like a flunky."

"You mean in your job?"

"That too," I said, following her out onto the street, "but I was thinking about my father."

Vicky gave me a questioning look.

"Tell you about it later."

We paused on the sidewalk across from Town Hall, a pretty Georgian two-story brick structure with granite quoins that had been put up in the 1930s. It would have made a realistic Disneyland representation of middle-American values, even though the town's median annual family income was nearly a quarter of a million dollars. They'd held teen dances in the parking lot behind it in our day. But the people around us didn't know that.

"How about we grab a Subway sandwich and head over to Mead Park," I suggested. "It may not be as trendy but has the benefit of being cheap."

"Okay, but back there in Cafe Cacophony I was going to ask if you're free to go to the symphony tomorrow night?"

"Maybe you won't want me there by then."

"That sounds ominous."

We spread the musty army blanket from the Saab's trunk on the hillside above the pond and soon found ourselves retreating from aggressive Canada geese. They left us alone higher up under the trees near the tennis courts. There, lying on my back, I saw that the September sun was already beginning to lower in the sky. It was just above the island's pine trees. Vicky sat cross-legged next to me, picking out excess shreds of lettuce mounded on her tuna grinder and dropping them onto the wrapper.

"What did you mean by 'I wouldn't want you' to go to the symphony?" she asked.

Ambivalence combined with cold feet as I weighed the total inappropriateness of the place and moment. I couldn't just dump her, out of the blue, at a picnic. "I was going to say that I have no appreciation for classical music," I said.

"Oh?"

"I'd rather go to a B. B. King concert."

"We can do that too." She abruptly shoved the remains of her sandwich back into the long plastic bag. "What's happening with restaurants these days?" she asked. "They're either too noisy, too expensive, or give you too much food."

"Overabundance," I said. "Decibels, calories, four million

dollars."

"Sometimes I feel like your straight man," she said. "What's four million dollars?"

"My disinheritance."

"Your what?"

I could have nipped the conversation to come in the bud— probably should have—with another jest. But apologizing to the waiter had opened up an emotional crack. Going against all my intentions, I found myself saying, "You said you wanted to get to know me better. So let me explain about my father."

"He was a bigshot wasn't he?"

"He was a bully. Our server at the restaurant got me thinking about him. Somebody once said that if you watch how a man treats a waiter, you're seeing his true character, how he's going to treat his wife. Dad got his jollies out of humiliating defenseless inferiors: waiters, clerks, salesmen. It made me squirm. I remember once he was buying me some fancy dress shoes that I didn't want, and he just belittled this young salesman for showing us 'shoddy merchandise.' He lectured him on how they were made with split leather, had mismatched hides, and whatever. The poor guy apologized. Can you imagine? For what? He didn't make them. So Dad stomped off in high dudgeon, head up and arms swinging self-righteously, and this kid says to me, 'And I am so sorry for *you*.'"

"Wow. Did you thank the clerk?"

"No. I told him to go fuck himself."

"But why?"

"Because I loved the old bastard." An unexpected surge of feeling washed over me. "And I wanted him to love me back."

There was a sweeter father long buried within the successful one, a younger man with long tapering hands who sometimes came home early enough to read Uncle Wiggly stories to me at bedtime. The way he turned pages with those elegant fingers he used on the piano produced a sense of being protected, as they did when he taught me how to ride a bike. Some inner amusement, maybe even lightheartedness, came into his eyes when he pronounced the name of the venerable rabbit's companion: Nurse Jane Fuzzy Wuzzy, the muskrat lady. He always got a kick out of those syllables, the penultimate word spoken at an upbeat tempo: *muskrat* lady. And when he'd put the illustrated book down, and I'd beg for more time, he'd tell me the Story of John McGorry: "And now my story's begun. I'll tell you another of his brother, and now my story is done." Almost always, he was still wearing his business suit trousers and white shirt as he turned out the light and left my room covered with its cowboy wallpaper.

I became aware of Vicky's pitying look.

"My loyalties were so fucked up. Pardon my repeated swearing. My high school buddies were scared to death of Dad. They called him Ming the Merciless. I'd laugh and then defend him, tell them about his achievements: Eagle Scout, a child prodigy on the piano, Harvard MBA at twenty-one, a co-inventor of offshore drilling. Oh, he was awesome, alright, and so very disappointed that I didn't measure up."

"But you were a class leader, went to Dartmouth."

"Not good enough. For him, it was Harvard, Yale, or death."

"Rit experienced the same treatment; he calls that a shame-based family, he lived in one too…"

"Uh, uh, no second-hand psychobabble from Rit. Not now. But do you want to know the craziest thing?"

"Only if it doesn't upset you." She was twisting the long sandwich bag, tying knot after knot in it.

"A few years ago, before Dad died and I was about to hock everything to move back to New Canaan, he had his secretary, Inez, book an appointment for me at his office. He wanted to talk about my inheritance, which I'd already bravely told him I didn't need, but really did. Crazy mixed-up kid, right? Anyway, there he sat behind his humongous mahogany desk with a picture of me in a football uniform on the credenza behind him. He said he had originally planned to set up a ten-year trust fund payout for me. Four million bucks, which is four hundred grand a year. But then when he and Lucille discussed it some more, they decided that was a bad idea."

"Who's Lucille?"

"My stepmother. Know what she'd told him?"

"You'd better tell me."

"That 'when a rich person tries to control his money from beyond the grave, the only people who benefit are the psychiatrists.' She'd read that someplace, and wouldn't it be far better for me to make my own way in the world, like he had? Become self-sufficient. And so Dad asked—with those gray eyes boring in—didn't I agree?"

I stopped talking. I'd never revealed this before. Not even to Libby, who probably would have understood my acquiescence, which I once thought had finally ended Father's power over me. Now, I didn't know if I'd been quietly defiant or a weakling. And why was I suddenly opening up to Vicky?

I tried to change the subject. I pointed to the duck pond's little island. "Did you ever notice that the setting sun appears larger near the horizon?"

"Yes, but what did you say to your father?"

"Do you suppose the denser air near the ground acts like a lens to magnify it?"

"It's an optical illusion. It's closer in comparison to buildings and trees. Please finish your story."

"So, in other words, if I could measure the sun with a caliper at noon and sunset, the spread would be the same?"

Vicky asked if I'd ever heard of the novel *The Moon and Six Pence*. It was the same idea: a coin held up at arms' length, like a miniature eclipse, will cover either celestial sphere at any point in the sky. "We see what we expect, not what's really there."

"That's very true."

"Are you going to leave me hanging?" She bugged out her eyes, as if to pull the words from me.

"Maybe I'm making what happened bigger in my mind too. Another illusion. So, I bet you can guess what happened."

"No, not at all."

"So I totally agreed with him. Right there in his office while he was getting a shoeshine from this old black guy who wore a brown cotton coat with his name stitched in white thread: Leroy. Leroy tried to be invisible. He put shoe polish on with his thumb and then made his rag snap. Yes sir, I said, I concurred absolutely, it *was* more character-building. And the fact is I suppose it really was. This was right after I married Libby, and he was still living here in town. Even though I was in debt up to my eyeballs, I told him I already had everything I wanted, earned it on my own, didn't need his help, thanks just the same."

"Oh, Pete," she said, "how devastating for you. Money is so tied to a man's self-worth, especially in your family. And it could have helped you so much"

"Actually, it was just that I didn't want to hurt his feelings. I tried to make it easy for him to do his tough love bit. Isn't that insane?"

Vicky took my hands in hers. "No, it's sad. More than the money, you wanted his respect, didn't you?"

I pulled my fingers away, realizing that I'd succeeded in drawing her closer to me, an outcome I didn't want at all—yet did.

"More like the other way around," I said, feeling barren. "After he cut me off I didn't care if he lived or died."

Chapter Twenty-Eight

Word Games

"Gusting," I said.

"High winds," Vicky answered.

"No, no. By the rules of grammar, that should also mean delightful, pleasant, appetizing. It's the missing positive of disgusting, get it?"

Vicky and I were in a dark-paneled Irish pub across the street from the Garde Theatre in New London. It was the night of her performance and, to my immense relief, she'd flawlessly played the flute solo in Debussy's *Prelude to The Afternoon of a Faun*. I'd been holding my breath as the spotlight rested on her, the orchestra waiting, the string section's bows upright in expectation, like a field of dried stalks. She threw back her head and filled the darkness with evocative melody.

Tonic water effervesced in my highball glass. Vicky had ordered white wine. We sat on high barstools with a thick pine table top between us. It was fashioned out of a ship's hatch with imbedded brass handles. The city was once a whaling center. They built submarines there nowadays. Honoring this history, paintings of sailing vessels and black-hulled attack subs hung on the walls. Behind Vicky hulked a massive walnut bar, complete with foot rail and ascending ranks of bottles, doubled in number by the mammoth mirror behind them. Overhead, the Victorian stamped-steel ceiling was blackened with the stain of a thousand cigars and cigarettes. It was past midnight and we were the only customers. Our cars waited outside at the curb.

"Oh I get it," she said. "Give me another one."

"Gruntled."

"Satisfied, pleased with the result?"

"Correct, and the same goes for combobulated; or, for that matter, sheveled."

"You're very sheveled tonight," Vicky said. "Nice yellow tie, *very* New Canaanish." She reached over and straightened the knot. "There, perfect."

"It's my so-called lucky foulard, and I wore it in your honor. But getting back to grammar, besides its meaningless prefixes, there's another reason English drives foreigners crazy: Synonyms out the ying yang. There's a historic reason. Did your father ever tell you about 'the three levels' of the English language?"

Vicky struggled not to smile. "You're cute when you get all professorial," she said.

I grinned back. "The three levels of the English language refer to the various synonyms introduced into the Germanic root language by the Romans and Normans. Take 'hut,' 'edifice,' and 'mansion,' their meanings vary slightly, but what about 'purchase' and 'buy'? The first is Germanic, the second Anglo-French. What's the difference?"

Vicky burst into laughter then looked guilty. "Excuse me," she said. "Keep telling me about synonyms. You're going to make a super English teacher."

"Nope. No more pedantry. And this teacher business you

keep harping about won't wash. It'll take years I don't have, and how will I support myself? Your father thinks I might starve."

"We'll find a way," she said, watching me through lowered eyelashes. "Love always does."

This was my opening, but I couldn't just give it to her right between the eyes. Nor was I sure I wanted to.

"Okay, be a sphinx, but since you're such a word guy, do you know what embouchure means?"

"Not a clue."

"I'll save you a trip to the dictionary." Elevating her chin, she pouted in a distinctive way. The pucker widened into a smile. "It's how we flute players form our lips to play. See? Oh, don't gape from way over there. Get closer."

I moved around the end of the thick tabletop to examine her mouth. Her lips were again flattened over her teeth.

"Amazing, all that beautiful sound comes from that teeny little gap? It's kind of the way you make noise from a Coke bottle, isn't it?"

Bobbing her head in assent, she leaned forward and, with a low growl, planted a big one on me. "It took me years to train these lips," she said when she was done.

"They're very talented," I said.

"I've been dying to do that ever since I saw you in the audience," she said. "You looked terrified."

"Well, I *was*. What you were doing looked so difficult. You were gulping breaths, glancing at the conductor, flipping sheet music, and moving your elbows around in circles."

"The last is called *affettuosamente*, playing with deep feeling."

"Yes, and it was just magical, as I've spent the last half hour telling you. You had the audience floating on a lavender cloud.

But you were all alone up there under the spotlight. The whole orchestra was hanging onto your intro. One sour note would have broken the spell, wrecked the whole performance."

"I thought you were going to pee in your pants, but observe these again." She put two fingers to her lips. "I don't worry when I use these, so why should you?" Vicky twisted the stem of her glass. "Pete, may I ask you something personal?"

"Personally, I prefer impersonal questions."

Undeterred, she wanted to know from whence came my fear of failure.

"That's easy, my father, the piano prodigy, who assumed I'd be one as well. For me, music was an agony of mistakes. I could never do it right."

"They say fear is caused by the absence of faith."

"So is the absence of talent. But, okay, I admit that I've always been morbidly self-conscious. I think it's one of the reasons I became a reporter, so I'd have a legitimate reason to talk with perfect strangers."

"Rit tells me shyness is a form of extreme egotism," Vicky said.

"No kidding. Is Rit some kind of expert on bashfulness?"

"He says shy people are convinced that everybody is scrutinizing their performance, keeping score of their failures. Life's all about you, the impression you leave."

"I never knew Varsity Rit was so sensitive. He swaggered around like Benito Mussolini."

"That was a protective shell; he worried people thought less of him because his family was poor. He says alcoholics are people with big egos and low self-esteem."

"What about people with low egos and big self-esteem? Is that the difference between an egoist and egotist? I ought to look that up."

"Rit's been trying to help you, hasn't he?"

"I don't need his help. I've told him that, repeatedly." Bent toward each other in the giant mirror's reflection, we appeared to be the image of intimacy.

"Maybe this is none of my business…"

I leaned away. "Maybe it's not."

"Rit tells me that in AA they ask God to 'rid them of the bondage of self,'" she persisted, "to lift their self-absorption."

"Just what *did* Rit say about me?"

"He thinks you have a drinking problem."

Regretting I'd opened up to her at the duck pond, I felt the old sullen resentment at criticism. I hated to be judged and needed to shut her up. "Drinking problem," I repeated, "isn't that somebody with a dribble glass?"

"Please don't turn this into a joke. I saw you knock back five drinks on our first date at the Silvermine."

"This whole conversation's become a joke."

"You seem upset."

"Duh, yeah. Wouldn't you be upset about being called a lush—especially since I'm drinking tonic water?" I tapped the glass. "Which has lost its fizz, by the way."

Vicky began sliding a finger back and forth across one of the table's embedded brass fixtures. "I push too hard sometimes," she said in a choked voice. "It used to drive Danny crazy. It's just that…"

"I know, you only want to help. Listen, the bartender looks like he wants to close up. He's wiping a hole in the counter." I eyed my new running watch. "It's time to shove off."

"Why won't you let me help you?" She straightened her shoulders and her words rushed out: "It just so happens I love you,

Mister self-conscious Hampton Wendell. I know this has been sudden, but I'd be good for you, could help you heal emotionally. And we're great together in bed."

I didn't respond. Inside my pocket, I fingered the worn Saab key, flipping it over and over with a snap.

"Why not let me in? It's so obvious that you've been struggling since your wife died."

"Don't talk about her."

Vicky opened her mouth but then shut it.

Something inside me let go. "I'll tell you why," I said. "Because, once you get to know me, you'll realize I'm a complete failure. I'll disappoint you like I did Libby. I disappoint everybody, especially myself."

"No you won't."

"Vicky, you cannot fix me. You're like some cheerful bulldozer. Know what my father's favorite line was? 'I'm disappointed in you.' I can't live up to *your* expectations, either. Don't you get it? I don't want to be a teacher. I don't love you in the way you need. I just want to be left alone."

Her expression froze.

"Hey, I'm sorry."

"I'm sorry, too." I could barely hear her voice. Swiveling off the high stool, she reached down to pick up her leather flute case and turned to walk out.

"And, oh by the way," I yelled after her, "did Rit tell you I might be charged with breaking and entering? That I could go to *jail!* You still sure you want to get involved with me?"

The barman gave me a curious look.

Vicky's heels clattered across the floor. She banged her broad shoulder into the entrance door and escaped into the night.

CHAPTER TWENTY-NINE

The Story Breaks

**Did Deceptive Sales
Create the Appearance
Of a Business Bestseller?**

By Thomas R. Dorsey
Staff Reporter of The Wall Street Bulletin

Over several weeks this summer, a carefully selected group of bookshops across the nation received telephone orders each totaling dozens of books for *Pulling the Right Tech Levers*, the new business opus from management maven Trevor Henshaw, CEO of Matrix Consulting.

Henshaw is the author of *Business Process Rationalization*—a prior blockbuster that created a boom in Matrix's business and a multibillion dollar shot in the arm for the entire consulting industry.

Bunny Rodriguez, owner of Miami's Dolphin Bookstore, said the requests were unique in her experience. By simply processing a credit card order from someone identifying herself as Nancy Donahue, Rodriguez would net as much as $1,200 in profit—all without having to touch a book. "It was like owning an oil well," she says. Other stores fulfilled similar orders from Matrix employees who, like Donahue, used company credit cards. The books were then shipped to various Matrix offices, the firm says.

What was going on? An investigation by the *Wall Street Bulletin* concludes that Donahue and other Matrix colleagues were part of a nationwide scheme to boost sales figures at targeted bookstores in order to breach the integrity of the *New York Transcript*'s prestigious bestseller list.

How? By systematically placing purchases at reporting bookstores, Henshaw's firm appears to have attempted to mimic a groundswell of demand, while avoiding detection by the *Transcript*.

Why? Bestseller status, especially from the *Transcript*, would guarantee fat consulting and speaking fees for Matrix. The expenditure of an estimated $350,000 to buy some 50,000 books in select locations is a pittance in order to gain a larger slice of the booming $100 billion global technology-consulting market. Matrix's share has been declining precipitously, according to industry analyst Booth Research. And that may explain the necessity for touting a new consulting fad.

Whether such deception violates mail fraud statutes is a matter for legal authorities, but publishing officials contacted by the *Bulletin* decried the tactics as clearly unethical. "It's akin to stealing intellectual property or trade secrets," added Robert Dunston, a professor at

Vanderbilt University School of Business. "This is their secret sauce."

But did the scheme really have an effect? In response to a *Bulletin* inquiry, The *New York Transcript* said it retains complete confidence in the integrity of its list. "Our systems spotted the bulk purchases of Pushing and discounted them," said Allan Krueger, a technology and survey editor for the paper's Book Section. "We have no reason to believe our rankings were manipulated." Nevertheless, *Pulling the Right Tech Levers* quickly rose to Number Four on its business-related list in the wake of what can be viewed as pump-priming sales.

Asked for comment, H. Peter Wendell, a Matrix spokesman, read a brief statement that the book's popularity was "generated by its own merit." The response also asserted that the bulk purchases were legitimately made to stockpile books for corporate events and mailings by different offices to potential clients. Wendell declined to respond to further questions.

The article was a nasty surprise. Why had it run at all? The *Transcript* had stoutly denied it had been hacked. Yet there it was—a much-ado-about-nothing article about allegations of a victimless crime, a non-story. I never thought I'd see printed the thrown-together statement I'd concocted early Friday. Yet as I stood in line in the Park Avenue deli reading it, I had to admit that I shouldn't have underestimated Tom Dorsey's determination. The deli's proprietor, a diminutive Korean woman, leaned forward in polite anticipation. "Sir," she prompted, "you want your lee-mon skare?"

"Oh sure," I said, reentering the world, "give me the usual."

In my office, I bit into the tart pastry and reread the ending. The story circled back to gather damaging quotes from other bookstores and a nettled comment from Henshaw's publisher, who denied any wrongdoing. Tom hadn't really made the case. Indeed, with big enough brass balls, one might even assert that the list's un-hackable safeguards only proved the book's rightful place on it. Could I say that without blushing?

A bus swooshed away from the curb a floor below me as I pried off the coffee lid. I sipped and wondered what Tom's second-day lede could possibly be.

Marianne, Henshaw's secretary, entered my office. "He wants to see you right now," she said.

Henshaw was outside his door when I got there. He was making an after-you-Alphonse gesture to someone inside. Dick Marin and Teddy deGruening exited on the double for the nearby elevators. Marin stopped to give me an empty look. "Just keep me out of the newspapers," he said. He joined deGruening, where he punched the down button three times.

"You had better come inside," said Henshaw. "And shut the door behind you."

Seated in the morning glare from his wall of windows, I offered him a temporizing opinion: "The story doesn't prove anything, Trevor."

Henshaw rose and adjusted the blinds to ease my squint. He squeezed my shoulder as he crossed back behind me. "Let's postpone discussing the story for a while," he said. "I want to talk about revenue."

He sat down on his low couch, flung an arm across the top,

and began: By some freak coincidence, Matrix had just started high-level strategy work for the *Transcript*, which was news to me. If our ideas were accepted, Henshaw went on, we'd launch an extremely lucrative development project aimed at making the paper more competitive in the dawning Internet Age. The preliminary concepts we'd come up with—so far shown only to the business side of the paper—had gone over well. The publisher had come around from his belief that a digitally delivered "paperless newspaper was about as likely as a paperless bathroom."

That was a joke and I gave the mandatory chuckle. Henshaw was a pretty cool customer. He moved from humor to the bottom line: He'd personally guaranteed a fivefold return on a six-month $2 million contract. If things continued on track, the *Transcript* could become Matrix's biggest client as, potentially, we advised it on everything from downloading news into internet-connected tablets to developing "push" advertising. I had only the thinnest grasp of these technological wonders. Supposedly, such features would reinvent newspaper publishing by allowing the *Transcript* to provide each reader with a "Daily Me," an electronic version of the paper with super-customized content. Gone, eventually, would be legions of costly workers manning composing rooms, presses, and trucks.

"We simply cannot lose this income," Henshaw said, drumming his fingers atop the couch. "And you're the key to making sure we don't."

Whether that largesse would continue was of course entirely up to our principal client, Adrian Adlinger, the Transcript's aged publisher. Henshaw said Adlinger had just summoned him for a meeting in his office at eleven that morning.

"A bit of a sticky wicket, eh? So how do we create—what do

you PR chaps call it—'plausible deniability' and hang on to our *Transcript* business?"

I brushed some powdered sugar from my trouser leg and gathered my thoughts. "First off, I think that's the least of your problems." I told Henshaw that he didn't have just a major PR crisis. Because of the possibility of contract termination and disputed fees, it could turn into a lawsuit. Larry Lieberman, the eastern-based corporation counsel, had to be called in.

"Not yet."

"Okay, but one big question remains," I ventured. "It'll take more than a mere denial to convince Adrian Adlinger or anybody else that we didn't do anything wrong. We have to prove it." I repeated Friday's question in a different way: "So, did somebody here do what we're accused of?"

Henshaw gave me a stony look. "The short answer is yes, but this time it was a sloppy job."

"This time?"

"Dick used the same tactic for my first book."

Disbelief overcame circumspection. "So is *that* what you're going to tell Adlinger? That having hoodwinked his paper's Book Section once already, we failed on the second try?"

"Steady on," Henshaw replied, "At my meeting with Adrian I'm going to unmask the real villain, Richard Marin, who dreamed up this whole wretched scheme. I just fired him. But no real harm has been done."

"'No real harm?'" This discussion was rapidly moving toward implausible deniability. "Adlinger will never buy that," I said. "Why should he cover for us? Their 'business model' isn't how they publish, it's what they publish. They think they're selling the truth."

Henshaw showed his incisors in a grim smile. "Who knows? His family-run company is in financial free fall. Massive amounts of advertising linage for little stuff—cars, apartment rentals, jobs wanted—are decamping to cheaper internet sites. The man really needs our help, and he knows it. I'll lay a wager I'll keep him as a client. Or at least he'll think better of me after I reveal that Marin's insider knowledge came from book industry contacts, not their computer files."

"Meaning deGruening?"

"This stays inside these walls."

"How did Dick take his dismissal?

"Not all that badly, as a matter of fact. He just agreed to take a very generous severance package for falling on his sword. In return, I guaranteed that we'd keep him and Ted out of any bad publicity."

"How?"

"We shield them, keep them out of stories. We limit our responses to your Q&A that Jock Connors agreed on Friday—'The book sold on its own merit, we always stockpile plenty of copies of our books for client calls and special forums.' Good God, man, the *Transcript* says nothing happened. We wholeheartedly agree." He regarded me with cold blue eyes. "So don't faff around. Make this disappear, you understand?"

"Yes, Trevor," I said, "I understand." I understood something else: Henshaw had to have known about this duplicity. Tom's story said people throughout the organization had participated. It also had to have cost a bundle, not an easy thing to hide in Matrix's cash-strapped state. And now, the unsavory job of protecting Dick Marin from the discovery he so richly deserved was my responsibility.

"One other question, Trevor: When did you find out about

this?" I was attempting to catch him in a lie. Friday, he'd said we weren't clever enough to have figured out such a scheme.

"This morning," he said, "when I confronted Dickie boy."

Three new emails had arrived by the time I got to my desk. Two were from business magazines, the other came from the AP. The phone's message light was blinking. My moment to take the press spears in the chest had come. I tried out a fairly plausible defense on myself: After all, Henshaw's book had sold on its own merits. The arithmetic of 200,000-plus additional sales beyond ours was all the evidence anybody needed. But didn't parroting that talking point amount to complicity on my part? Whether Marin's bamboozling had been needed or not to make a genuine bestseller, wasn't it still wrong? And what if somebody wanted to know about our consulting work at the *Transcript*, the real deep secret? How to duck that? I'm not at liberty to reveal client names? That was true enough. And there was a whole other consideration: lots of livelihoods were at stake. Scandals destroy companies. A single derivatives trader in Shanghai had just brought down Barings Bank. He'd been hiding $1.3 billion in losses, not stealing a piffling confidential list of bookstores. But the loss of trust—the sticky impression of sleaziness—could be just as fatal to our little "Tinkerbell" operation.

What to do? I could make a clean breast of things and bring the walls down around my ears—the nuclear option. I could prevaricate and wait for the facts to come out, as they always did, and try to postpone the day of reckoning. Or, maybe I could walk an ethical tightrope, really earn my pay, admit only what I had to.

Another email popped up. The header read vgingerella@l-hschool.edu. I opened it.

Dear Hampton,

I want to just hate you. It would make things far simpler, but I guess pity is more appropriate. You have a lower opinion of yourself than I ever could, and it's so completely undeserved!

Anyway, here's today's etymology lesson for the word guy: your unused first name means "little town" or "home settlement." Bet you didn't know that.

Did you also know you can get pretty touchy? So alright, forget about teaching, bad idea from moi. And forgive me for coming on so strong. It's a family trait, like big hands.

My well-known failings are know-it-all-ism and not listening. A large part of this comes from the certainty I have in my faith, which seems to irritate you. They're not great traits for someone in a one-sided relationship with a very private person.

But you weren't honest. It was as if you were afraid being truthful would hurt me. Honesty is really the ultimate gift, along with—as you said on our first date—emotional generosity. So thanks for finally setting me straight. And don't worry, I'm a tough broad.

You'll know what to do with your life, without any help from me, when you know who you are. I think you came home to find out. I pray that you do.

Vicky

Little town? Pray for me? She was saying her final goodbye. I took a sip of cold deli coffee that tasted like medicine. Now that I'd succeeded so well in pushing her away, I felt bereft.

Nancy Donahue entered my office. Dick Marin's administrative assistant didn't look so haughty this morning. She held up a copy of the *Bulletin* and smacked it with the back of her hand. "How can they *do* this?" she wailed.

I closed Vicky's email and mentally changed gears. "I'm afraid they have every right, Nancy. Like it says in the First Amendment, it's a free press."

"But it's not fair! I have to *agree* to talk to them before they can write about me, don't I?" In her anxiety, she was tugging some strands of her long brown hair.

"Is it accurate?"

"Yes. But I didn't do anything wrong. I was just doing what Dick told me to do! He said other consulting firms do this all the time. How come they didn't print *that*? You have to make them print a retraction!"

"Do you want your name in another story that repeats the allegations?"

"No," she said grudgingly, "no I don't. But this isn't right. I could lose my job like Dick just did. And then who'd hire me?"

I had no answer.

After she left, I found an empty conference room to return my press calls. I wanted no more interruptions. Before I could begin, Henshaw's admin Marianne entered, tight-faced and flustered.

"We can't go on meeting like this, Marianne. People will talk."

"Thank God I found you. Trevor asked me to transfer a call to you."

"Who's it from?"

"The *New York Transcript*."

Marianne stepped to the phone's console and briskly tapped buttons. She passed me the receiver like it was a rattlesnake.

"Here."

I put it to my ear as the door eased shut behind her. "Hello?"

"Mr. Wendell? Tim Carson, media reporter for the *Transcript*. I'm calling about certain allegations in this morning's *Wall Street Bulletin*." Carson had a mellifluous almost jolly broadcaster's voice. "Can *you* get Mr. Henshaw on the line for me?"

"You can talk to me."

"Are you authorized to speak for Matrix on this matter?"

"Yes."

"Can you answer my questions?"

"I have a prepared statement."

"Which is?"

"Trevor Henshaw's book became a bestseller based on its own merits."

"Is that your all-purpose response?"

"We bought several thousand copies to stockpile for mailings and client events, if that's what you're getting at."

"Can we go a little deeper into the manner of those purchases?"

"My statement covers that."

"Did you know our Book Section has done an investigation and now admits that the safeguards on its bestseller list were breached?

"No I did not." I felt a cold drop of sweat run down my side.

"Any comment?"

"All told, two hundred fifty thousand copies of *Pulling the Right Tech Levers* have been sold. That overwhelming popularity is clearly based on the book's merits. Have you read the reviews?"

"And the specific cherry-picking of reporting bookstores is a coincidence?"

"We always purchase books for internal purposes."

"That's it?

"That's it."

Carson snickered and my face baked.

"Mr. Wendell, I'm giving you another opportunity to own up."

"Mr. Henshaw's book sold well based on its merits."

"What about the fifty thousand copies Matrix bought? Isn't that an awful lot to keep on hand?

"As I said, we bought several thousand copies to stockpile for mass mailings and for the scores of client events we hold."

"And you see nothing untoward in any of this?"

I kept quiet, not wanting to be quoted denying an accusation.

"Hello?"

"Mr. Henshaw's book sold well based on its merits."

CHAPTER THIRTY

Larry Lieberman's Sleuthing

Steam poured out of a big steel pipe in the middle of Broadway as
I crossed with Larry Lieberman. Skirting the orange plastic bar-
rier around it, Larry stopped to peer into the manhole. "There's
some schmuck down there in a hardhat," he shouted over the
high-pitched whine. He removed his glasses the better to see.
"Can you believe that? The guy must be roasting."

We'd left the office to avoid being overheard. His learned legal
opinion about criminal prosecution was to scoff at the idea. It
was all legal, just not ethical. Tom was just huffing and puffing,
Larry assured me. "Editorial fulminating," he called it.

"Okay, so nobody goes to the slammer, but what can I say
from now on that's honest and still defensible? You've seen the
Q&A. It's a shriveling fig leaf. I can't bullshit the *Bulletin* reporter
anymore. He used to be one of my best friends."

I was awaiting his guidance when the crosswalk light's red
hand started to flash its countdown. People flowed around us
faster as Larry lingered, gaping. "That guy needs asbestos U-trow."

The light changed. "Come on, we're holding up traffic," I said,
thinking the utility worker wasn't the only guy taking heat.

"Understanding the context is worth twenty-five IQ points,"

said Larry, once on the other side of the street. "Forget that Henshaw had to be involved. What I can't figure is how slick Dick Marin could spend more than a quarter of a million bucks to amass books without Connors going ape-shit. Our combustible CEO has been *all over us* about costs. Remember the last revenue forecast meeting?"

"How could I forget?"

"Something doesn't add up." He mouth formed a wide grin. "Literally."

"You're saying Jock Connors knew about this, that he approved the spending?"

"Most likely, but maybe he figured it was just another unsavory cost of doing business."

"What do you mean, 'just another?'"

"Rumor has it we pay bribes to foreign powers who buy our defense equipment."

"Do you believe that?

Larry shrugged. "It's not for me to say as an officer of the court. If I knew for sure and didn't report it I could get disbarred. But that's kind of off point."

"So what should I say?" My weak left foot clanged on a pair of metal doors set flush into the sidewalk.

"Talmudic scholars believe that lying is permissible," he said, "in situations where, quote, 'honesty might cause oneself or another person harm,' unquote."

"That's not particularly helpful," I said.

"How about this: Do they pay you enough to lie?"

"No, not even close."

"Let me see if I can find out something," Larry said. "Meantime, you'd better tap dance very carefully." His vision dropped to my legs. "Speaking about dancing, why are you shambling along like a zombie?"

"My feet hurt."

"Well, get some new shoes."

We arrived back in the building's narrow marble lobby with its gilt beaux-arts pilasters surrounding the brass-fronted elevators. We jotted our return times on the register and the sleepy uniformed guard nodded our admittance.

Upstairs in my office, I hid behind my talking points in phone grillings with reporters from *BusinessWeek*, *Forbes*, the *Financial Times*, and the wire services. It was easy enough. None had heard about the *Transcript*'s change of heart, and it wasn't my job to update them. Then, with a giddy existential feeling, I called Tom Dorsey to say I needed to talk with him in some place that was private. We agreed to meet at the Greek sub shop where I'd courted Libby with dripping takeout sandwiches. I promised to be there at one o'clock. My course was clear: It was time to grow up.

Larry Lieberman was leaning against my office doorframe as I put the phone down. "How're you doing?" he asked. "Taking the strain okay?"

"I'm having a ball. You ought to try this sometime."

He pulled up the visitor's chair. "You should know that the natives around here are getting restless."

"Not my problem."

Always strenuously unfashionable, he hoisted a hairy arm to inspect his Mickey Mouse watch, attached by a red plastic strap. "It's only eleven o'clock and I've talked with three partners who've told me the same thing: They're getting phone calls from recruiters and business school buddies telling them this might be a very opportune time to find another job."

"So?"

"Our assets are about to depart down the elevators in droves."

"Meaning the rats are leaving the ship?"

"Meaning the whole ship might sink, drowning ordinary employees chained to the oars below deck."

Shifting his shoulders in his ill-fitting Moe Ginsberg suit, Larry gave me a tutorial: At the highest levels, our senior partners counsel inherently insecure CEOs with an intimacy approaching psychiatry. They not only devise competitive strategy, they help specific client executives succeed against internal rivals. Such trust solidifies and becomes portable. With scandal in the air and bonuses in doubt, the ablest and most highly compensated partners can become unsure of their place of employment, but not their future. They study their options, they test the waters. This is when their deep relationships pay off, when old job offers are reconsidered, and new ones weighed. The precipitate departure of the best and brightest was in the offing.

"There's something else," Larry added, looking around furtively in an elaborate show of not wanting to be overheard. "I found out how this all went down. Turns out it's a pretty common technique in the book industry. In fact, we did it before with Trevor's last book."

"Yeah, he told me that."

"Good for him, but it's a well-guarded secret inside the company. I found out that Jock Connors has a big recurring line item in his personal budget that covers 'book promotion.'"

"How'd you find that out?"

"Spies in Los Angeles. And that's not all. Your nemesis Dick Marin had the book's ideas focus-group tested, revised, and then retested by a marketing firm—just like in preparation for a TV ad campaign. That's how they came up with that godawful title. Nothing illegal there, but that cost tens of thousands more, exactly when we were all trying to scrimp and save to make our earnings projections. What's more, deGruening wrote drafts of dust-jacket blurbs for our top clients to approve, working with PR guys at these companies. Bet you never heard about that either, did you? They pushed every angle. I had no idea how much was riding on this book launch. What's really interesting is that I'm told that your boss Jim Phillips knew nothing about this, either."

"So Trevor was inside this?"

Larry shrugged. "I wouldn't doubt it for a moment."

As I headed for my rendezvous with Tom Dorsey, Kitsie Schoemacher stopped me in the hallway in front of the elevator. "I'm in awe of you," she said. "You did a masterful job of turning around the allegations in the *Bulletin* this morning. Millions of dollars couldn't buy that kind of free promotion for Trevor's new book. 'Two-hundred-fifty-thousand volumes sold on their own merit.' And right there on the front page of the Bible of Business. We're going to be top-of-mind when senior executives think about hiring consulting firms. Keep up the good work."

"Thanks," I said, wondering what kind of mind share we'd have with CEOs after I got through talking with Tom.

Before she left, Kitsie asked the day's bottom-line question: "Did we really do what they're accusing us of?"

"Seems so."

"Too bad that part of it leaked out, because it was really sharp marketing. Your idea?"

"I'm, not that bloody clever."

BOOK FIVE

AFOGs

Chapter Thirty-One
Keeping the Biggest Secret

The sub shop looked smaller and dirtier than I remembered. The Greek proprietor was older and more subdued than when Libby and I bought grinders here eight years before.

I ordered two cups of coffee and a slice of baklava from George, the owner, who offered to microwave the pastry and bring it over to his establishment's solitary, chrome-legged dining table. His line of takeout customers represented Wall Street's lower rungs: secretaries in sneakers, Gordon Gekko wannabees with slicked back hair and gaudy silk ties, floor traders in blue jackets, a bicycle messenger wearing pant-leg clips. The same big menu that Libby had so carefully studied—greasier now and with some selections covered by masking tape—was still on the wall.

Outside on the sidewalk, the financial district's lunchtime parade marched on in random interweaving patterns. A car horn blared twice and somebody shouted a curse. Tom walked through the open door and acknowledged me with a chin thrust. "Where's your helmet and flak jacket?" he asked.

I pushed the cardboard cup toward him as he sat down. "Black, like you like it."

"No thanks," he said. He adjusted his John Lennon glasses

and leaned back, his face twisted in a sneer. "Surprised we ran the story?"

"Flabbergasted. Why did you in the face of the *Transcript*'s pooh poohing the whole idea?"

"When all was said and done, I just didn't believe you."

"I guess I wouldn't either in your shoes."

"So whadd'ya got for me?"

"Well, first off, I can tell you that you were absolutely right, we did snooker the *Transcript*."

"Damn straight."

"I can tell you we did it before. I can tell you who did it then and now, and why. I can tell you that they've been fired. It was also probably authorized from the top of the food chain. Frankly, I wish you could leave that part alone, because you could put Matrix out of business."

"Tough shit."

"You can speculate all you want in your story, but this whole plot was dreamed up and orchestrated by two guys in Matrix's marketing department. The other thing is that no matter how worthless the book seems, there were no shortcuts in our research or interviews with business executives to come up with our findings. Our sin is like the L.A. cops who tried to frame an already-guilty O.J. Simpson. I mean, we didn't *have* to cheat. Our last book launched a business revolution."

"'Business revolution?' You're beginning to believe your own PR, aren't you?" Tom said. His glasses glistened. "Why the hell should I worry about the consequences of your trickery? You should have thought of that beforehand."

"I'm trying to defend the thousands of little people who knew nothing about this deception."

"Really? There had to be lots of 'little people' in the know, ordering books, covering up the reason, fully understanding the company was trying to get away with something underhanded. Why didn't any of them raise the alarm? Why? Because they're guilty as hell. Let's go further: why didn't *you* know about this? You're supposed to be the big honcho of corporate communications. You could have nipped this in the bud, but you looked the other way, didn't you?"

"I guess I was guilty of not wanting to know. Thinking back, there were plenty of signs."

"Speaking about guilt, this isn't your first whopper to me, is it? Apparently, I looked nonplussed.

"You don't remember do you? Well, Libby told me all about how you misled me but good when you were at NCC. Did you know she did that?"

"No. When did she do that and in what context?"

"Years ago, back when those PCs electrocuted a bunch of users. The RISC machines? Remember when you guys had me for dinner in New Canaan? Afterward, she said you cooked up this scheme to spring the news on me just on deadline and deny that people got hurt; that was pretty slimy. "

"I'm surprised she told you. She knew I was ashamed of that."

"You 'shocked' her too, Pete."

"As you no doubt remember, it was Jason Dinsmore who skated around the truth," I said. "But you're right. I could have called and set the record straight."

"Libby wasn't entirely straight with you, either. We kept in contact after you guys got married. I told her I was still in love with her; that you weren't good enough, just a spoiled rich boy. We met up the night before her interview with Deke Malloy. She was staying at the Carleton Hotel; we talked up in her room. She said your marriage wasn't so hot."

My breath grew shallow. "Hold on a minute!" People waiting to order turned their heads. "Are you claiming that Libby was unfaithful? Because if you are, you're a fucking liar!"

Tom released a harsh laugh. "Such language from the slick PR exec. No, I'm not impugning Libby's behavior, though I wish to hell I could. She was worried about you, thought you'd gone off the deep end with this junior-executive thing, and that you were trying to live some deranged lost dream out there in Newkie land. She wanted to know how she could save you from yourself. Your joining the golf club was the last straw." He turned to thrust his chin out at an eavesdropper. "Getting this all down, buddy? Want me to talk louder?"

Embarrassed, the man shook his head and faced forward.

Tom went on. "I told her one sure way to get your attention was to threaten a divorce. That nearly always gets couples talking. Or, if you were as stupid as I hoped you were, get her back in my arms. "

"You're right, I didn't deserve her," I said. "Maybe you *would* have been better for her."

"No… frigg'n… way, asshole. She said she loved you 'googolplex times the universe,' a direct quote. Wanted to bring you to your senses, 'cause you were so kind and sensitive and a lot of other happy horseshit."

He grabbed the coffee cup, sloshing some of its contents on the table top. "I think I *will* take some of this crap. Let's get back to Topic A. So make with the facts, who are the bad guys?"

I'd forgotten for a moment why I was there. "Sure, we can start with Dick Marin."

He pulled out his pocket notepad and flipped back though pages covered with writing to a fresh one. "Go," he commanded.

The little man and deGruening quickly got sold down the river. I said the latter had learned this technique from flacking in the book industry. Tom's story had the mechanics right, but I gave him some new details: thousands of excess books were stockpiled in a storage facility in Bayonne, New Jersey, not all sent to Matrix branches. To save money, the plotters tried to return as many as possible for credit once they were counted in the weekly *Transcript* tallies.

"Those are nice little tidbits; I'm going to have to quote you on this."

"Sure, why not? My Amsys days are numbered."

"By the way, the names of the bad guys confirmed what I heard from a separate source inside your firm."

"Who was that?"

"None of your business."

"You said 'firm.' That suggests someone at Matrix. Is his name Lieberman?"

"I don't reveal my sources."

"Surely not Henshaw!"

"Nice try. Anything else you want to tell me?"

"When the *Transcript* called to grill me this morning, they admitted their list was compromised. I have to assume that will be in their story tomorrow."

"Thanks. I really miss working with you," Tom said. "We found out the same thing an hour ago. By the way, Deke was plenty worried about going with the story when their Book Section said it couldn't happen. He gave me that 'I'm-putting-my-balls-in-the-wringer-for-your-sake' speech."

"I remember that speech. But what I don't understand is why this never came to light until now. Apparently bulk buying is an open industry secret."

"Because that would have messed up a good thing for publishers. The list is supposed to be confidential, but everybody involved starts with the knowledge that there's just a single reporting bookstore in every city. It wasn't hard to figure out which, because that bookstore has a huge financial incentive to whisper its status to every publisher and book agent in the U.S."

"Why?"

"It took us a while to figure that out. It's because they want to hold public book signings, and they need the publisher's permission."

"I don't follow."

"Each appearance is a colossal moneymaker," Tom explained. "A big-name author can sell hundreds of books at full retail price in just an hour; it's a huge windfall for the store. So, they quietly let the agents and publishers know the score, the signing events get scheduled, and everybody rubs their hands in anticipation. Henshaw's second book was supposed to be another big payday."

"So the publishers are the true culprits?"

"They'll deny it, but every big book publisher in America has cobbled together a list of reporting bookstores for its use. And they let it be known to certain parties. Supposedly, presidential candidates do this all the time with their ghosted memoirs."

"So wait a minute, isn't *that* the real story, an industrywide scam combined with a national political scandal? That's really juicy. Why are you picking on poor little Matrix?"

"Because you guys were so blatant that one store owner called us to complain. He wasn't getting his fair share of the illicit benefits. He said he'd shop the story around to other business pubs if we didn't bite, so we had to go with it."

"Why didn't he call the *Transcript*?"

"They laughed in his face. I think he was honestly upset by the manipulation. Cheer up, Pete. My article is what Libby wanted for your sake—it's going to force you into honest work."

"I always wanted to be honest for her."

"I know that and after talking to you, I'm convinced you weren't in on this."

"Thanks for the belated vote of confidence."

"Any time."

"I've got one final plea, Can I be 'Pete Wendell' in your next piece instead of 'H. Peter?'

Tom's eyebrows went up. "What for?"

"I want all my friends to know me as part of my atonement."

"No problem. Speaking about bylines, it should come as no surprise that Deke cancelled Henshaw's management column."

"I figured. But I'm curious about something else. How did your meeting with NCC's 'Lurch' Devlin go the other day? Did you get your exclusive?"

"How'd you know about *that*?"

"None of *your* business."

We grinned at each other.

George arrived. He put the heated baklava, floating in syrup, in front of me. "Where's the pretty woman you used to come in here with?" A disgusting leer covered his face. "You no mind I say I liked watching her walk out the door? Ha, ha. She home raising lots of babies?" With an anticipatory grin, he held out a white plastic fork wrapped in cellophane.

Tom put his head down and pinched his pug nose. Misery

must have shown on my own face as well. George looked confused, then embarrassed, as he stood there offering the fork. Wordlessly, Tom rose and walked out. I followed.

"I wasn't expecting he'd remember her," I said, as I shook Tom's hand out on the street.

"She was a beautiful person," Tom replied, holding onto my hand for an extra moment, "not someone easy to forget. I'm sorry for your loss."

"Our loss."

We turned away from each other and headed in opposite directions.

CHAPTER THIRTY-TWO
Dry Drunk

The world moved on and I was left behind. I'd kept the momentous secret about business relations between Matrix and the *New York Transcript*, but it didn't much matter. I learned that after the paper's courtly publisher Adrian Adlinger fired him, he gave Henshaw about thirty seconds before showing him the door. Larry Lieberman informed of that, adding that he'd landed a new job with a law firm that represented the indigent.

I was unemployed the next day, sacked by Jim Phillips and cut dead by Trevor Henshaw, who refused to even acknowledge me after Tom wrote that Henshaw had paid hush money to Marin and deGruening. I got no severance package from Amsys. Nobody called, nobody threw me a rope. I felt like I was bobbing in a cold midnight ocean, watching my ship recede into the night, a shrinking cluster of twinkling lights. Not surprisingly, I never heard from Kitsie Schoemacher, who stood me up for our long-postponed date for drinks the day I got the boot. That was fortunate. I might have fallen off the wagon.

After several weeks, what I noticed most was my body odor. I let my beard grow, jogged compulsively—deathly afraid of another bender that might not stop—and slept late in the same rank-smelling running shorts. Result: When I came in after a run, the tiny house had the sour jockstrappy smell of a football locker room. I was a man without a job or the self-definition that work provided. Nights were the worst. The TV was broken and I couldn't concentrate on books, even the English mysteries Libby enjoyed. The plots didn't grab, I couldn't remember character names, got angry with poor word choices and silly descriptions. In one, the handle of a suitcase carrying body parts had "creaked forlornly" when the murderer picked it up. A particularly pathetic fallacy. After rereading a page several times and getting nothing out of it, I'd drift out on the porch. The river made its musical murmur and the night sky, smeared with stars and the occasional silent jet blinking rhythmically miles up, pulled me toward a contemplation of creation's vast mystery. She'd loved me, she said, as big as this universe, times googolplex. Shivers from the early fall air, or pain from a cricked neck, would return me to earth. She was out there, untouchable, unreachable—maybe still sentient in a spiritual way, and hopefully at peace.

Somehow, I hung on by will power alone, staying away from even alcohol-free beer, certain that this was how I could redeem myself. I learned later that recovering alcoholics call this brutal state of self-denial being "dry drunk." But no matter how bad things get, I discovered that they could always get worse. Unable to pay the mortgage, I received a final notice for a foreclosure in one month. My realtor hung a "price reduced" placard beneath the for sale sign and I buckled down to work on further repairs to make the house more attractive.

I was replacing rotten studs on either side of a new porch door when Rit stopped by in his wife Gail's gleaming red Mercedes.

"Slumming?" I asked, when he barged right in without knocking. "Or on a raid?"

"Looking for a guy who's hiding out, who avoids people. What's the word for that kind of dude?"

"Misanthrope? Hermit? Fugitive?"

"'Pete' is a better one." The large cardboard box containing a new French door caught his attention. "You planning to hang that monster by yourself? Looks like Hampton the hermit could use some company."

Rit and I worked together to position it for more than an hour, getting it in plumb with a carpenter's level and using the package of shims I'd bought years before to steady the camelback couch.

"There you go," he said as he countersank the last finish nail, and handed back my claw hammer and nail punch. "That's done right." He gave it a test, opening and shutting it several times. "See? Swings like a California wife swapper."

"Or like your home run stroke in high school."

"Those were the days, weren't they? But let's talk about the here and now. Real reason I came over is 'cause we're having a family barbecue tonight; Gail wants you to come."

"Oh, I don't want to impose…"

"Don't be a *stunod*. Show up at six." Rit sniffed the air and then made a show of holding his nose. "And take a shower, will you?"

CHAPTER THIRTY-THREE

Frog Man

Gail Carrington DeMarco, Rit's patrician blond wife, was dressed in an expensive lime and pink summer frock. Standing at the door of her ivy-covered place, she greeted me with a loud smacking kiss near my ear. "You never change, do you?" she said.

"If you mean my maturity level, no I don't."

Painted white, her elegant brick dwelling was tucked at the bottom of a hill on a short country cul de sac. Below, beyond a rock wall, was a hayfield. I'd never been there before, never found time to socialize with the DeMarcos when Libby was alive. Gail brought me though a large, low-ceilinged living room strewn with toys and overstuffed furniture. Rit was seated on the stone terrace behind the house.

"Yeah, it is a pretty nice spread," Rit agreed after I took a chair. He let his eyes wander over the well-groomed property. "Nothing like marrying bucks." Belching, he put his glass of club soda back on the cast-iron table between us. "I know," he said. "You're wondering why I don't just clip coupons and play golf? Because a man's got to do something meaningful; preferably something he loves and is good at."

"I wouldn't know."

"Speaking about meaningful, you going back to PR?"

"Like I told you, I was fired. I can't imagine anyone hiring me."

"Good for you. You weren't cut out for that life."

"So what am I cut out for?"

"I don't know, just not that."

We watched Rit's two children scamper around on a lawn that sloped on and on. The smell of mown hay came up from the lower field. Mark and Lisa DeMarco were carrying glass jars. A perfect division of their parents' genetics, Mark was dark and brown eyed; Lisa was fair and trailed maize-hued tresses as she chased after her taunting brother. A pair of columnar tulip poplar trees towered above them, framing the pastoral view, their big yellow-orange flowers catching the evening light like electric ornaments.

"Maybe I can be your gardener," I said. "Bucolic, safe, and there's a whole career out there on that lawn."

"Already got one."

"Or your tree surgeon."

"Same guy.

"You know I'm broke, right? Living on an almost maxed-out credit card."

"I *do* know that, you just told me."

"Not funny, Rit. I'm going inside to get an iced tea or something."

"Stay put, drinks are on the way." He looked over my shoulder and waved. "Hey there, cousin!"

I turned to see Vicky, shadowy behind the porch screening, balancing a tray of glasses and soda bottles. She pushed down the handle with an elbow and opened the door with her toe. Behind her came Gail DeMarco, holding a platter heaped with hamburger patties, buns, and potato salad. "Look who stopped by, Pete!" Gail trilled. The door slapped shut behind her like a pistol shot.

"This is no good, Chooch," I said under my breath. "I've let it be known I don't want to see her anymore."

"'Let it be known?' That sounds—what was your fancy PR word?—'oleaginous?'"

"Okay, okay, I told her I was a complete failure, not good for her, and wanted to be left alone."

"She came over to be with my kids; they adore her. You just happen to be here tonight. Maybe she'll snub you."

"Auntie Vicky! Auntie Vicky!" screamed the children. Charging across the lawn in no time flat, they jumped up and down in front of her, demanding attention.

"Come with us!"

"Yes, hurry!"

"We're going to catch frogs!"

"Mommy, give her a jar."

"Now!"

"Hold on," said Vicky. I stood to greet her. She put down the tray with a tentative smile. "Auntie Vicky has to say hello to an old high school friend."

"Do that *later*," shrieked Lisa, who was seven. "It's getting dark out."

"Please, please!" Mark, two years older, shouted.

"Stop that incessant yammering," barked Gail, "*right now*." The children fell silent.

In the sudden hush Vicky said, "So, hello there, classmate."

We stood regarding each other across the metal mesh tabletop. She was wearing white shorts and a coral tank top. She seemed a bit stouter at the waist, perhaps. As ever, her luxuriant hair bulged out over her forehead like a breaking wave: Paint Brush Face.

"Go Rams," I said.

Vicky laced her fingers backwards as if embarrassed and said nothing. The silence lengthened.

Little Lisa shook her jar in the air. "Earth to Aunt Victoria!"

Vicky broke off eye contact with an effort. She bent down and addressed her second cousins. "How about you guys start and I'll catch up?"

"But it's no fun without you!"

Vicky looked at me helplessly.

"Want some company?" I said. "Where're we going, anyway?"

"There's a little pond in the stream down past the big tulip tree on the left," answered Rit, as he knotted an apron around his waist. Across his chest it read: *Ain't I Barba-Cute?* "You can get to it through the opening in the wall. Why don't you guys go explore while I warm up the grill?" He traded meaningful looks with his wife. "Take all the time you like."

"I want to go with Pete!" Mark erupted. His small palm slid into mine.

Lisa grabbed the tips of Vicky's fingers, as if we were choosing teams. "Hurry, hurry!" she pleaded. "We have to be the *first* to catch a froggy!"

"Yeah, come on!" Mark yanked at my hand with surprising strength.

"Know why frogs say needeep, needeep?" I asked the children. "They're telling each other the water's depth."

Lisa snorted. "I heard that joke in first grade."

We started walking in a line four abreast, but the capering children quickly pulled us into a yearning bow. I let go of Mark and he and Lisa surged forward.

"You limping, Pete?" Vicky asked, as we continued after them. "You're kind of dragging your left foot."

"Just slowing down due to my advancing old age."

Beyond the wall lay a miniature pond choked with lily pads abloom with white blossoms resembling floating tea cups. A stand of eight-foot high phragmites grass bent forward over the still water on one side. The only direct access was via an apron of lawn that I soon discovered was wet and spongy underfoot. I could see two big bullfrogs on pads on the far side, but the only way I could imagine capturing one was to hit it with the glass jar I was holding and then swim out to get it. As I contemplated my mission, one of the glistening amphibians slipped into the water with a plop. Eyes awash, he floated there in the middle of expanding rings.

"Is there some technique to catching these critters?" I asked Vicky. "Shouldn't we have nets on poles?"

"That's not the real game," she answered. "Usually, we just count the frogs we see and then give them names. There are any number of Aunt Vickys out there."

"We skate here in the winter," Mark informed me, spinning the top of his empty peanut butter jar back and forth with an impatient grinding.

"Daddy makes a fire on the shore and we toast marshmallows," Lisa joined in. "Aunt Vicky can skate on one leg, can you do that?"

"No, I can't do much of anything on one leg these days. But maybe I can tell you a story about those two froggies out there. See them? What shall we name them?"

"Aunt Vicky and Pete," announced Lisa.

"No, Skeltor and Aquaman," countered Mark.

"Let's go with Nikki and Zeke," I said.

"Are they in love?" Lisa wanted to know.

"They used to swim in the same circles but never met. But then one day Zeke saves Nikki from a big bad water moccasin that tries to sneak up on her."

"What's the snake's name? Skeltor?" asked Mark.

"No," said Vicky, "it's Big Mouth. He's always telling people what to do. He's a butinsky."

Mark tried to interpret his cousin's assertion. "Do snakes talk?"

"This one does," said Vicky, "a whole lot, and he's actually a she."

"So anyway," I said, "Nikki is sunning herself in a string bikini on a big water lily, when from below in the water Big Mouth sees her shadow. He starts to rise stealthily."

"What's 'stealthily' mean?" asked Lisa.

"It means she's sneaking up on Nikki, who's wearing a modest two-piece," said Vicky.

"What happens?" Mark demanded.

"Zeke jumps in the water and swims toward Nikki," I said.

"He does the butterfly, because he was a state swim champ," Vicky said.

"County champ," I said.

"This is confusing," Lisa said.

"It gets exciting when Zeke swims right over Big Mouth's big mouth and dangles a tasty webbed foot down at him," I said.

From Mark: "Does Big Mouth bite it off?"

"No, but he chases Zeke around the pond, who swims in circles faster and faster until Big Mouth gets dizzy. And then Zeke pushes him, or I guess I mean her, over the dam."

"We don't have a dam," Mark pointed out.

"And that's how Nikki gets saved."

"Then, Nikki thanks Zeke profusely and lets him go back to his own lily pad," said Vicky, "where he lives happily ever after in splendid isolation. The End."

"What's profusely mean? Lisa asked.

Mark shook his head in dissatisfaction. "You're dumb Lisa, and so was that story," he said. "Everybody knows that profusely means like a pro. Anyway, I was hoping you'd catch a real frog, Pete. Aren't you even going to try?" It was a question that led me, over Vicky's protests, into the tangle of stiff stalks. After about twenty minutes of motionless waiting in the increasing gloom, I saw one big fellow hop out from under debris. Scrambling to block him, I snared the frog at the expense of a wet loafer.

The children had drifted back to the house by then, but Vicky had waited. Holding up my trophy I said, "Maybe you should kiss this guy if you want a real prince. Listen, I owe you an apology. I would have done it sooner, but I was feeling sorry for myself after getting fired. Did Rit tell you that?"

"Yes, but that's okay, we've both been through a rough time lately. I'm now on my parents' ultra-bad poopy list."

"What happened?"

"Family spat. They'll get over it."

"Well, let me know if I can help. And can we remain friends, maybe talk some time when either of us needs an ear to listen?"

"Of course."

Transferring a layer of frog slime to her palm, I shook her hand very formally. Standing out there on the dark lawn, I wanted to say something more, like maybe we could still work things out. But that scenario felt as cruelly conditional as my father's approval—only if she proved worthy to me.

Before dinner, the children named my catch "Pete." I held him in two hands as they cautiously petted the back of his head. His bulbous eyes closed with each stroke.

"Let's eat," said Rit. "How about some frog legs?"

"Noooo!" wailed Lisa.

Vicky and Gail had removed the meal's aftermath from the now-darkened terrace. I could see them rinsing the plates through the glowing kitchen window. Vicky seemed preoccupied, though she made a labored joke during the meal: "To paraphrase Yogi Berra," she said, "Since Pete can catch frogs with either hand, he's 'naturally amphibious.'"

"What's that mean?" asked Mark.

Now, Rit lit a cigar and waved out the match. "Gail won't let me smoke these things inside," he explained.

"That's because they smell bad." I batted away the drifting smoke.

Rit blew the rest over his shoulder. "Okay, so what'd you and Vicky talk about?"

"We agreed to be friends. The rest was just interaction with your kids. Makes me feel heartless, but I don't want to be recruited as some kind of pre-husband in training. The thing is, I miss her. Like you once said, she's got a good heart. She's also smart, funny, one-hundred percent honest, and even wise. What's not to like?"

"You tell me?"

"The real problem is all I *really* want to do with her is put my face between her breasts."

"Sex rears its ugly head."

"There's nothing ugly about it, but she's got this Catholic prohibition against just 'doing it.' And why is she so eager to get married, anyway?"

"Besides your irresistible charms, she has another reason."

"She wants children?"

"You got that right." Rit tossed his cigar in a sparkling parabola out onto the dark lawn. "But there's a little more to it."

"Like what?"

"Use your imagination."

"I have no idea. Look, I like happy endings as much as anybody. Falling in love, courtship, taking her out to dinner and the movies, roses in the moonlight, asking Enzo for her hand in marriage; it would be sweet and right, a romance novel. It'd probably work out if I were a better man. But I can't feel anything right now, have nothing to give. Libby's still in all my thoughts and I'm also crawling with nerves from not drinking. All I can do to keep from going nuts is to run my ass off."

"You're white-knuckling it."

"Meaning?"

"As in you are hanging on by your fingernails. You're not sober—ergo happy, joyous, and free—you're just not drinking."

"Well, I guess I'll muddle through."

"Actually, you've been given a great gift."

"Oh yeah?"

"The gift of desperation.'"

"Is this AA-speak?"

"We also refer to troubles that force us to act as AFOGs"

"Decoded?"

"Another fucking opportunity for growth."

Rit pushed the stem on his watch to make it glow. "We still

got time to get to a meeting tonight. There's one at the Episcopal Church, your old stomping grounds.

A light came on in the porch. "Good night, Pete!" Vicky called from inside. "I don't want to go out there and get Rit's stogie stench on my clothes. The kids thank you again for catching Froggy Pete. We just put them to bed. Your namesake is in a Tupperware box on Lisa's dresser. We punched holes in the top with a screw driver. Tomorrow it goes to Mark's room."

"Hope he doesn't croak," Rit said under his breath.

"Sorry about your shoe," she added. "Wad some newspaper inside it when you get home, it'll be fine."

"Will do."

"Night, Rit!"

"Night, Cuz!"

Vicky withdrew into the house. I saw her hug Gail and then slowly shake her head in response to a final question.

"You ready to live a new life?" Rit asked.

I didn't answer.

"Hey paison, don't give me that pained face. You might just learn how to live comfortably in your own skin, claim your real destiny. Look at me: From Ritaldo the Thug to police chief soon. Yeah, that's right. That's what the chairman of the Police Commission tells me. Another Carm Triola who, by the way, arrested me once for breach of the peace. Talk about a one-hundred-eighty degree personality change. So it's up to you, my brooding Hamlet: 'To be or not to be sober,' that is the question."

"I guess I don't have much to lose, do I?"

"Not a frigg'n thing."

CHAPTER THIRTY-FOUR

Hello, Hampton!

Rit steered his big Ford pickup truck in silence as I imagined what my former professional peers would think if they knew I was going to a meeting of Alcoholics Anonymous: suspicions confirmed. We turned into the church's wide circular driveway.

"How long do these things last?" I asked, seeing the filled parking lot.

"Tell you an alky joke," Rit said, his eyes on the windshield. "Old Shamus finally succumbed to the drink, and at his wake people were trying to console his widow."

"I don't find funeral jokes funny," I said.

"This one is. So anyway, Mary McGurk comes up and asks Shamus's widow if he'd ever tried AA. And the old woman replies, 'Oh, no, he was never *that* bad.'... Ba dum, bum."

"I don't get it."

"You will."

The basement of the church was unchanged from my choir-boy days. Fitted into the dark brown linoleum floor were lighter tiles forming shuffleboard triangles pointing at each other from across the room. Several four-by-eight-foot framed cork boards on castors were pushed up against the wall, their ragged surfaces looking like they'd been used as BB gun targets. Slender Doric columns held up a Homasote ceiling of patterned perforations, where a dozen fluorescent fixtures resembling aluminum ice trays provided buzzing illumination.

A cheerful elderly man sat behind a wide table with collapsible legs at the front of a group of perhaps forty seated people, who were talking and laughing. Beside him was a sandwich board listing the Twelve Steps in bold script, with smaller explanatory verbiage under each. Its blurriness made me I realize I was beginning to need glasses. A whole anthology of individually framed platitudes was on view: *One Day at a Time; Easy Does It; Let Go and Let God; Think, Think, Think.*

"That last saying's not for you," said Rit, following my gaze.

The chairman was named Bob. He banged a gavel and read from a card: "Welcome to this meeting of the Hair of the Dog group. Also, every day in this room, we hold the Loony Noony meeting. This is a one-hour speaker discussion meeting. Members of AA, and anyone wanting to stop drinking, are welcome."

The gathering didn't jibe with the bleak portrayal of Jack Lemmon's filmic AA meeting in *Days of Wine and Roses*, where everyone appeared baggy-faced and ruined.

The leader asked someone to read a preamble, whose gist was that their fellowship was not allied with any other groups, was self-sufficient, and sought only to help keep other alcoholics from drinking.

"Are there any anniversaries?"

A matron arose, dressed as my mother once did in a scarlet, boiled-wool coat with pewter buttons. Diamond-and-sapphire tennis bracelets jangling, she said, "Hi, I'm Pamela and I'm an alcoholic."

"Hi, Pamela!" everyone said but me.

"Thanks to God and this fellowship, I have five years, as of last Saturday."

She received enthusiastic applause, along with a coin and a hug from the animated chairman. I shifted uncomfortably in my metal chair. The atmosphere felt contrived, cultish, dependent on magical thinking. There were no other anniversaries. Bob read down a list. "Any out-of-town visitors? No? Anybody here for the first time?"

Rit elbowed my side. "Stand up," he hissed.

I did and somebody yelled, "What's your name?"

"Tell them your name," prompted Rit.

"My name is Hampton," I said, "and my buddy here thinks I'm a dipsomaniac."

"Hi, Hampton!"

"Yup, we've been saving a seat especially for you," somebody said.

"Keep coming, pal," said another. "You need it."

"Is this your first meeting, Hampton?" asked Bob,

"Yes, but I'm just auditing this course."

"Come on up here and get a man-hug," said the cheery chairman. He handed me an aluminum chip for 24 hours. His bear-like embrace came with a rasping encounter with his stubbly cheek. Releasing me, he said, "Nobody can tell you if you're an alcoholic. You have to be completely and thoroughly honest with yourself. If you don't think you belong here, you can go out and experiment some more."

I laughed but nobody joined me.

Bob moved on to the main event, the speaker. Rit was introduced and smirked at me as he strode forward to sit down at the chairman's table.

Rit's began his sharing by talking about his life as a boy, a period when I'd known him, yet hadn't really. Its main theme was resentment toward his father. Dom DeMarco had been the head groundskeeper at the same country club where I'd taken ballroom dancing lessons, swam on the club team, and snapped at girls' bottoms with a rolled towel.

Dom had been a Jekyll and Hyde figure, a man proud of his son, who tossed balls with Rit, but who became violent when he'd had too much to drink. Rit never knew which man would arrive home at night, the caring, easygoing man, or the wife beater. Terrified and filled with guilt, Rit had been unable to defend his mother. Then one day Dom deserted the family. Rit vowed he'd never become an alcoholic, never touch the stuff; indeed, never be anything like his worthless dad. But you can't make a positive by focusing on a negative. It was, Rit said, like the old story about the baseball coach who called time out to talk to his pitcher on the mound in the bottom of the ninth at a tied championship game. *Whatever* you do, the coach said, do *not* throw it low and outside, which was, of course, what he did, resulting in a home run.

Rit offered a grim smile. "Then again, nobody poured alcohol down my throat. I had what the Big Book calls an 'allergy' to alcohol, a physical craving to keep on drinking once I started. Thanks to my genes, I was spring-loaded to become an alcoholic. It wasn't my fault, or yours, or my dad's. It runs in families, though I sometimes wonder if this would have happened if I grew up in a happy one."

He discovered in high school that not only couldn't he stop, he didn't want to—which, he said, is the obsessional component of the disease. He was having too much of a good time, or at least he was at the beginning. "First it was fun, then it was fun mixed with trouble, then it was just trouble," Rit said.

"All this manifested itself in barroom brawls, crashed cars, and my uncles on the police force letting me off easy. But they weren't doing me any favors. Then, after I got tossed out of Syracuse and came back home, I tried to stop for my new wife's sake, but I couldn't. By that time, Gail said she'd had enough. She wound up leaving me. And there I was working as a part-time tree surgeon, living in a motel room full of empties, and too ashamed to cash them at the liquor store. I mean, somebody might get the idea I had a drinking problem, right?"

Rit paused for a moment. "So that's enough of my 'drunk-alogue.' Let me turn to a happier tale—my life after alcohol. I always like to hear speakers talk about how they're now living lives beyond their wildest dreams. It encourages newcomers like Hampton there to know that this mysterious thing called spirituality allows us to regain our sanity.

"So how does spirituality give us a reprieve from physical addiction? The answer is I have no idea. All I know is that I'm not the same person I was fifteen years ago. There's been a complete but slow character transformation—one day at a time. Other people noticed it before I did. As I changed, I went back and got my degree in criminal justice at New Haven College, joined the town's police force, and began working with other alcoholics. Am I cured? No. It's a chronic disease. I'm still powerless over 'people, places and things,' as it says in the Big Book. But I don't drink over my troubles, and I now have a purpose in life.

"It all started when this old-timer started twelve-stepping me, a friend of my father's, Ed Kerrigan, who ran the Shell station here in town in the old days. You remember him, Pete. You used to work for him."

I acknowledged that I had as everyone eyed me with curiosity.

"Ed's dead now, but he saved my life. How he got me to my first meeting is kind of a funny story, because he'd been pestering me to come for months. And I remember finally showing up one night, and he motioned me to an empty seat next to him. 'What took you so long?' he asked. And I was confused. I told him it had only taken a couple of minutes to walk over. But Ed meant why had I been in denial so long? I used to call him 'Special Ed' because he finally helped me to make peace with my father.

"In the end I prayed for the old guy and forgave him, for my own sake. Dad was still in the area, alone, broke, very overweight, and bedridden at the VA hospital with congestive heart failure. When his condition turned terminal, my wife and I brought him home for Hospice care. I went through my Ninth Step with him, apologizing for hating him when I was a boy. He never confessed regret about hurting my mom. He didn't say he was sorry. That would have been nice. But I was okay with that, because my side of the street was nice and clean. He died in my arms."

Rit peered out at us. "I know what you're thinking. You see a normal, reasonably contented guy with years of sobriety in the rooms and think, 'Is this really the same person he's describing?' And then you do the comparison thing: I never got arrested, lost a job, crashed cars, or whatever. Ergo, I don't belong here. But remember, the model is not preaching, it's testifying about a common human identity, and not denying who you really are. The difference is between denial and acceptance. It's your choice.

"So if there's anyone in this room who wants a new way of life, give us a try. As the old-timers say, if it doesn't work, we'll cheerfully refund your misery. "

There was a long round of applause.

Afterwards, Rit drove me back to his house, where we sat in his driveway, the diesel engine of his hulking truck ticking and clinking as it cooled. "So, what did you think?" he asked.

"Did you know you'd be speaking?"

"Yeah, I called Bob, the chairman, to set it up. Want to try some step work?"

"With you?"

"I can be your temporary sponsor and get you started."

"I'm not sure. I don't know about this God thing."

"You don't like the capital-G God? Create one of your own understanding; make it stand for 'Group of Drunks,' if you like. Just have faith that if the program works for us, it'll work for you."

"I still need convincing."

"Know what it says on the medallion you got tonight?"

I pulled it out of my pocket to see and he pointed a fat finger at the saying on its face: *To thine own self be true.*

"Ralph Waldo Emerson," I said.

"It's Shakespeare. Polonius in *Hamlet.*"

"How do you know that?"

"Vicky told me."

"That figures. Thanks to her dad, she's very well-read."

"Thanks to you, she's also very pregnant," Rit said.

My head whirled. "What did you just say?"

Rit remained in profile. "She doesn't want you to find out. She and Gail have been talking with adoption agencies." He turned toward me. "I figured you had a right to know."

CHAPTER THIRTY-FIVE

I Am Sentenced

October 24, 1995
2 Tamarack Tree Road
New Canaan, CT 06840

Judge Leonard W. Sweeney
Connecticut Superior Court
123 Hoyt Street
Stamford, CT 06905

Dear Judge Sweeney:

I am writing you as a character witness for Hampton P. Wendell, who will be appearing in your court as a defendant at a trial set for Oct. 31. The charge is criminal trespass and operating a vehicle under the influence. The latter would be his second offense. I am doing this as a private citizen and his first sponsor in Alcoholics Anonymous.

As you may know, Mr. Wendell has not contested responsibility for these crimes, as part of a plea for lenience being offered by his lawyer to Prosecutor Henry Dandridge. However, as you may not yet know, Mr. Wendell was not arrested at the scene, or in response to a warrant. He was not picked up by the police at all. Rather, because he simply thought it was the right thing to do, he voluntarily went to make restitution to Mr. Loring Davies, who was a former Police Commissioner here in New Canaan, and who decided to press charges. Also, in a small irony, decades ago he was Mr. Wendell's scout master. Mr. Davies had no idea who entered his home at the time and apparently, because of increasing dementia, has only a limited recollection of the incident, itself. In other words, Mr. Wendell placed himself in jeopardy of a prison sentence because of his own moral values.

Judge Sweeney, you know me as a Police Lieutenant in the Town of New Canaan, and through our interactions, I have come to respect you as a person who balances the letter with spirit of the law, as someone who fits the punishment to the crime. I have known "Pete" Wendell from the time we were boys together, and I take him to be an exceptionally honest person. I don't understand why he did what he is charged with, but I do understand the larger context. Just like me, he is a sick and suffering alcoholic. Add to that the emotional agony of the tragic death of his wife, and I think you might more fully understand his situation. He is not a bad man. The only difference between him and me is that I am in recovery from this chronic disease, which also killed his mother. Certainly, his sad condition is not a valid excuse for total leniency, but it offers mitigating factors to put him in a wholly seperate category of being a perpetrator without true criminal volition.

I pledge to you that regardless of the outcome of the sentencing phase of his trial, I will take him through the 12 Steps of Alcoholics Anonymous. He has agreed to do this and looks forward to a new life of spirituality and, perhaps, regaining his former life as an award-winning journalist.

Sincerely,
Ritaldo N. DeMarco

"How's that, Pete? Not bad for the English class dumbbell, huh?"

Rit had authored the note he'd just handed me because—addled though Loring Davies was—he didn't forget to file a criminal complaint against me. After all, I'd helpfully written Rit's name and number on a pad as an aid memoire. In the legal cascade that followed, Rit had served me with a warrant, driven me to Stamford to sign a statement that I'd appear in court as summoned, and gotten me a lawyer named Salvatore Tarzia, another one of his cousins, who had started negotiating a plea deal for a reduced sentence on my behalf. Rit amounted to a one-stop-shopping guide through the Connecticut judicial system

"Well, you misspelled separate," I said. "Remember, 'there's a rat in separate."

"I meant the content, lamebrain. Screw the spelling. How's it read?"

"I don't know. I sound like Little Boy Blue, kind of a pitiable, a hopeless victim of forces beyond my control. And I can't swear

Mom died of alcoholism; I think it was really clinical depression. Is the judge going to laugh out loud at this?"

"But you are hopeless, pal," replied Rit, and slapped me on the back. "Accept it, you're a hopeless alcoholic, powerless over booze. You need lots of help, not time in stir. The judge has seen plenty of guys just like you, they keep him in business; he knows the score from drunks. I'm just trying to convince him not to let that hard-ass Dandridge put you away forever when my cousin Sal offers to nolo contender the case.

"Nolo contender, as in no contest?"

"Yes. You agree to accept the ruling of the court without admitting guilt."

"Isn't that giving up without a fight?"

"What do you have to fight with? You've got bupkis. We're throwing ourselves on the mercy of the court. You contest this like Perry Mason and you'll just piss Sweeney off."

"I hope what you say makes sense."

"Me too," said Rit.

"By the way, I didn't know your middle initial was 'N', what's it stand for?"

"Nunzio."

"Huh, sounds like somebody high up in the Vatican."

"I think it translates as Hampton."

"All rise!" shouted the uniformed clerk. "Department A-Two of the Superior Court of the Stamford/Norwalk jurisdiction is now in session, the honorable Leonard W. Sweeney, judge presiding. All those having business before the court may approach the bench."

It was the day of my trial. Though I was breathless with apprehension, it all felt so small bore and humdrum. Loring Davies was sitting with a smattering of spectators who looked as if they had nothing better to do than watch the entertainment from the hard seats. The court's minimalist décor included American and state flags, along with 1970s dark walnut trim that matched the finish on the judge's high perch.

State Prosecutor Dandridge and my lawyer, Sal Tarzia, moved forward to stand with hunched shoulders, talking in low voices to His Honor. I could overhear everything they were saying:

Judge Sweeney: "Okay, gentlemen, let's get this over with before lunch, if we can. You gents still haggling over the terms of the sentence agreement?"

Prosecutor Dandridge: "Yes, Your Honor, this is egregiously serious. Just on the basis of his second DUI, alone, under the state's uniform code..."

Attorney Tarzia: "Hold it a second, Hank. Lenny, do you think this unfortunate young man will be improved by two years in jail?"

Judge Sweeney: "What's so 'unfortunate' about him? I was looking at his sheet again in chambers. New Canaan toff, Dartmouth grad, ex-NCC; he's been anything but unfortunate. He looks like a dissipated party boy."

Prosecutor Dandridge: "I agree. The real issue is that he broke into the home of that poor 75-year-old man back there—the genuine unfortunate in this case—and scared him half to death. Good grief, the old boy could have died of a coronary. Then we'd have had no disagreement at all about a nice long sentence."

Attorney Tarzia: "Aren't you forgetting that my client turned himself in? He could have avoided this whole hassle entirely if he'd just kept his lip zipped. More to the legal point, Mr. Davies was in no way hurt."

Judge Sweeney: "Okay, okay, I've read both your briefs thoroughly; we've batted this around in legal theory long enough. I want to ask some questions of the principals involved. Can we please move on to that?"

Prosecutor Dandridge: "Yes, Your Honor."

Attorney Tarzia: "Of course, Your Honor."

Mr. Davies was sworn and went first. His responses were vague and tentative: "I heard somebody laughing downstairs in the front hall. Seemed pretty odd. I lay there for a while thinking I was dreaming, but had to get up and go to the bathroom, anyway." He paused as if thinking hard, then explained, "My prostate kills me." He wore an ancient tweed coat with large lapels and leather patches at the elbows. His open shirt collar gaped away from his scrawny neck.

"And then?" prompted Judge Sweeney. "Tell me in your own words."

"Then? Why, I went downstairs because it sounded like someone was walking around." There was another long gap in his narration.

"And who, or what, did you see?"

"Saw this shadowy guy standing there. But he ran away and knocked over an old oil lamp. Tore off in his car like hell. Kind of looked like somebody I knew."

"Who?"

"I don't recollect, exactly. Later, the young man there," he pointed at me, "came to my house and confessed he was the one. Told me he was a drunkard, which made me mad. My wife was killed by a drunk driver. I told him I wanted him to face his consequences, get some help as a result, maybe. Turns out he was one of my scouts. He took it well, offered to pay for the lamp. So that's why we're here."

"It says in the police report that you stated that your front door was not latched," stated the judge, "is that true?"

"Never lock it, 'cause I'm always losing my keys,' replied the old gentleman.

"Anything else you'd like to add?"

"Sorry this had to happen to him. But sometimes you've got to face the music. Like we used to say in the Navy, the Wailing Wall is right around the corner."

"Thank you, Mr. Davies."

Since this was an administrative hearing, there were no questions from the lawyers. I was next.

"Was Mr. Davies' testimony substantially correct, Mr. Wendall?"

"Yes sir, entirely," I responded.

"What were you doing there that night?"

"I don't really know. As I told the detective who interviewed me, I'd stopped to examine Mr. Davies' nineteenth century entryway. I live in an old house and have an interest in antique home architecture and adornments."

"Yes, I read that. But why did you go inside without knocking?"

My breath grew short. Here was the matter of criminal intent, the crux of my guilt or not. Was the safe in the bookcase the reason? Yes or no? I really didn't remember. Rit had told me to leave that out. Reason being, that in my fogged state of mind I wasn't thinking rationally, and why speculate on something I didn't do?

"Mr. Wendell? We're waiting."

"I think I was recalling or reliving a moment when I'd attended a party there decades before, held by Mr. Davies' daughter." I said. "I remember we had a conversation in the den about a picture of her father in a silver frame. In it, he was standing next to a warplane, a dive bomber named 'The Flying Hydraulic Leak.'"

"What a memory," marveled Loring Davies, audibly from his seat.

"So, is that your defense for trespassing, an unauthorized stroll into the past?"

"I have none, sir."

"And you admit that you drove there in a drunken state, even though you were on probation from a DUI conviction two years before?"

"Yes."

"You do know a second DUI is a felony in this state? With a maximum sentence of two years and a minimum fine of one-thousand dollars."

"Yes. I'm not proud of my behavior, judge."

"Wouldn't it also seem criminally worse that despite the fact your wife had been killed by a drunken driver—indeed, you fully understood more than most people the danger you posed to others—that you still operated a vehicle in that impaired condition?"

Davies rose to his feet. "Hold on a minute there!" he shouted. "Your wife was killed by a drunk driver? Why didn't you tell me that, boy? This is dreadful. You have to stop this proceeding, judge. Good Lord, he's been punished enough. I want to withdraw my complaint. I know my rights. I used to be the Police Commissioner right here in this town."

In the end, Judge Sweeney dropped the trespass charge at Davies' insistence, and over the strenuous objections of Prosecutor Dandridge. But I'd convicted myself out of my own mouth of driving under the influence. For that offense, the judge sentenced me to two years at a minimum security prison, but suspended to 120 days with the possibility of fewer as part of a program to help ease overpopulation in state prisons called the Accelerated Release Program (ARP). I was also ordered to pay the fine, reimburse court costs, report regularly to a parole officer for three years, submit to periodic drug and alcohol testing, go to at least ninety consecutive AA meetings after release, and put in one hundred hours of community service. A week later I began to serve my time.

At the prison, they assigned me to a work detail of ten short-timers. Traveling to work sites in Correctional Department buses, we did a variety of service chores. We repaired homes and did schlep jobs, mostly for low-income senior citizens, guarded by two correction officers who smoked cigarettes and made idle suggestions on how to make the repairs. Climbing a ladder with heavy bundles of asphalt shingles over my shoulder, I learned how to roof a house in a slum neighborhood, using a chalk line to keep the rows as straight as I intended to go after gaining my freedom. I dug drainage ditches and trimmed tree branches. We cleared clogged toilets or replaced them altogether. Sometimes, we ladled out food in warm shelters, where I saw a preview of my future if I kept drinking.

My cellmate was another white-collar felon named Stoughton Walker, a stock broker for Merrill Lynch. Walker had been arrested multiple times for driving drunk. He was my roofing partner and took meticulous measurements in order to accurately snap the "whappy string" chalk line across the tarpaper underlay we'd stapled down. During my confinement, the little house on the river was sold in foreclosure. Sal Tarzia the lawyer handled the paperwork, as well as managed an auction of my furnishings, which paid the state fine and helped defray some of his fees. He briefed me on these developments in a windowless basement visitors' room that smelled of disinfectant. Between us ran a long oak table with a low plastic divider running down the middle of its surface. Sal's swarthy face bore a morose cast as he ran through his points, as if he was wondering if he'd ever get paid in full.

Keeping my head down and my mouth shut, good behavior reduced my sentence to four weeks. An unexpected highlight was, while wearing an orange plastic convict vest and picking up trash with a pointed stick along Route 206 in New Canaan, the Rev. Elway drove past. He waved in recognition before opening his mouth in surprise. He was gone before I could react.

"Who's the crusty old dude with the dog collar?" asked Stoughton Walker.

"My priest when I was a little kid?"

"He had a great and lasting influence on you, didn't he?"

"Stoughton, refresh my memory: How many DUIs do you have?"

"Ten. They're going to put me away until the next century."

"Based on that, wouldn't you have to admit you've got a drinking problem?"

"I've got a police problem."

"Want to read from my copy of the Big Book?"

"N-F-W."

I emerged dried out and physically fitter, but also bankrupt, homeless, and with a permanent criminal record. I was allowed to keep my Saab, which was essentially worthless. But I couldn't drive it. I checked into a seedy no-tell motel in Norwalk and called Rit.

"Are you drinking?" he immediately wanted to know.

Chapter Thirty-Six

Cold Truth

Vicky opened her condo door wearing a thick sweater. A cold front had moved in overnight. She folded her arms across her waist, pivoted one hand upward to support her chin, and raised quizzical eyebrows. "Didn't I get rid of you a couple of months ago?"

"I had a yen to go for a walk on the beach at Calf's Pasture and wanted company. You up for it?" Vicky's baby bump was beginning to show, despite the bulky garment.

"As a matter of fact, I was just making a list to go to the grocery store. You know, to stock up on pasta e fagioli ingredients?"

"You'd better wear a coat and a hat. It'll be chilly out by the water."

"I much prefer to go to the store, alone, if you don't mind."

"Oh, come on, you'll love it."

"What's with you? Don't you remember that you politely dumped me? Do you think I'm some kind of emotional yo-yo?"

"I've had my ups and downs too, you know. I had to ride my bike over here, and there were all these great big hills."

Exasperation contorted her face.

"What's wrong?"

"You can ride it right back." She started to close the door.

"No, wait, please! I need to tell you something."

She gave me a bleak smile. "Oh alright, come on inside. You look like you're bursting to unburden yourself. Rit told me about your suspended sentence, glad you were sprung early; is that what you want to confess, your treatment of Mr. Davies? Because I really don't care anymore."

"Can we take a trip, instead? I want to show you the spark-plug lighthouse that's off Calf Pasture. When I was a kid, I swam there and back; it was half a mile each way."

"More nostalgia."

"It was flashing out there the night we danced on the sand, remember?"

"Mmmff."

"You'll have to drive us because my license is suspended."

"Oh, for God's sake.

At the shore, I realized I'd made a mistake. The tide was dead low, the rippled mud plain strewn with brown kelp and limp braids of yellowy-green bladder wrack, fingered with flotation pods. A herring gull glided from left to right, gazing down with bent neck. He honked at us, as if upset he was no longer alone along the leaden-clouded shoreline. Vicky raised her collar and pulled her fuzzy blue woolen cap down over her ears. The site of our first date felt all wrong. Its ebb-tide setting was the epitome of barrenness. The little lighthouse continued to flash red and white, making real again a remembrance of myself as a little boy, rising and swooping sickeningly in translucent green swells, do-ing a chopping racing crawl, gagging on seawater, then resting and estimating the remaining distance, gathering the energy and courage to prove something to myself.

"I'm surprised I didn't drown," I said, staring out at the distant light.

"In my car, you said you had an announcement to make," she reminded me, "one that you'd only reveal here. Now would be a good time, before your lips freeze shut."

"Two announcements," I amended. "One: I'm going to AA meetings. To be honest, it's that or go back to the clink. I've asked Rit to be my sponsor."

"Congratulations," Vicky said. "Rit mentioned that. It's done him a world of good." She stuffed her bare hands beneath her armpits to warm them. "What's the other momentous revelation? Chop, chop, Hampton, I'm chilly."

I got down on one knee. "So, I'm asking you—right here in the great outdoors—to marry me."

Vicky's eyelids narrowed. "Somebody told you, didn't they? Who blabbed?"

"Blabbed what?"

"That I'm pregnant."

"Are you?"

"Stop this charade, will you?" She kicked my bent leg out from under me, and for a few seconds I listened to her diatribe on my hands and knees. "You're a *stunod*, alright. You don't want to marry me, and I certainly don't want to marry you!"

I scrambled back to my feet. Her eyes were big and dark, her face pale, despite her olive skin. "What kind of marriage would that make—everyone thinking that the townie slut had trapped the socialite?"

"It's the other way around: Town cad takes advantage of saintly woman."

"Not for nothing are you in PR, Hamp-ton." My name

sounded like an expletive. "That was a very slick line. I can see you're practiced in the art of deception. But you forgot to mention one crucial thing in your quest to make an honest woman out of me: Do you love me?"

"What's not to love? You're great for me."

"On a scale of one to ten, what is it?"

The words googolplex times the universe automatically came to mind, but I said, "I trust you with my life, that's the God's honest truth."

She compressed her lips. "You're weaseling. Anyway, you don't believe in God. The real truth is that you're still in love with your wife and all that vanished past you carry around in your head."

I realized I was completely transparent to her, always had been. And she was absolutely correct. I didn't love her like Libby, perhaps never would, but I wanted to very much. Wasn't that enough? "Vicky," I began, but got no further.

"Take me home, I'm freezing my keister off."

I grabbed her right wrist and tried to extend her arm, as if to dance, but she wrenched it away. "There's no music out here anymore," she said. "The band went home, which is where I'm headed. And if you don't want to drive there with me, you can walk back to your bike."

"But you're carrying our child. I want to protect him and undo my family curse. I want to encourage him in his own desires, not mine; tickle his little tummy and make him laugh for joy."

"It's a her," Vicky snapped, eyes brimming. "And how do you know it's yours? My ex-husband Danny visited me a couple of months ago. And I'm still a woman with certain appetites."

"I don't believe that."

"Okay, nothing happened, but it could have, because he wants to marry me too. He phoned again the other night to press his case. He even knows I'm expecting. So you can withdraw your proposal in good conscience and go sit on your wife's headstone for the rest of your life. And don't look so stunned. Rit told me all about dragging you home drunk from the cemetery. He wants me to forget you and move on."

"Good for him, but I'll ask you the same question you asked me: Do you love Danny?"

"I saw something in him once, thought I loved him. But I didn't support him when he needed me. I still feel bad about that."

"Then..."

"Then, nothing. What a lame pair of suitors I've got: two drunks without jobs, one now with a criminal record." She savagely wiped away a tear. "Mary, Joseph, and Jesus."

"Mary was unmarried with a child, too."

"You think I don't know that, you idiot?"

Gusting wind hurled a stinging rattle of sand across our faces. Vicky rubbed her wet eyes.

"Okay, home you go," I relented. "But I'm going to support you and our child as best as I can. That's a solemn promise."

"You don't have to. I'm making no claims on you."

"Understood."

"Good."

I put my hand on her back and rubbed it to warm her. She didn't wriggle away, which was encouraging. "Do you want to go to a movie tonight?" I asked softly.

Her glance was a wordless question.

"Let's start the rituals of courtship and do things right," I said. "I need you; please help me redeem myself. I'm lost without you."

She gazed out at the choppy water. "Who needs to go to a movie with cheesy dialogue like that? Got any more?"

"What's the answer, Queen Victoria?"

"Okay, maybe, but please get me off this beach. I'm so cold, my brain is numb."

"There's just one more thing I need to confess to you," I said, "which might affect your decision about marrying me."

"So now all the dirt comes out in the wash, eh? What is it; you've got another woman pregnant in New York?"

"I've been diagnosed with Parkinson's disease. It won't kill me, but you could wind up being my caregiver. So that's a perfect out for you if you want one."

CHAPTER THIRTY-SEVEN
Tree of Life

Father Elway married Vicky and me in a mercifully short service in his chapel. Rit and Gail were our only witnesses. Vicky, short-tempered and bulging at the waist like a Schmoo, picked out a garish spread-collar shirt for me to wear with my yellow tie.

"But I'll look like I'm going for a job interview."

"You are. If we're going to apply to be Episcopalians we've got to play the part."

"Yes, ma'am," I said.

I took a job editing an alumni magazine at a Catholic university near Newark, New Jersey, the only Protestant in the administration's non-academic staff. Tom Dorsey, an influential alumnus, recommended me. I didn't wear my foulard there. I couldn't. I'd donated it to the Goodwill. Out of curiosity, I also approached the Journalism Department, where the professor in charge—a former local broadcasting celebrity—acted like I was quite a catch. He offered me a position as a non-paid adjunct professor, while I took free courses as an employee toward a degree in education. I was becoming a teacher after all. My lectures centered on interviewing techniques and ethics. Written up, my misadventures as a flack became a popular J-School case history.

Meantime, we found an apartment in South Orange, where I started attending AA meetings with truly desperate guys, blue-collar types, blacks, and Hispanics who—like me—wanted to stay out of prison. My new sponsor was nicknamed Payroll. I didn't want to guess why. He picked me, not the other way around, and told me in no uncertain terms that I had to call him every day. I continued to contact my parole officer in Connecticut, and went back for periodic drug and alcohol tests. Nearby Newark was where little Camille Wendell came into the world. Concetta Gingerella—who along with Enzo boycotted the wedding— had wanted her granddaughter named Olga or, if a boy, Barton—which seemed an odd pairing. Vicky, fortunately, had a mind of her own.

One sparkling July day, while Camille was still only months old, we returned to New Canaan without informing Vicky's parents, even though the arrival of a granddaughter had returned us nearly back to their good graces. Instead, we picnicked at the Nature Center on the old Bliss estate on Oenoke Ridge. It encompasses a botanical garden, arboretum, nature preserve, and pathways covered with bark mulch through acres of fields and woods. Vicky had worked there in high school as a volunteer in its then-rudimentary glass greenhouse. Since then, all kinds of expensive and architecturally significant structures for growing plants had arisen. She told me that, because her parents didn't have the money for a second car back then, she'd ridden to work there on her bike.

"Pedaling down Garibaldi Road and up Parade Hill—and then back again—was like an ant crawling across the middle of a bathtub, twice," she said. "Where do you think I got my great calves?"

"Yes, I've noticed those. Wobbly Stork Legs is mighty jealous."

For an instant, Vicky appeared stricken. "I like your legs, too, and with a lot of exercise they're going to keep you going just fine until they come up with a cure for Parkinson's disease. So let's go stretch them, right now. Here, take the basket and blanket and head down there." She pointed down the driveway. "And remember, keep swinging your left arm."

"You make me self-conscious."

"Heel toe, heel toe, that's it, you're doing fine."

"I'm walking like a wind-up toy."

Below us, the refurbished yellow-clapboard estate housed a series of exhibits of local wildlife and plants, but Vicky wanted to take me out onto the trails that wound past snaking stone walls and through a hemlock forest. She had a favorite spot. It was a clearing with a giant gnarled tree with low hanging rough-barked limbs. They radiated out twenty feet and bore the wear marks of the countless children who'd climbed on them. We spread my old woolen blanket under the intricate pinnate leaves of its canopy. I sat down with a thump. Camille joyously pumped her arms and legs like an overturned turtle.

"They told me this was a cork tree that was more than one hundred years old. There was another myth that it came from India as a seedling." She unpacked a thermos and some wax paper-wrapped sandwiches from a woven basket as she spoke; it was the same one she'd used to bring me lasagna the night Camille was conceived. "Some people back then called it the Bodhi Tree and said it had a link with Buddhist belief systems. But I just called it the Tree of Life."

"It's some tree, alright." I pulled up Camille's side-snap T-shirt and blew fuzz on her belly button. She squirmed and squealed, spreading drool that looked like watery cottage cheese.

"Now, don't get her all riled up," Vicky warned, handing me a clean cloth diaper to wipe Camille's cheek. "I just nursed her, you know."

"I do know that," I said. "I just saw you. What a lucky little *bambino* she is."

"*Bambina*," Vicky corrected. "And there's nothing 'lucky' about it. She's blessed. You and I are blessed too. Why can't you get that into your head, make it part of your world view?"

I responded that I'd try for all our sakes. I really wanted to believe.

CPSIA information can be obtained
at www.ICGtesting.com
Printed in the USA
JSHW010724150120
3603JS00001B/4